Fierce

James Kemp

Copyright © 2024 James Kemp
All rights reserved.
ISBN: 978-1-909951-25-9

1 3 5 7 9 10 8 6 4 2

Castlegreen Publishing
http://www.castlegreen.org.uk/
Forfar, Scotland

GUDRID'S PROPHECY

Lost yet found, he stands tall far from the sea
In among the ghosts of fallen spear carriers
Where, women witness and are spared to bear
daughters descended from god's fire made flesh.

The father's myriad faces are bent on
elevation making kings, princes, cities.
His lover's fierce flame flowers vigorously
when her sacred sword sings in the old ways.

Sacrifice to the old gods, blood in rivers,
smoke skywards. Worship her righteously,
seek perfection, embrace the bird filled trees.

She brings justice by night and ends empires,
oppression by northerners, faith restored.

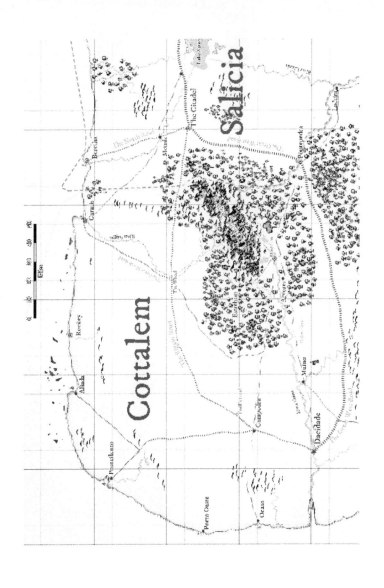

DEDICATION

To my wife, who took me to Bergen,
which started all this off!

ONE

ᛋᛏᚱᚨᚡᛖᚾ

STRAVEN

'Noren! What's keeping you?' I peered round the door of the boat shed.

'I'm stowing the nets, Yngvild.'

'Can't you just throw them back in the boat like everyone else?'

Noren stopped sorting out the net and looked up at me. 'Because, Yngvild, you can't throw them well if they're tangled.'

'It's a waste of time, we could be doing something more enjoyable!'

'If they're stowed well I catch fish faster, so I get to come home sooner. That means I get to spend time with you.' Noren smiled widely, his blue eyes gleaming.

I stuck out my chin and pouted. 'Well it's time you showed me how much you appreciate my company.' I reached out to grab Noren's neatly patched sailcloth smock and pull him closer.

'Noren! Yngvild! Dinner!'

'Gods, her timing is terrible!' I ran a finger down Noren's sleeve and across his back. 'later.' I turned to leave.

'Tell her I'll be in as soon as I've finished stowing the nets.'

'You are such a stickler.' I blew Noren a kiss over my shoulder as I left the boat shed.

~

The light from the open doorway eclipsed as Noren joined the rest of us in the main hall. The day's work done, he'd hung his smock in the boat shed. He came in, dressed in his distinctive linen shirt with the extra wide panels under his muscled arms.

Noren crossed the space between door and table in two strides. He sat in his usual space in the middle of the bench nearest the door. I sat opposite him. Everyone else was already here, waiting for his arrival before starting.

The table was laden with bread, beer, bowls, and serving dishes with butter, eggs, peas, barley and salt. We had some fried fish fresh from today's catch, the rest of which had filled the smoke house.

'Let us pray in thanks.' Old Bjorn stood at the head of the table. Helga the Red sitting on his right. Arne the Slow, the steersman, sat at the other end. Down the table there were ten others on each side, a third of the boat crew plus their family members shared the main hall. The rest were either in the old hall or the barn with the younger children.

'Let us give thanks that we are all here today,' Old Bjorn said. 'and that we have a bounteous catch to eat and plenty to trade.'

'I give thanks to the Gods for the health of all our children.' Helga the Red said.

I stood. As the youngest adult present it was my duty to finish the prayers.

'I give thanks to the Gods for the food we are about to eat.'

'I give thanks'. The adults chanted in unison.

Dinner started with a rattling of dishes and utensils. Two fish dishes went round the table, one from Old Bjorn and the other from Arne the Slow. Others helped themselves to the side dishes while we waited for the fish to come round.

'Have you picked out a lamb for First Night yet?' Gunnar asked as he stuck his knife into a loaf.

'Yes, the first one born.' I chose a piece of fish from the dish that Leif passed to me before passing it on to Birgitta.

'So are you going to do it this year?' Leif put a piece of the fish in his mouth and started chewing.

'I've done it several times already, as you well know.' I stuck my tongue out at Leif.

Gunnar laughed. 'You walked into that one, old friend.'

Leif's cheeks went red above his blond beard.

'You've embarrassed him.' I slowly sucked the grease off each of my fingers, looking at him.

Gunnar almost choked on the ale he was drinking, and Noren slapped him on the back.

I added some butter to the bread I'd torn off the loaf. 'Yes, I'm doing the sacrifice to Malfin. Are you helping me?'

'Me and Leif were planning to.' Gunnar put the tankard down. 'What about you Noren?'

'Yngvild has sorted out a job for me.' Noren put his knife down. 'I've got to chop the wood for the fire on the hill.'

'You could do some for us too.' Leif said.

'Why not.' Noren ate a boiled egg whole.

~

After dinner I followed Noren from the hall, there was unfinished business to attend to. I enjoyed watching him move, seeing the smooth strides. His woollen hose clung to his legs and showed his muscles rippling as he walked. He was V shaped, tapering down from his broad shoulders.
He rolled across the landscape like a thundercloud towards our favourite outcrop over the beach.

I couldn't keep up with him when he moved with a purpose, but I knew where he was going and I could enjoy the view. He stopped on the top of the smooth rock and stood looking out at the sun low on the horizon across the fjord.

I took my time getting to him, he wasn't going anywhere else tonight and I thought about my dreams of being with Noren in the forest. All our work was done and the evening meal eaten. There was nothing else to do but enjoy the sun, and each other's company, before bed.

'Good weather again tomorrow.' Noren said as I arrived.

I climbed onto the rock and, tucking my skirt behind my knees, sat at the edge, my feet dangling over the beach. 'Come, sit with me.' I patted the edge of the rock next to me.

Noren took the cue and sat beside me. I put my arm round his waist and leant into him, resting my head on the side of his chest. I thrilled at his scent, there was something about the combination of salt, sea, wool and Noren that enticed me to be near him and, if I'm honest, melted my insides a little.

He hugged me with his left arm, pulling me into him. 'It's a beautiful evening.'

We sat in silence, watching the waves hit the beach and straggly pink clouds scudding on a horizon flecked with tiny islets and white foam where rocks broached the surface. Gulls swooped and heeled into the sea, emerging moments later with fish in their beaks glinting in the sun.

'You ever wonder about going away?' I said.

'One day I'll have my own boat. Who knows where my haven will be.'

'I've been dreaming about us in a forest.'

'Boats aren't great in forests.'

'The seagulls took us to the forest, so the bear could find us.'

'Is this like the dreams you had about the raiders?'

'Maybe, although Old Bjorn says that sometimes dreams are just dreams. But I keep having this one.'

'How exactly does it go?'

'A giant seagull picks us up and carries us off. It drops us into a forest, and there's a bear looking for us. It can't find us, but it wants to help us.'

'How do you know the bear wants to help us?'

'I just know. There are ravens everywhere in the forest, but they're not friendly, and they're scared of the bear. I get flashes of them trying to peck out the bear's eyes.'

Noren stiffened. I stopped talking, slightly annoyed that he wasn't listening properly.

Noren pointed. I couldn't see anything where he was pointing, even though I squinted into the setting sun.

A speck on the horizon broadened. 'Is that a ship?' Noren said.

'What?'

'Over there, between Portree and Brevik.' Noren indicated both places as he mentioned them.

'Oh. I see it now. Isn't it a bit late for being out?'

'Well it's not like it's getting dark soon, is it?'

I laughed. 'Not for a fortnight at least' I squinted at the smudge on the horizon 'I wonder who it is and where they're going?'

'They're a bit far away, but it doesn't look like one of the fishing boats I know'

'How can you tell? It's so small'

'The sail is wrong, we've just got the one mast with a square rig.'

The ship approached, becoming clearer. Two masts were under sail, and a third furled. The fore mast had a huge triangular sheet. Above it a smaller rectangular sail bulged ahead of the ship. Both sails had the large blue circle of the King's Ships painted on an otherwise plain sail. It seemed to be coming straight towards us.

'I think we ought to go tell the others about the King's Ship' Noren said.

'Won't someone else have seen it?'

Noren looked back at the houses, two parallel tenements running inland from the jetty. 'I can't see anyone, if they'd seen the ship then they'd be getting ready to welcome it.'

'We've got a few more minutes.'

'We have. But others might have gone to bed, you know what Old Bjorn and Helga the Red are like.' Noren disentangled himself from me and rolled away, launching himself off the rock.

'Wait for me!' I scrambled after him with my skirts hiked above my knees so that I could crawl.

Noren didn't wait for me. He broke into a run towards the houses.

'Ships!' he yelled. 'Ships!'

I turned to look back out to sea, surely there was just one ship?

There, behind the first ship, and obscured by its sails, were two others. They were much further out, but following the same course. Neither had the blue pennant nor the blue circles on the sails. One had a red pennant with patched sails. The other a green pennant with green and white vertically striped sails.

'Gods above! Raiders!' I swore under my breath and hurried to the houses. I could see that Noren had already reached the decking ahead of me. He was shouting to wake up the households.

'Raiders! Raiders! To arms!' Noren shouted. He reached the horn hanging on the front of the building, next to the alley entrance.

FFFRROOOUUU! The horn sounded.

An upstairs shutter thumped open against the thick wooden boards of the tenement. Arne the Slow glowered down at Noren.

'What's the panic, dwarf?'

'Ships! Raiders! Coming here.' Noren pointed at the incoming ships. 'First one is a King's Ship, but the two behind look like raiders.'

Arne looked out at the ships. 'Best get tha battle gear on, then.' he ducked back inside, leaving the window shutter open.

The thudding of my feet on the planking echoed off the walls as I dashed down the alley. My room was upstairs at the back of the alley. As I ran full pelt along the alley people began to appear.

'Raiders, get ready!' I shouted as I passed them.

Noren's footsteps rang on the boards behind me.

No-one was asleep now, children hollered and cried as they were grabbed from their beds.

I took the stairs two at a time and crashed through the door into my room.

I tore off my skirts, stepping out of them as they fell to the floor. My shield came out from under the bed, with mail, dagger and helmet.

A bright red padded woollen coat covered me to mid-thigh. I bent my head forwards to catch my braids in a bright red knitted woollen cap. Once they were safely enclosed I threw the mail shirt over my head and shrugged it down over my body.

My dagger and a quiver of arrows were on the broad leather belt that pulled the mail tight around my waist.

I took my bow from the corner, it's string loose, and bent it against my foot with one hand while stringing it with the other.

Then the helmet went on my head, hinged cheek

pieces and a human featured face plate covered everywhere except my eyes and mouth.

The shield and a sharpened stake were taken in my left arm and I ran back out the door.

We'd practised weekly since the beginning of last winter. The alley had two way traffic. Young mothers and oldsters herded children inland. Everyone else moved towards the jetty. Not all were wearing battle gear. Some carried it to dress on the jetty.

On the jetty Noren had a pile of battle gear in front of him. His padded jerkin discarded behind him, he was pulling a mail shirt over his head. Noren's arms flailed above his head, the mail clanking loudly.

'No point continuing, dwarf, tha's too large for yer mail.' drawled Arne, who stood close by, already clad in armour. His shield bore a black snail on a blue field, with two wavy lines below.

A loud splash drew my attention to the King's Ship. Both sails were furled and sailors stood ready to throw lines. The ship was at least three times as long and twice the width and height of any of the fishing boats on Straven. The people on the King's Ship were mostly unarmoured, although an armed contingent was assembling on deck.

The other ships were closing in too, sails furled and under oars. There were archers in the prows.

'I'm not going back with the bairns!' Noren said. 'My place is here with you, mail or no mail'

'Stay in middle of th' back row, dwarf. Tha's too good a fisher to lose just cause tha's too large for yer mail.' Arne said.

Old Bjorn, in plain black battle rig minus helmet, stood on the jetty to meet the King's Ship. Many white tally marks covered his shield.

'Hello there!' Old Bjorn waved at the ship.

A man in a blue cloak waved back.

'Bjorn Johansson, the Counter of Battles?'

'Aye, that was me. Who are you?'

'Captain Ragnar Ragnarsson, of the King's Ship, Seagull."

'Ragnar the Ready! Have you got any better at finding your gear?'

'Much better, sir.'

'Wouldn't have been hard to improve. Why have you brought me a battle at midnight?'

'I was going to ask you the same thing, sir.'

'No need to sir me any more, Ragnar. All I'm in charge of is a fishing boat.' Old Bjorn gestured at the other ships. 'Who are your friends?'

The Seagull thudded gently into the side of the jetty. While Bjorn had been talking to the captain, Erik the Dark, Leif, Gunnar and Freya had caught ropes thrown by the Seagull's sailors and tied it off.

'The green sails are merchant venturers from the Aelfheim Company. But I don't know the other.' Ragnar said.

'We reckoned them as raiders on first sight, chasing you down perhaps.'

'That would be a bold move, but at two to one it might pay off.' Ragnar stroked his black beard. 'I guess we might stay trimmed for battle until they've docked.'

The boat crew formed a shield wall across the end of the jetty, the only place larger boats could land. Noren was in the middle at the back, with two full rows in front of him. I stood to the side with three other archers ready to shoot into the flanks of anyone attempting to force the shield wall. Old Bjorn stayed at the end of the jetty with Captain Ragnar. The sailors formed a group on the jetty, with their archers in the stern of the ship.

We didn't have long to wait. The two ships rowed towards them. Fifty yards out the leading vessel shipped oars and hailed Old Bjorn.

'Ho there! Permission to dock?'

'Who are you?' Old Bjorn shouted back.

'Merchants from the Aelfheim Company out of Kronstadt.'

'You don't look like Aelfheim.'

'No. We ran into a raider early this morning. We captured their ship. I've got a prize crew and some prisoners.'

Old Bjorn looked at Captain Ragnar and raised an eyebrow. Ragnar nodded.

'Why have you come here rather than Portree?' said Bjorn.

'We saw the King's Ship and thought we'd be better off handing over the prisoners to the King.'

'One ship at a time, and we don't want to see anyone armed on deck.' Said Bjorn.

'Of course.'

Ragnar gestured to some of his sailors. They disappeared from deck. Moments later a second contingent of armed and mailed people came out of the King's Ship and surrounded Bjorn, facing the other side of the jetty.

The first ship, the alleged former raider, slowly drifted towards the jetty. It was shorter and wider than the Seagull, and higher than the jetty. The man that had hailed them still in the prow. As he approached it became clear the shields around the ship were identical.

'How many have you?' one of Ragnar's crew shouted.

'Ten as prize crew, and thirty two prisoners.'

'How are you holding them?'

'They're lashed to the oars.'

'When you tie up I want you down here on your own. Then we'll come aboard and take control.'

'Fine by me. Can I have a receipt for the ship please?'

Bjorn laughed. 'Don't worry lad, I'll see they don't do you out of your prize money'.

Bjorn stood back and let Ragnar's crew deal with the raider. They filled the deck with their crew while the locals stood on guard at the end of the jetty. Once the ship was secured they started bringing out prisoners an oar at a time. Two came out on their own, the raider captain and steersman.

As the raider was emptied the locals took the oars, each with three prisoners lashed to it, down the beach. Each oar was spaced out along the beach front and guarded by a spearman or archer. The raider captain was taken into the main hall by Old Bjorn, and I was set to watch him. His steersman went with Arne into the old hall. Ragnar's crew stayed back to land the other ship.

'This is Yngvild the Fierce, you'll not be her first kill.' Bjorn said to the raider captain. He turned to me, saying 'If he tries anything put an arrow through his heart.' Old Bjorn winked at me as he turned away from the captain.

I knocked an arrow and took a good look at the raider captain. He looked tired and worn out, but his hair was dark to match his weather beaten skin. The cold blue eyes showed intelligence and darted around appraisingly. His clothes were rich, proper loom woven wool, with an even felt. Not the home worsted we all wore on Straven. The colours were bright, twice or thrice dyed, and with lots of braid and ribbon. His buttons were bright too, silver most likely, and he had rings on his fingers. He was shorter than Noren, but only a little. He'd ducked slightly to get under the door lintel.

Bjorn got himself a tankard of beer from the keg we'd broached at dinner. The foam piled over the top of the rim like shorn wool. He set it down on the end of the table and collected some leftover fried fish from the sideboard. Replacing the cover he sat down in his usual seat and ate half the fish, washing down each mouthful with some beer.

Old Bjorn looked up at the raider captain and broke the silence. 'Do you know who I am?'

The raider captain looked hard at Old Bjorn for a moment before replying. 'Should I?'

'Not especially, I'm just a fishing boat captain. How about you?'

'Pretty similar really. My company are independent traders, not as successful as we'd like. Small fry. Not worth attacking. Yet that's exactly what those elvish bastards did.'

Bjorn raised an eyebrow, watched the raider captain and ate more fish.

'They're taking out the small competition by claiming that we're raiders. They get prize money and they sell more stuff.'

Bjorn stayed stubbornly silent and swigged some beer.

'Look we're legitimate traders, and it's a scandal that we've been attacked and then held prisoner.'

Bjorn stood up and left the room.

I watched the captain closely. Was what he said true? Why would you make up a story like that? He certainly looked like he could be legitimate, his clothes were finer than any I'd seen in Straven. Or even at Portree, which was the richest port with a day's return trip. But those eyes searched like he was looking to escape, maybe the clothes and jewellery were his ill gotten gains from raiding?

Old Bjorn returned, with Captain Ragnar. Bjorn sat back down, leaving Ragnar on the corner bench.

'I'm Captain Ragnar Ragnarsson of the King's Ship Seagull. Who might you be?'

'Captain Ranald Magnusson, an independent trader and co-owner of the Flower of Skyss.'

'Ranald, I have reason to believe that you have been acting as a raider. What do you say to this?' said Ragnar.

'I've already told the old man there that I'm the victim. The elves attacked us and took me and my crew prisoner. They're the raiders.'

'That's not what your steersman told me.'

'Either he's lying or you are. Ask the rest of the crew.'

'My crew are doing that as we speak. I'll have the truth, one way or the other.'

'I certainly hope so. What about the elvish crew? Have you made them prisoners?'

'Are you aware of the penalty for leading a raiding crew?'

'Yes. That's why I'm not a raider. Besides you'd need a King's Justice to pass sentence, you don't have that authority in Skyssian waters.'

'Correct. But the old man here is a King's Justice. He can pass sentence any time he likes.'

Ranald's face drained of colour.

They say that you cannot lie to a King's Justice and live. This isn't quite true. You cannot lie to a King's Justice without them knowing about it. You only die if they decide that sparing you isn't helpful. Or so Old Bjorn had told us.

'You can confess now, or I can compel you. It's less

painful if you confess voluntarily.' Bjorn said to Ranald.

Ranald confessed. His crew hadn't attacked the Aelfheim Company ship, he'd been telling the truth about that. However the Aelfheim Company was large, well resourced and had a long memory. Ranald's crew had boarded one of their smaller ships in the spring. The crew had given a description of the pennant and the distinctive patching on the sails. That had been enough for the larger ship to identify them and deliberately take them.

The trial was brief, and Bjorn told Ranald that he was being spared for crown service, as was his crew. There was relief on his face as Bjorn and Ragnar performed the geas binding him to the King's Service. Ranald volunteered to speak the words.

'I pledge my life in atonement to the service of the Crown. I will follow all orders given to me by the King and officers appointed over me, even unto death, as diligently as possible.'

'Ragnar, ask Arne to find Ranald the Raider a room up the middle stairs. Put his steersman in with him.' Bjorn said.

'What about the crew?'

'Any that freely confess can be bound to service and put in the barn. They won't run. The others can be put in the hold pending questions from a King's Justice.'

'Yes, sir.' Ragnar and Ranald left me alone with Old Bjorn in the main hall.

'Why didn't you tell us you were a King's Justice?' I asked.

'That's my old life, I've retired to live peacefully.'

'Does anyone else know?'

'Helga does. Arne too. No-one else. And you won't tell them.'

'I promise.'

'Why did you tell Ranald that he wouldn't be my first kill?'

'Because it was the truth.'

'I haven't killed anyone.'

'And you didn't kill him. So he wasn't your first.'

'You couldn't possibly have known that when you said it?'

'Couldn't I?'

I was perplexed. What powers did the King's Justices have? Could they see people's fates? What else did he know?

Bjorn stood to leave.

'Wait! Can you see our fates?'

'I see a future. It's bed shaped.' Bjorn left the hall.

~

The Aelfheim Company left at noon, after they'd slept off the previous day's exertions. It took the whole crew to warp their ship out far enough to row away from the jetty.

Noren was busy with Captain Ragnar, and Freya was busy too. So I found Noren's discarded mail and took out my frustration by opening its links with a hammer and chisel in the forge. Straven didn't have a smith these days, Aksel the Steel came through every now and then to do repairs, but he wasn't due soon.

If Noren needed armour then he could lace it up the back with some rawhide strips until Ragnar visited to make it big enough. It was better that than not wearing anything and praying to Meniaxter not to be hit. Noren was too big a target to be missed. I took Noren's armour with me to dinner. The sooner I could make it work for him the better.

'Noren, I've adjusted your armour. Please try it on so that I can see if I've done enough.'

'Thank you Yngvild' Noren took the armour. 'Here, or in the forge?'

'Here will do.' Noren unfolded the mail and put his arms into the sleeves. 'I'll need some help doing it up.'

'I thought it was better to make it usable than to wait.' I threaded the rawhide through the iron rings and laced it up Noren's back.

'Thank you. We were lucky yesterday.'

'I think you were foolish you know.'

'It was all fine in the end.'

'It might not have been. I don't want you fighting, especially not without armour.'

'I'll keep myself safe, there's no rush to die.'

I stepped round Noren looking for pinch points in the mail. I tugged in a couple of places.

'My point exactly Noren. What did he want with you?'

'Nothing much.'

'Took a long time for nothing.' I tested the left sleeve by bending Noren's arm into a shield hold.

'He was extolling the benefits of being a King's Messenger, he thought I might like it.'

'What did you say?'

'I turned him down. I'm happy here, and one day soon I'll have my own boat to captain.'

'You know that Old Bjorn used to be a King's Messenger?' I moved Noren's right arm up and down, like he might use a spear.

'Ragnar mentioned it.'

'He knew Old Bjorn didn't he?' I pulled at a loose flap of mail at Noren's behind.

'Ragnar said he was still a midshipman when Old Bjorn retired, although not long before he got promoted.'

'Old Bjorn must be unspeakably ancient then, Ragnar didn't look that young.' I started to unlace the mail so he could take it off.

'They don't call him Old Bjorn for nothing.'

'I heard Ragnar call him the Counter of Battles.'

'I heard that too. The older folk joke about the tally marks on his shield, some say it's his kills, others his women. Never heard anyone talk about his battles.'

'You can take it off now.'

Noren shrugged himself out of the armour.

'Does anyone recall him adding a tally marks to his shield?'

'Not that I know, but he's been the captain here since before I can remember.'

TWO

ᛋᛏᚱᚠᛉᚲᛗ ᛋᚾᛁᚲᛋ
STRANGE SHIPS

Noren and I went out for our customary after dinner
walk. I carried a blanket with me as we walked up
the hill to the highest point on the island. We were
going to watch the sun finally set over the sea to the
West of Straven. As we approached the trees the
ravens' caws echoed round the island, the birds
flapping round the copse. We carried on up the hill,
others followed behind us, and I could see a few
could already on top of lookout hill.

'I suppose we'd better bring a few branches up
with us.' Noren said as we got to the trees.

'That one there looks like it might keep us warm
for a bit.' I pointed out a fallen branch, leg thick, that
had splintered away from a tree. 'Did you bring an
axe with you?'

'Yes.' Noren drew an axe from his belt and with a
few swift strokes cut the remaining splinters and
freed it from the tree.

I gathered up some fallen sticks from close under
the trees and bunched them in my overskirt. We'd
need kindling.

'I think that will do. Let's go up.' I said.

Noren carried the large branch over his shoulder
to the top of the hill. It barely slowed him down.

'Tha'll need to chop it a bit dwarf, we're not firing
the whole hill!' Arne said when he saw us.

Arne and Alwilda were already at the top of the hill
and had started to build a fire with wood they and
Alwilda's children had brought up. It wasn't lit yet,

that would come later.

'What about mine?' Yngvild asked.

'Put yours here, dear. They're just right for the next layer.' Alwilda said. 'Would you mind keeping the children away from Noren's axe?'

'Of course.'

Noren dragged his half-tree sized bough out of the path and set to it with his axe. Pieces of wood chip flew off like the first blizzard of the winter.

'Tha could play a tune to your chopping, dwarf' Arne said.

'Did you bring your pipes up?' I said.

'Do fish swim in the sea?' Arne uncovered a basket and picked his pipes up. Tucking them under his arm he inflated the bag with a few large breaths. The music was a jaunty tune that Noren's rhythmic chopping accompanied well.

Old Bjorn and Helga the Red were coming up the hill at a stately pace. They alone of the others on the path between the houses and the top of Lookout Hill had empty hands. Everyone else was bringing wood, food, drink, musical instruments or something for the party.

'Sun will be down soon.' Noren said. Behind him was a sea of wood chips, and a neat pile of logs the length of his forearm.

'You chopped that fast!' I said.

'It was only a small tree.' He shrugged.

'Come, let's get a space and sit together.' I grabbed Noren's hand to tow him to the southern side of the hill.

'Here looks good, not too far from the fire.' Noren said.

I shook out my blanket before letting it billow down onto the grass. Noren sat down first, and I sat next to him, burrowing in under his arm and putting my arm round his back. I rested my head on his chest as we watched the others come up the hill.

The whole community assembled on the hilltop. Erik the Dark had brought a barrel of beer up. Freya some bread and cheese, Birgitta had made some cakes. Gunnar and Leif had brought the lamb we'd killed in honour of Malfin. They'd cooked it earlier or it wouldn't have been ready to eat before dawn. It would go back on the fire when we lit it.

'Gather round! Gather round!' Arne stood next to the fire he'd built and waved people to assemble. 'Sun's on the horizon.'

We all stopped what we were doing and formed a loose horseshoe round the fire, facing the sun. Parents carried their smaller children, and the older ones were pushed to the front.

Old Bjorn, as the boat captain and community leader, stood with the sun to his back facing the fire at the mouth of the horseshoe.

'People of Straven! We gather to celebrate the return of the dark of night. And to make homage to Malfin, our Lady of Darkness.' Bjorn turned to face the sun.

We all watched the sun drop below the horizon. Old Bjorn lead us in praying to the Gods.

As the last part of the sun fell below the horizon Arne struck sparks on his flint and the fire breathed into life. Arne prayed to Aeolf, Malfin's twin sister and Goddess of Flames, and the fire grew rapidly to a huge blaze. I could feel the heat on my face.

Slowly the sky darkened and we were able to see the other fires from the other settlements. Gunnar and Leif lifted the lamb onto the spit assembled on either side of Arne's fire.

Noren and I sat on the blanket I'd brought up, drank beer and ate some scones. We enjoyed the short night, it wouldn't truly be dark, nor would the sun be below the horizon for long.

'Look, out there, another light.' Noren said, pointing to the South.

'Isn't that out on the open sea?' I asked.

'Yes, it must be a ship.' Noren said.

I wasn't used to the summer ale Erik had brewed for the festival. I snuggled into Noren and let the drowsiness overcome me.

~

Wide gnarled pillars support the verdant sky. Skeletal brown fingers and arms rise out of the leaf litter. Nothing moves, except the dappling shadows. A susurration of leaves in the wind provides a backing to invisible birdsong. The forest smells damp, yet fresh, a feeling of reassuring calm.

I walk through the wood. Stepping round fallen branches and patches of bracken. There are deer somewhere in the woods. Also a bear. I can't see any of them, but there are tracks on the ground, and there's a sense of a benevolent watcher. There are no branches with leaves below my head height. So I don't need to duck and I can see a fair distance ahead.

Nothing moves, yet I am aware of someone behind my left shoulder. Turning, I see a dark skinned woman with lustrous straight black hair. Her eyes are totally black, the pupils expanded past colour. Her eyes suck in my gaze. She smiles. I feel a thrill that sends shivers through me.

~

The following day the light out to sea grew from a small speck on the horizon into a strange shaped ship heading straight for Straven.

The first night was always short, less than an hourglass. The following day the fishing boat always stayed home. The community celebrated the coming of winter by starting preparations for the dark time, even though it was still several moons off.

I spent my day checking cheese and skyr barrels in the barn and bringing out the empty casks for cleaning and refilling. Noren was in the smoke-house checking the fish. Soon the early catches would be packed in barrels and sent to market. The money they brought would bring dried herbs and spices, iron work and other essentials that Straven was too small to provide for itself.

It was when we broke for lunch that Arne spotted the strange vessel.

'By the Gods, I haven't seen a rig like that before!' Arne said, nodding seawards.

'Where?' said Old Bjorn.

'Out South East of Brevik in the open water.' Arne indicated the direction with his arm.

'Aye. That's a strange one, alright.' said Old Bjorn.

Many eyes swivelled to pick up the ship, Old Bjorn had seen a lot, anything he thought was odd was worth watching.

'It's got a house built on at the back, can't be stable.' said Gunnar.

'Those sails are neither square nor triangles. How do they work?' said Leif.

'They catch the wind and push the ship. Same as ours.' said Arne.

'He asked for that!' Freya laughed, as did several others.

'Think they're coming here?' said Gunnar.

'Not likely, they'll be on course for Portree.' said Arne. 'but we'll get a good look as they pass by.'

'It's come back to me. The ship, I've seen that sort before. They're from Mangandlay.' said Old Bjorn.

'Where's that then?' Yngvild said.

'Long way south of here. I didn't know they came this far north. I've only seen them near Kronstadt and to the South.'

'Have you been to Mangandlay?' Yngvild said.

'No lass, but I've heard a bit about it.' Old Bjorn said. 'Mangandlay is a port at the mouth of the river Mangand. It's hot, humid and full of flies and biting insects.'

'Biting insects?'

'Oh yes, they've got leeches that would suck the blood out of a man if they're not knocked off. Also lots of small flying things, leave pink spots all over your body. Makes my skin crawl just thinking about it.' said Old Bjorn.

'Why would anyone want to live in a place like that?' Gunnar said.

'Why would anyone want to live in a place that could freeze you to death and stays dark for two moons?' said Arne.

'Time we got on with things, there's a lot to get done before dinner. I want to take the boat out tomorrow.' said Old Bjorn.

~

I was moving a stack of empty barrels that needed repairs to the forge when the horn blared. I put down the barrel I was carrying, and dashed back up the alley to my room to prepare for raiders.

The horn sounded again, I stopped, turned and leant against the wall of the alley. I closed my eyes and let out my breath in relief. After a moment I went back along the alley towards the jetty to see if anything was visible. Gunnar stood on the decking with the horn in his hand. Freya and Leif were further down the Jetty, Birgitta and Alwilda appeared as I watched. The strange Mangandlay ship was taking up its sails as it headed straight for Straven.

I went back to collect the barrel I'd dropped, and joined the reception party on the jetty when I'd stowed it by the forge. By the time I got there almost all of the adults were present and many of the older children.

Leif, Alwilda, Gunnar and Noren stood at the seaward end of the jetty with Old Bjorn. Arne had another party half way down the Jetty with Freya, Birgitta and Helga. Arne waved me over to join him.

The ship drifted in closer. The Mangandlese sailors were tall and darker skinned than most of us. They also had shaved heads and faces. They stood with ropes ready to throw to us. Some stood down the sides of the ship holding rope fenders in place. Others had poles to steady the approach to the jetty. All of them were men, not a single woman among them. I wondered how they managed to come so far from their homes without women.

'Can we land?' one of the shaven headed sailors in the prow shouted.

'Who are you?' Old Bjorn shouted.

'Chantara, out of Mangandlay.'

'What business do you have?'

'We are traders, and we seek some fresh water too.'

'You are welcome to tie up.' Old Bjorn shouted.

Moments later the ropes were thrown. Gunnar caught the first one and the tying up process began.

Just before I had to start hauling on a rope myself, I spotted a black haired person at a window in the house at the back of the Chantara.

~

The Chantara stayed with us for nearly two whole days. Most of the crew stayed on board when they weren't filling casks from our spring.

Three men came ashore and stayed with us in our houses. Two were shaven headed Mangandlese, and the other was the black haired man I'd seen at the window.

Bo Thu Myat was their captain, he was only a little shorter than Noren. His clothes were a strange shimmering fabric. The other Mangandlese, Maung Yaza Lin, was their translator. Maung told me that it was a special kind of silk. Both of them had brown eyes and skin the colour of the old hall's panels. Maung was perhaps a little younger than Bo, it was hard to tell how old they were without any sign from their hair. Neither were old enough to be wrinkled.

Most of the talking was by the black haired man. He was not Mangandlese at all. He spoke our tongue like he had a bad head cold. He claimed to be interested in how people lived in different places and he asked a lot of questions.

During the second day I took the sheep up the side of lookout hill. He was sitting with an open leather roll across his knees, sketching with thin pieces of charcoal.

'Hello there, how are you?' he said.

'I am well, and you?' I said.

'Passing fair. Please, let me introduce myself. My name is Arald.'

'Pleased to meet you Arald. I am Yngvild the Fierce, Helgasdottir.'

'The Fierce?'

'I'm good as any with weapons, and hold no fear.'

'They call Arne the Slow, and Noren the Dwarf. Arne is quicker than most, and Noren is one of the tallest men I've ever met.'

'Nicknames aren't always the opposite of how people are, sometimes they're accurate.'

'So why are you Yngvild the Fierce?'

'When I was 14 we were attacked by raiders. I didn't run with the children like I was supposed to. Instead I picked up the bow I'd been practising with and shot arrows at the raiders.'

'Did you hit any of them?'

'I had the wrong sort of arrow heads. But I bounced an arrow off the helmet of the raider captain. Twice. It was enough to make them go away.'

'Yet you are tending the sheep?'

'Sheep need guarded from the wolves.'

'I suppose they do.'

'What brings you up here then?'

'I came to see the whole island, and to speak with you.'

'Well this is all we have. The houses, the barn, and some workshops next to the jetty. Behind them we have a paddock and a couple of small fields. Other than that there's just some woodland and the two hills.'

'You forgot to mention the stream that runs from this hill to the jetty.'

'I did. Didn't I.'

'And the pretty shepherdess.'

'It's Birgitta's day off today.'

'Well played.' Arald laughed.

'Can I see your picture?'

'It's not very good, just a rough impression of the landscape.' Arald held up a piece of paper he'd been drawing on.

'You're right, not nearly enough trees.' I said. 'Why come here?'

'Because I've never been here before. I've travelled much of the world seeing it for myself. I came here because I'm interested in how different people live in different places.'

'Don't you have a home?'

'Yes. I have a home, and a family. How about you?'

'I've not travelled far, just some hunting trips and to the annual fisher-meet.'

'The fisher-meet.?'

'All the fishing communities gather around mid-summer over on Portree, it's the largest island we inhabit. There are weddings, feasts, games, and the captains all talk business and do elections. As a child it's a wonderful time, because you get to meet other kids your own age.'

'So everyone goes to the fisher-meet.?'

'Every single one of us, although we are close enough by that we can manage it. Other communities sometimes just send the boat crews and the older children.'

'Why the older children?'

'It's all about binding us as a single community, and we form friendships that last. Many of us will move community when we come of age, so it's best that we are known to each other and the prospective boat captains.'

'Is that so that the captains can pick their new crew?'

'Sort of, but really the crew pick each other, and then they pick their captain.'

'Now I'm confused.'

'It's quite simple. A boat needs a crew, maybe ten to sixteen adults, including the captain and steersman. The boats are small and the crew live closely together. So they need to be sure that they are all happy with each other and get along.'

'So the crew forms by mutual agreement?'

'Yes, and then they choose who the captain and steersman are.'

'I see. So are you part of the crew?'

'I'm a reserve. We're thinking about whether to build a second boat on Straven. When we do I will be part of Noren's crew.'

~

Old Bjorn met me when I brought the sheep back in from the hill.

'Lass, we need to talk. Come inside.' he said.

I followed him into the main hall, but he carried on through the main hall and up the stairs at the back. At the top of the stairs we turned into the room that he shared with Helga the Red. He opened a door and we went up another set of stairs. Without another word said he ushered me into his sanctum in the roof space.

I'd never been in here before, it was a given that the community leader had a private space, but no-one but their closest would ever see it. Old Bjorn's had a skylight with glass in it, covered by a shutter. When the shutter was closed you couldn't tell where it was from the hill. I'd known it was up here because I'd seen the shutter open when I was tending the sheep. There were eight shutters in total, four on each of the tenements. As far as I knew none of the others had glass.

Old Bjorn's sanctum was a treasure trove. It wasn't a large space, barely room enough for two. There was a small table covered in pieces of paper, a chair, and two shelves. Candles were piled under the table, and two candlesticks sat on the back of the table. On the top most shelf sat a gilded full face helmet. It bore a passing resemblance to Old Bjorn, and was clearly a fine piece of metalwork. Leaning in the corner was a black silk banner, the folds hinting at the blue circle denoting someone working for the King. It also had white tally marks on it, just like Old Bjorn's Shield.

The lower shelf had seven books on it, a king's ransom worth. Unlike the others, the largest was about four inches of papers bound together with leather thongs between two black leather covered boards. They were propped up with a fragment of rock with teeth shaped crystals in it. A large broken axe head cracked across the blade, still with a splintered wooden haft sticking out of the collar, formed the other bookend. There was also a small wooden chest, bound with iron, on the shelf.

'Sit down, lass.' Old Bjorn pulled down a seat that was hinged to the wall.

I sat down, still wondering why he'd brought me in here.

'You were never in here, and I haven't said what I'm about to say.' he said.

More secrets. I nodded.

'I've had word from the King, Arald is not to be trusted.'

'There haven't been any other boats.'

'Don't worry about that. What was Arald doing up the hill?'

'He was drawing pictures when I met him. Then he asked me lots of questions.'

'What did he ask you about?'

'He wanted to know why I am called Fierce. Then he asked about the second boat and Noren.'

'What did you tell him about Noren?'

'Only what everyone knows. That he's a foundling, he grew up here and everyone likes him because he's really good at being a fisherman.'

'Then what?'

'That was all, he decided to go back down the hill.'

'Did you see his drawing?'

'Yes, he showed me it. It wasn't very good, not enough trees.'

Old Bjorn turned to the papers on the table and ruffled through them. He picked one and held it up. 'Did it look anything like this?'

'A bit like that, but he'd drawn the houses on and written some strange runes on the sheet. I could clearly see the shape of the island and the hills from his picture.'

'Looks like he was drawing a panorama.'

'Is there something wrong?'

'Relax, lass, you've done nothing wrong.' Old Bjorn

pulled down the wooden chest from the shelf and put it on his table. He fiddled with it for a moment, muttering under his breath, and then opened the lid with a single touch from his index finger.

I couldn't see what was in the box, my seat was lower than Old Bjorn's table. All I could see was a faint glow from whatever was inside. Light reflected from the open skylight. Old Bjorn pulled a silver coin out from the box, attached to a silver chain.

'This is for you Yngvild, I should probably have given it to you earlier, when we decided you were an adult, but I had hoped you'd not need it so soon.'

Old Bjorn held the silver chain by the clasps, and the coin dangled below. He held it so that the coin was in front of my eyes. I

t looked freshly minted and polished, shinier than most silver coins I'd seen. Not that I'd seen very many.

The side facing me had the standard crest of Skyss, a circle of nine circles, gold coins when painted, and crossed axes in the middle with a boat prow underneath. Usually a blue circle with coloured paint. The boat was green and the axes red. This coin had a small hole drilled where the top-most of the nine coins went.

Old Bjorn turned the coin round. The other side had the face of the Goddess Malfin. The runes Bjorn had cut round the edge read "Malfin, guide and protect your loyal servant and champion Yngvild the Fierce, Helgasdottir and Keeper of Secrets".

'It's beautiful.'

'Yngvild, before I give you this I need you to make a promise.'

'Are you laying a geas on me?'

'Yes, but not an onerous one.'

'What do you want me to promise?'

'For this amulet to protect you from harm you need

to follow the guidance and teaching of Malfin, and pray to her first amongst the Gods. Can you accept this?'

'Yes. I promise to follow the guidance and teaching of Malfin, and make prayer to her first amongst the Gods.'

'Can you keep the secrets that you will be entrusted with, and only share them when others need to know?'

'I promise to keep the secrets that I am given, and only to share them with friends that need to know.'

Old Bjorn shut the clasp on the amulet behind my neck. He held both hands over the clasp and said 'In the name of Malfin I deem you worthy of protection, and of service.'

I felt the amulet grow warm against my chest where a moment ago it had been cool. 'It's warm!'

'Aye, lass. Keep it against your skin at all times. It'll give you protection, and sometimes the goddess will speak to you directly when she needs a service done. Always listen to her. Help all those that pray to her as best you can.'

'I will, father.'

~

Just before the Mangandlese ship left another sail was spotted on the Southern horizon. Several of the crew recognised it as the King's Ship Seagull. It bore a direct course for Straven. The sailors on the Chantara seemed to step up their pace for departure when the sail was seen.

The Seagull tacked a couple of miles out of Straven to follow the Chantara. It pursued the Mangandlese ship towards Portree. The Seagull had a clear speed advantage with its extra mast and cleaner lines.

'Boat!' shouted Leif.

Eyes left the spectacle of the pursuit to search for the boat. In the wake of the Seagull a small boat was being rowed to shore. Two crew pulling oars on each side, with a steersman in the back and a woman in the prow.

'Should we launch to pick them up?' said Gunnar.

'No point. By the time we get the boat in the water and meet them they'll be more than half way here.' said Noren.

'Maybe we should get them a room and some hot food.' said Alwilda.

'and some beer.' said Arne.

'We could help them land on the beach.' said Noren.

'in a little while, dwarf. In a little while.' said Arne.

'Do you know who the woman is?' I asked Arne.

He peered a little more conspicuously at the boat. The woman in the prow wasn't rowing or steering. She had auburn hair and was wearing a pale sea green cloak over her clothes. It was too far to be sure, but she didn't look armed or armoured.

'No idea. She looks important though, maybe someone should fetch Old Bjorn.'

'I'll go.' I said, and walked back up the alley to find Old Bjorn.

When the boat reached the shore Noren and Gunnar helped the crew drag it up the beach above the tide lines. Old Bjorn had sent everyone else back to their normal duties. So there were just ten of us on the beach.

'Greetings, my lady! We were not expecting you, hence the lack of reception.' Old Bjorn bowed lower than I'd ever seen him do before.

'It is nice to see you again old man. You age well.' she said, returning the bow, although not so deeply as Old Bjorn.

'Noren. Gunnar. Why don't you take the sailors to the old hall to rest. I'll take our esteemed visitor to where we can talk.'

'Aye, captain.' Gunnar said, herding the sailors away.

A few moments passed in total silence with Bjorn and the Lady looking at each other. I watched her closely, trying to discern the relationship between her and Bjorn. They clearly knew each other, but how?

'What about her?' she said.

'She's a Keeper of Secrets.'

'How can you be sure?'

'Guess.'

'I don't have time for games.'

'You had time to come all the way here'

'but not enough to wait for the boat to turn round after it's dealt with the spies.'

'I thought that was just your usual flair for the dramatic.'

'Better than hiding out in the islands.'

'I think we're pretty much done with hiding.'

'I hope so. Are you going to introduce me, or have you not got out of the habit of keeping secrets?'

'My apologies. This is Yngvild the Fierce, Helgasdottir.' Old Bjorn pointed his open hand at me. Then he turned to me and said 'and this, my lass, is Helga Trollslayer, for whom you are named.'

Both of us stared with shock at Old Bjorn. Lady Helga spoke first.

'You old bastard. That was too low.' Lady Helga stepped forward and embraced Yngvild. 'Child, woman. I cannot believe that he'd never told you.'

'I knew my mother was Helga, and I knew his partner was Helga. So I sort of assumed that she was my mother.' I said.

'Yes, he's a devious one. I'd not trust him to tell

someone it was daylight in summertime.' Helga said.

'So is he my father?' I said.

Lady Helga laughed.

'No lass, he's not your father. Although I'll grant he's been more of one for you than anyone.' she said.

'So who is my father?'

'It's a long story Yngvild, the sort that skalds sing sagas about, but I'll tell you before I have to take my leave again. I promise.'

'What does bring you here?' Old Bjorn said.

'Things are kicking off down south. You know who is up to his old tricks again.'

'That doesn't mean you need me.'

'It's not you that I've come for. I've come to invite the children to stay with me for a bit, and to finish their education.'

'Finish their education?' I asked.

'Maybe start it, if my suspicions about what Old Bjorn has taught you are correct.' she said.

'They might not want to go.' said Old Bjorn. 'They've been getting on well up here, and Noren is going to captain the new boat.'

Lady Helga arched an eyebrow at Old Bjorn.

'Well, you should at least ask them.' he said.

'Yngvild. Would you like to come to Kronstadt with me and learn about your family history?'

'Yes, if Noren comes.'

'Let's find Noren and ask him too.'

THREE

ᚱᚠᛗᚢ ᚢᛁᚾᚷᛁᚱᛗ
THE LADY YNGVILD

We went up to the houses, and into the main hall. It was as I'd always remembered it, familiar carvings and paintings, with the marks I remembered from helping decorate it.

Yet it was now also alien and strange. No longer home.

Now that I knew Lady Helga Trollslayer was my real mother, and Old Bjorn and Helga the Red were not actually my parents. It didn't seem to matter that Bjorn and Helga the Red had loved me as their own. My whole world had been turned upside down.

Every step dragged me closer and further away at the same time. I needed Noren more than ever. At least he had always known that he was a foundling.

'I'll get Noren.' I heard myself say as we approached the alley.

I went left, into the old hall. For a moment I just stood. The old hall was more ornate, yet plainer. There were more winters of carving wood, more tales of the gods and heroes of old engraved into the panels, but the paint had faded and gilding worn away.

Noren sat talking to the sailors. They were all drinking beer. Food was on the table, cheese that I'd made from the sheep's milk. Bread, fish, some sliced lamb. The lamb I'd slaughtered after the feast because it was too skinny to make it through the winter.

Reminders were everywhere here. I needed to go.

Silently I slid up behind Noren and hugged him. Sitting down the top of his head touched my chin. I waited until he turned, and then lead him without speaking out into the alley.

'I love you Noren, and I need you to come with me to Kronstadt.' I said when we got into the alley.

Noren blinked and looked at me.

'Something's changed. What happened?'

'Come into the main hall and I'll tell you.' I lead him by the hand in the main hall.

'Noren. I brought you here as a baby.' Lady Helga was waiting for us to come in.

'Sorry. I don't remember that far back.' he said. 'Pleased to meet you again though.' Noren said.

'Noren, this is Lady Helga Trollslayer, she's my mother.' I said. 'She wants us to go to Kronstadt with her.'

'Why Kronstadt?' he asked.

'To find out about our family history.' I said. 'I need to go. I need you to come with me.'

'Can I think about it?'

'Take as long as you like, lad. Don't let the women bounce you into a decision.' said Old Bjorn.

'I've thought about it. Captain Ragnar asked me to go to Kronstadt a few weeks ago. I said no, because I wanted to be a boat captain, and I didn't want to leave Straven before it was ready for the winter.' Noren looked at me in the eyes. 'But I can see how important it is to you that we go. We've done well in the last three weeks with our preparations. If I'm good enough, then I'll have a boat to captain when we get back.'

'Get your gear together lad, and you lass. Be on the jetty as soon as you can.' Noren and I went to our rooms, to gather what we needed. Old Bjorn gathered the crew to launch the boat.

I took all my battle gear, and my spare shift. I picked out my two best ribbons and left the rest, along with my apron and smock for Birgitta to do with as she would. I made sure not to leave the shirt I'd been making for Noren, nor my winter gear. I laid it all out on the shield and then wrapped it in a spare piece of linen canvas that had been destined to be a new smock for Noren.

Out on the jetty the boat was ready. The whole crew were present, along with the sailors from the Seagull and Lady Helga.

~

The boat from Straven caught up with the Seagull and the Chantara off Portree. Noren, Old Bjorn and I transferred onto the Seagull, along with Arald, who was in chains, and we set sail for Kronstadt.

Old Bjorn passed his captaincy on to Arne for the time being and the fishing boat returned to Straven without us. The Chantara was ordered to return home, the Seagull escorted her South.

It was a four day trip to Kronstadt. I was put in a tiny cabin in the stern with Lady Helga. Noren was with the crew and Old Bjorn shared with the officers. Arald was kept in chains in a rope locker in the bows.

The Seagull had two decks above the hold. Our cabin was in the upper deck. We had windows and a couple of gratings overhead that let the air circulate when the weather wasn't heavy.

Noren and I continued our evening routine of sitting together and watching the sunset after the evening meal. We sat out of the way of the crew on the grating above the cabin that I shared with Lady Helga.

After we'd been there a while I heard Old Bjorn speaking to Lady Helga below. At first they spoke too softly to make out the words, but then they got louder.

'... just isn't ready for this.' Old Bjorn said.

'you said the same about me when I was their age.' Lady Helga said.

'and look how that went.'

'that's not what I meant, and I'd had a few years to learn before I chose to do it.'

'It isn't the same. You were brought up for it, I haven't trained them for it.'

'Why in Malfin's name not?'

'I was maintaining our cover. They got brought up to be boat captains and deal with raiders.'

'What, exactly, did you teach them?'

'Boat handling, people handling, weapons and small group tactics.'

'What about the mysteries?'

'Only what everyone knows, I didn't give them any special instruction.'

'Right. The first thing we'll need to do when we get to Kronstadt is to initiate them.'

'Ah! Maybe not.'

'They need to understand the mysteries to have a chance of survival.'

'I agree. But I've already bound Yngvild to Malfin.'

'Oh. Really?'

'She got involved in some interrogation, so--'

'--you thought it would be a good idea to shut her up to keep your secrets?'

'Helga, you always make me sound so awful.'

'That's because you are awful Old Bjorn.'

'That's not why I did it. I think she's ready to learn, and I was about to start when the Chantara turned up with your friend Arald on board.'

'That's good. What about the boy?'

'Noren is strong and very capable. But I think he will need a different approach given his lineage.'

'Right, you two! Time you cleared off the deck.' said Leif Nine-fingers, Ragnar's steersman. He'd just come up onto the rear deck where the rudder control was. The King's Ship ran three watches and was crewed day and night.

~

We arrived at Kronstadt sooner than I had expected, on the morning of the fourth day. We'd been sailing with the coast on our larboard side most of the way from Straven. The hills were green and mostly heavily wooded. As we neared settlements the woods thinned and fields and pastures appeared.

On the approach to Kronstadt the trees started to appear in blocks all the same size. They'd get progressively larger, and then there would be a bare patch. A little along from it would be some saplings. Strips lead up from the coast for about two hours before I first glimpsed Kronstadt.

I'd never been there before. Old Bjorn had told us that Kronstadt was the largest city in the world, and that you could buy anything there. I didn't believe him. Kronstadt was where fjords met. There were two main approaches to it, each guarded by stone forts that could throw flaming pitch at any ship that tried to attack.

I was on the prow all morning, because Captain Ragnar had told me it was a sight to behold. We came in on the Western Approach. A King's Ship stood out in the fjord ahead of us. As we approached it pulled down some flags, and hoisted others.

A horn sounded on the other ship, and was answered by someone on the rear deck near the steersman.

'What's going on?' I said to Snorri, one of Ragnar's Lieutenants.

'We're being challenged to make sure we are who we appear to be.' he said.

'How do they know if you've been taken over?'

'Watch and find out.'

No sooner had he said it than another set of horn blasts bounced over the water. This time from the Seagull. The off-duty sailors below deck came swarming onto the main deck. One watch lined the rail on the upside of the ship, and the other climbed into the rigging above them. In moments the deck went from almost empty to crowded with the entire crew.

When I looked over at the other ship they'd done the same, although their crew was smaller than ours. The ships passed close enough to each other to see the faces of the crew on the other ship. Many of the Seagull's crew yelled the names of people they recognised on the other vessel and cheered in response to their own names being shouted back.

'That's how we recognise each other. If we'd been boarded then we'd stay silent, or shout the wrong names.' Snorri said.

As soon as we passed the other ship the crew mostly went back down below. Only those on watch stayed on deck, or in the rigging.

The next sign of Kronstadt was the watch tower on Castle Rock, in the middle of the two fjords opposite Kronstadt. The high watch tower was visible over the horizon. A fortified keep and stone built batteries housed iron reinforced catapults, next to them stood glowing braziers.

As we approached Castle Rock the captain ordered the sails furled and the Seagull switched to oars. The crew, excluding those on the oars, came onto deck again. This time they lined the rail on both sides of the ship. I could see the smoke from the braziers on the battery, keeping the pitch warm.

'Look, on the other side' said Snorri.

I looked where he was indicating. Another battery, also with smoking braziers. The crews were closer, and I could see stacks of pottery jars next to each brazier. The crews looked relaxed, although they were stood watching us rather than lazing about.

'They put hot coals in the jars just before they release the catapults.' Snorri said.

'Isn't that dangerous?'

'Extremely. That's why they do it. Keeps the air from snuffing out the flames.'

'I see. And the jars break when they hit a boat?'

'Exactly.'

Once past the batteries I could see Kronstadt on the headland, or rather I could see part of Kronstadt. Right in front of me there was a headland, with fjord on either side. The Eastern fjord was slightly starboard of our course. The Northern fjord to our larboard, and out of view behind a hill.

Kronstadt was at the foot of a mountain that grew out of the sea. The fjord I could see was lined with stone and wooden jetties on both sides. It was longer than the entire isle of Straven. I could see several tiered rows of houses leading away from the jetties along the entire length of both sides of the fjord. At the far end of the fjord the houses continued round.

The jetties had dozens and dozens of ships, most the familiar shape of Skyssian ships, but others with unusual designs and pennants I couldn't place. I couldn't count how many, but more ships than I'd ever thought possible in one place.

We didn't land there though.

As we came to the mouth of the Northern Fjord we turned into it. A grand white stoned wharf lined part of the Eastern side of the fjord. There were fewer buildings on this side, but they were huge. A large stone built palace stood in the middle of a park. Although I hadn't see it before, I instinctively knew it was the King's official palace.

We carried on down the fjord. At the end, and down the western side, was a shipyard. I counted fourteen slipways as the Seagull rowed past. All with ships, or the skeletons of hulls in them with people hammering, sawing, and painting them.

A second grey stone jetty had two King's Ships moored against it. We tied up against it, aided by an army of dock workers hauling on ropes and with a bridge to emplace against the Seagull when we were tied up.

~

Just as the Seagull was tying up Old Bjorn appeared, dressed in his armour.

'Yngvild! Noren! Go put your battle gear on.'

'Are we in danger?' I asked.

'No lass, easier to carry that way, and we're going to escort Arald to Lady Helga's house.'

I had my bags with me. So I shirked out of my skirts and put the battle gear on. Woollen jacket, mail over my head, belted on my dagger and quiver. Then I rolled my skirt round my bag and threw it over my left shoulder onto my back.

Lady Helga came on deck, also wearing mail and with a sword at her hip. Her shield was slung over her back. Over the mail she had a sea green tabard with two blue ships. In her hands she had another sword belt. She looked around until she spotted me, and then strode over. The crew rapidly got out of her way.

'Yngvild, I have something for you.' Lady Helga held the sword flat in both hands. The scabbard was a midnight blue leather, with black enamel fittings. The sword belt was black leather, with a black enamelled clasp, on which a full moon was embedded in mother of pearl.

'That's a beautiful sword.'

'Take it, please.'

I took the sword and strapped it round my waist, over the other belts. It was still way too large. I needed to pull it in a whole foot to get it to fit.

'Thank you.' I said.

'You do know how to use a sword?'

'I've had some practice, but I'm way better with my bow.' I said.

'Sometimes you need a sword.' she said. 'That one is a family heirloom, it belonged to your father. It's yours by right.'

Lady Helga turned to the crew.

'Time we got going. People will have seen us come in.' she said.

About twenty crew were in identical battle gear. They had sea green padded jackets under their mail. The shields were sea green with the King's blue circle in the middle, surmounted by a Seagull on the wing. The blue circle had Skyss's green ship in it.

At Lady Helga's speech all but three filed down the bridge to the jetty and formed into two lines with a single crew member between them.

Lieutenant Snorri bowed to Lady Helga. 'Escort ready to proceed, my Lady.'

'Carry on, Lieutenant.' she said. Lady Helga nodded to Old Bjorn, Noren and I accompanied her onto the jetty. Behind us two crew escorted the still chained Arald. Lieutenant Snorri brought up the rear.

The procession set off with Arald in a hollow square of crew, then Lady Helga and us, and then another group of crew in the rear. Snorri was at the back.

We turned North and marched away from the Seagull. The dock area was relatively quiet. Buildings lined the edge of the jetty, just like Straven, but these weren't houses.

Each building had a large number painted in the rook gable, and underneath the runes told us what it contained. Rope, Sails, pitch, planking, spars, masts, food, beer (that one had a guard on it), mail, shields, bows, weapons, and more that I was too far away from to read.

Back down the jetty there was a steady stream of sailors moving between the warehouses and their ships. As we got past the warehouses I could see that the dock area was fenced off.

Almost as soon as we left the docks the smell of the city hit me. It replaced the salt and fish with a more powerful odour. There were a lot of people living close together in Kronstadt, and the waste wasn't as easy to get rid of. Rot, faeces and sweat assaulted my nose, and made me gag. It was like being punched in the gut, and I fought back nausea. Kronstadt might be the biggest city on the planet, but it certainly wasn't the sweetest smelling. Now I understood why the palace had such a large park surrounding it. It was to keep the stench at bay.

We went through streets, just wide enough for a couple of people to pass us as we marched three abreast. The upper stories of the houses and shops overlapped, just as our alley did in Straven. No-one walked under the upper stories though without first looking up, and then down.

It puzzled me at first, then I realised that many of the upper floors had round holes cut into the overlap. Excrement and rubbish dropped through them onto the street, which accounted for the stink.

Other than the smell, Kronstadt was much like Portree, but on a much larger scale. There were workshops and inns facing onto the street we went down. Housing above, and alleys running off to the side.

'Where are we going?' I said.

'We're taking Arald to the House of the Justices, and then we'll be going to my official residence.' Said Lady Helga.

'Is it a long way?' Noren said.

'Not far, you see the sign with the Blue Boat up ahead?' Lady Helga said.

'Yes.'

'We turn right when we get to it and the House of Justice is 100 yards down that road.'

Just ahead of us a cart filled with night-soil and rubbish started to come out of an alley. My amulet throbbed. I looked round, people with shields came running out of the alleys we'd just passed on both sides of the street.

'AMBUSH!' I yelled.

We all stopped moving.

The sailors in the rear turned to face the shieldwall that blocked the street behind us.

The sailors in front formed their own shield wall facing the cart, which now blocked the street. Arald was thrust into the middle with us. Old Bjorn grabbed him.

We all stood looking at each other. The numbers were even, but I expected help would arrive for us soon.

'Helga. Noren. Yngvild. If they try to get him away I need you to kill him.' Old Bjorn said.

I drew my new sword, we were too close in for arrows. Lady Helga had been right that I'd find it useful. I was only slightly surprised to discover that the blade was completely black, like a slice of darkness.

'That alley is empty.' Noren said.

'Too obvious. Must be a trap' said Old Bjorn.

The opposing shieldwall started taking slow paces towards us, beating on their shields.

'Let's spring that trap.' Lady Helga stepped towards the alley.

Buckets of human waste and rubbish started coming out of the upstairs windows towards us. I held my shield over my head and pushed Arald with my sword pommel into the alley to our right.

'Go! Down the alley! Go!' yelled Lady Helga.

Noren and Lady Helga went first. I pushed Arald ahead of me, Old Bjorn was behind me. I could hear Snorri shouting commands to the sailors to bring their shield walls in behind us in an orderly fashion.

'Stop! Be ready!' An unfamiliar woman's voice spoke to me inside my head. I stopped. Arald kept moving.

'Still!' I said. Noren and Lady Helga both stopped, preventing Arald from moving any further forward. I glanced back, some of the crew were coming into the alley, shields above their heads.

'You must not let Arald escape, it will spell your doom.' The woman's voice again.

Arald lunged forwards, pushing Helga into the wall. A door opened between us, I stepped towards Arald as it swung out, blocking the Alley behind me.

'Kill Arald before he escapes.' The voice said.

Hands reached for Arald from the open door.

Noren blocked another door from opening by pushing it with his shield. Helga struggled back to her feet.

I stabbed with the black blade.

There was no resistance to my blow. It went straight through the arm nearest me and sunk into the chest of my target.

Blood soaked his jacket round the blade, and gushed out of his mouth as he coughed out his last breath.

As he fell I pushed Arald off balance with my shield and thrust again at the other would-be rescuer. His beard was scraggly and he soiled himself as I stamped forward.

I pulled the blade up and hit him in the face with the guard. He went down. Others behind him ran.

'Good work, now leave here quickly.' Said the voice.

Helga grabbed Arald, 'Yngvild, with me.' she said.

We ran down the alley, pulling and pushing Arald with us. I heard Noren follow behind.

'Keep going ' he said.

'Left!' Helga said as we approached the junction.

Round the corner and we kept going. There was no sign of pursuit, nor of other people.

We broke out into another street with a stone building in front of us with guards posted.

The guards were startled by our headlong rush down the alley, with weapons drawn. But they were alert enough to draw swords and close up in front of the door. Once they saw Helga's tabard they hailed us.

'Still! Who goes?'

'Second Sea Lord, and party.' Helga said.

'Advance and be recognised.'

Helga lowered her sword and stepped forward.

'What happened?' the guard said.

'We were attacked bringing this prisoner in for questioning.' Helga pointed to Arald.

'Are you hale, lass?' the guard asked.

It took a moment to register that he was asking after me. 'I'm fine.' I said.

'Can we get the prisoner inside?' Lady Helga said.

The guard banged a rhythm on the door. In response it opened, disgorging more guards out into the street, shields and weapons ready.

'In you go, my lady.' the guard said.

We went in.

I felt surprisingly calm. The point of danger seemed to have passed for me. But Old Bjorn, Snorri and his crew were still out there.

Arald was forcibly sat on the floor by Lady Helga and Noren. I watched through the still open doors where I could see down the alley we'd come.

Guards had blocked the street out front on both sides of the door, and some had gone round to get behind the cart that had blocked our way.

A few more had gone down the alley and I could see four blocking the other paths on the junction. While we'd been waiting just inside the doors even more guards had gone out.

Where was Old Bjorn? Had Snorri and the sailors escaped, or had the attackers cut them down?

'Calm, child. They are fine. You did well, and I'm pleased.' The voice said.

'Who are you?'

'Think about it.'

I thought. Hearing voices wasn't normal. Perhaps it was a reaction to the battle? But I hadn't had it before, that's what got me nicknamed 'Yngvild the Fierce'.

My amulet throbbed. Of course.

'Clever girl. You'll make an excellent hero.'

Just then Old Bjorn came round the corner, with some sailors carrying a body. Who was it?

Not a sailor, the clothing was wrong, so an attacker. More sailors followed. I counted them. Snorri appeared at the back. No casualties for us.

~

It took a while to finish up at the House of Justice. We counted heads, and then handed the prisoners over to a King's Justice in person. Or rather we had them taken into custody. The attackers had lost three people. One dead, one knocked out, and a third grabbed by the Guards as she tried to leave the building the dead man was in.

'I think we're done here. Let's go.' said Lady Helga.

'I need to stay and clear up a couple of things.' said

Old Bjorn.

'Will it be safe?' I asked.

'Not for anyone that tries to attack us.' said Noren.

'That's not what I meant.' I said.

'News will have got round about the ambush. The guards and everyone nearby knows your name. They know me too.' said Lady Helga.

'On you go. I'll catch you up later.' said Old Bjorn.

Noren, Helga and I walked to her official residence. As predicted it was uneventful. We went in the back door, because it was closer. As soon as we were inside people descended on us.

Friendly people.

Lady Helga's household. She introduced us, but there were too many and I forgot who most of them were. Except Linhildr. She was a little older and plumper than me, with long blonde pigtails and green eyes. She wore a blue skirt with a red body over her heavily embroidered shift. She was clearly keen on needlework, all of her clothes were well decorated, with ships, flowers, birds, waves, and other patterns.

Linhildr looked after me. She took me upstairs to a room with a stone fireplace in one wall, and a large bed with curtains round it. There were two chests against the wall on either side of the bed and also a cupboard next to the chimney breast. There was a shuttered window on the wall opposite the door. The walls were wood panelling, decorated with carvings of ancient sea battles and the saga tales of trolls, elves, and dragons.

'This will be your room while you are staying here, my lady.' Linhildr said.

'Yngvild will do.' I said.

Linhildr smiled. 'Let's get you out of that filthy battle gear and dressed properly.'

I'd left my shield downstairs, so I took my helmet off. It was only when I saw the visor, browned with blood, that I realised how fearsome I must look. I stared at it in disbelief for a moment before Linhildr gently took it from me and set it aside on the long low bench that ran the length of the room under the window.

I unbuckled the sword belt and put it on the bed. I'd need to clean that too. Linhildr took my skirt and bag that had been slung over my back. She wrinkled her nose. It was encrusted with rubbish, and I guess it smelt like the streets. Somehow my nose had filtered it all out.

When I pulled the mail over my head it left a litter of fragments on the floor. Bits of things that had been thrown at us had stuck between the links. Linhildr helped me shake it out, but it would still need a good brush to clean it.

'Don't move.' said Linhildr. 'I'll get a brush.'

She opened one of the chests and pulled out a brush, which she then used to clean off my padded jacket.

'You can take it off now.'

'Thank you.' A wave of tiredness suddenly washed over me. I dropped the jacket on the floor. Then I let myself fall into the bed.

Linhildr stacked my jacket and mail on the bench with the helmet. She also moved the sword there.

Linhildr shook my shoulder gently.

'Wake up, my lady. It's too early for bed.'

'mm tired. Sleep.'

She shook me a little more.

'Sorry.' I shook my head in an attempt to wake myself up.

'Nothing to be sorry about, my lady.' she helped me back to my feet.

The floor was clean, and some clothes were laid out. Not my clothes. I had nothing but what I wore, a spare shift and hose, and the skirt I'd slung over my back.

'Hands up, please.'

I lifted my hands.

Linhildr threw a red silk skirt over my head. It rustled down and she fastened it around my waist. Then she picked up a matching bodice made from the same cloth and helped me put it on.

'Time for a bath I think.' she said.

'That would be fantastic.'

I followed Linhildr back down to the basement. She brought a fresh shift and a bag with her.

In the basement a large wooden tub filled with water sat in the middle of a steam filled room. Slatted wood benches on two of the walls, with pegs above to hang our clothes on. I couldn't see the fire, maybe it was next door. Two young women were tending the tub when we entered.

'This is Aelfdis and Sigrun, my lady. They will help you bathe.' Linhildr said.

'Thank you.' I said.

The women were both about my age and dressed in shifts with rolled up sleeves, underskirts with bare feet and armed with soap, cloths and brushes. It was hot and steamy in the bath room. I was glad to get out of my clothes and into the bath.

'My lady, your necklace.' Sigrun pointed to my amulet.

'It's fine, I never take it off.' Old Bjorn had told me to keep it next to my skin to ensure protection by Malfin. I didn't feel safe enough yet to want to remove it.

The water was fragranced and Sigrun took a brush and soap to my back. Then she undid my braids. Aelfdis brought jugs of warm water and poured them over me while Sigrun washed my hair.

The bath invigorated me, and I felt clean again. While I'd been getting washed Linhildr had been getting ready to dress me. This was beyond my experience. Back in Straven I bathed and dressed myself, usually in company with others, but not like this. Here I was being washed and dressed by other people.

Linhildr put a new shift on me. Not my spare one, it was softer material and much more ornately decorated round the wider square neck-line and sleeves, as well as along the bottom hem where no-one would see it but me. The red silk skirt and bodice went back on, but not before I was squeezed into a boned under-bodice. I also had a heavily pleated underskirt made of linen. It weighed more than my old woollen skirt. These two garments changed my shape. My waist was smaller, and my hips much wider. It also pushed me up and created cleavage on my chest.

Dressing wasn't done yet though. Sigrun and Aelfdis combed and braided my hair, weaving red ribbons into the plaits. Linhildr placed some jewellery on me. First there was a double line of pearls, which sat tight enough to feel around my throat. Then Linhildr put rings on two fingers of each hand. She looked forlorn when she felt my ears.

'You haven't had them pierced?'

'Should I have?'

'You could have worn the earrings to match the necklace.' Linhildr held up a large teardrop pearl dangling from a silver wire hook for me to see.

'Maybe another time.'

She put the earring back in the box she'd taken it from and pulled out a wide ribboned necklace, with silver filigree along the edges of the dark blue ribbon, and a heavy egg shaped pendant with a sword enamelled on it.

'This shows you wield the legendary sword,

Jafnadr.' Linhildr held the ribbon reverently above me.

I bowed my head to make it easier for her to place the ribbon over my head and rest it on my shoulders. She straightened it in a couple of places, and pinned through the ribbon on both shoulders to make sure that it wouldn't move.

'Now, you are ready.' Linhildr said.

'Ready for what?' I said.

'Dinner.'

'Do you need to get ready too?'

'No, I'm not eating with you.'

'Do people here always get dressed like this for dinner?'

'No. Tonight is a special occasion. Other nights are probably more what you are used to.'

~

I was the last of our little group to be ready for dinner. The building was bigger than I had expected. Linhildr lead me from the basement, along a corridor, past the stairs we'd used on the way in. Lady Helga was dressed in a sea green dress embroidered with two ships, the same as her shield. White lace made waves under the ships. She had blue ribbons tied in bows holding back her auburn hair.

Old Bjorn was all in black, in an unfamiliar plush fabric. His hose were tight around his legs and the tunic came to mid thigh. It was edged and embroidered in black.

Noren was still in his green tunic with blue hose, although it looked like he'd been well washed and shaved. I guessed they didn't have spare clothes to fit him. His eyes widened and his jaw fell open when he saw me. I hoped he liked what he saw.

'You scrub up well, lass.' said Old Bjorn.

'You're beautiful, Yngvild.' Noren recovered the power of speech.

'You do look good dear, but we need to go in now.' said Lady Helga. 'Noren. Take Yngvild's left arm and follow me. Bjorn, you bring up the rear.'

Lady Helga lead us through some doors into a paved courtyard. We crossed diagonally and through another set of doors into a polished stone hallway. A pair of imposingly large polished wood doors were flanked by armed guards in blue livery. Each armed with a long, spiked axe.

As we approached they stiffened up and the doors opened inwards. Ahead was a blue carpet leading to a table laden with food that sat across the hall. Chairs were arranged around one side of the table and at both ends. None were occupied. Men and women stood behind six of the chairs at the furthest point from the door we'd come in. To our left was a roped off area. Noren and I followed Lady Helga.

Her pace slowed down as we went through the door. I glanced up, the ceiling was painted like the summer sky at one end, fading to winter night at the other. Images of the Gods were superimposed on the skyscape. I was so overawed that I stopped walking. Noren pulled me on.

Lady Helga stopped three seats short of the larger central chair. She turned to face us.

'Noren, you sit there.' she indicated the seat two from the central chair. 'Yngvild, you sit on the other side of Noren from me.'

I was next to the main chair.

'Stand behind the chairs until you get the signal to sit.' she said.

Old Bjorn stood behind the chair on the other side of Lady Helga.

I wondered why, in her official residence, that Lady Helga wasn't sitting in the main chair. More people came in and stood behind the other seats, although none behind the central one.

Other people came in and stood in the roped off area. None quite as well dressed as the people at the table, but still mostly better than I was used to.

Next people came in with plates of food and started setting them down on the table. The aromas reminded me that I was famished. Lots of plates, more than the people stood round the table could have eaten. In front of me was a chicken, a plate of fish fried in breadcrumbs, some boiled eggs, carrots, cabbage and peas. In front of the centre seat a whole roast animal was set steaming on a couple of trestles in front of the table. A drip tray set under it to catch the juices.

Two high pitched horns sounded in tandem. The people in the roped off area all swivelled to watch the door. Four armoured men with blue shields and shining helmets came in and stood either side of the carpeted walkway, revealing an average height man with plaited white hair and beard. He wore a blue tunic with nine gold coins sewn onto it and gold and silver threads picking out the rest of the Skyssian crest. A plain gold circlet was held onto his head by the plaits in his hair.

King Thirfinn walked round the table and took the centre seat. Four more of his King's Guard had followed him in. Six stood between the table and the roped off area. The other two stood one behind each of the King's shoulders.

'They're waiting for you to sit next.' the guard behind me whispered.

I pulled the chair out and sat down. Everyone else followed suit.

'We had not expected the new bearer of Jafnadr to be quite so young and so beautiful.' King Thirfinn looked me in the eye as he spoke.

Jafnadr? I looked back at the King and saw mischief in his eyes. He was playing with me.

'I'm glad to have exceeded expectations, your majesty.' I smiled back.

'Tell me, how long have you had the famed sword Jafnadr?' he said.

Not me. Someone else. He's playing with someone else.

'I believe it's been mine for a while.' I didn't think it was worth telling people that I'd got it about ten minutes before I got off the boat this morning.

'Indeed it has. We hear that you use it well. Our enemies should tremble.'

'They don't call me Yngvild the Fierce for nothing!'

The King laughed, and it rippled across the room.

~

After we'd finished eating, an orderly queue formed on the carpet. The guards kept them from approaching until the remaining food was cleared onto tables at the back of the hall. Some of the spectators started on the food while it was still being moved.

The first to approach was the Mangandlese Ambassador. I recognised his allegiance from his shaved head, clothing and complexion. He was tall like the crew members of the Chantara. His clothes were a little more ornate than those worn by their captain, but then everyone here was more ornate than I'd ever seen anywhere else.

'Your Majesty.' he bowed deeply 'May I beg your indulgences to ask for the release of a prisoner.' he said.

The King nodded at him and indicated for the Mangandlese to continue.

'I have had a message from Bo Thu Myat of the Mangandlese ship Chantara. One of his paying passengers was taken from the Chantara by the crew of the Seagull. I am lead to believe that he is being held here since the Seagull arrived earlier today.'

'We see. Do you know on what basis this passenger was taken?' said the King.

'I am given to understand that the captain of the Seagull believed the passenger had not been authorised by the Board of Trade.'

'Your petition has been heard.'

'Thank you, your majesty. Can we also suggest that the passenger is given parole to live in the Mangandlese Embassy pending his return home.'

'If he will give it, and if the reason was as you suggest then we may feel that might be appropriate.' the King said.

The tall Mangandlese bowed low. When he came back up he looked at me and smiled before taking two steps backwards. On reaching the pair of King's Guard he turned and strode from the room.

The next petitioner wanted permission to appeal against the Board of Trade denying her a licence to trade with Cottalem in iron and timber. Three others followed, an inheritance dispute over a merchant ship, a request for clemency on a convicted criminal and a contractual dispute between the steersmen of a merchant company. None of these petitions were explained in any detail, the petitioner simply stated what they wanted and handed over a paper to the King's Clerk, who stood just to the left of the petitioners. The petitioners were all well dressed, but there were others in just to finish off our food, they'd eaten ravenously all the way through the petitioning. They weren't well dressed at all.

'Are there any more petitions for His Majesty!' the King's Guard said.

The room looked like all the well-dressed petitioners had left.

'Begging your pardons, mister. I got one.' A woman with an unbleached grey, or perhaps very grubby white apron, over her homespun skirt and bodice stepped forward. Her eyes were bloodshot, and there were bruises on her sunken cheeked face. Her hair was red, and braided well. The ends were tied off with scraps of cloth. Her skirt and jacket were patched in places and hung unflatteringly from her bony frame. She'd missed too many meals, no doubt why she'd taken the opportunity here to eat her fill.

'Approach.' The King's Guard said.

She wiped her hands on the apron, stood up a little straighter, and approached slowly, like a frightened child. Her eyes darted about with each step. Silence descended on the hall. Everyone seemed to be watching and waiting for what she had to say. Poor people petitioning the King couldn't be an every day occurrence.

She stopped where all the others had stopped. I saw her eyes widen as she looked at me.

'Meniaxter protect me.' She spoke so quietly I doubt none but the King and I heard.

She fell on her knees. 'Your Majesty.'

'Rise, child, and speak to us.' The King said.

She pushed herself up onto her feet. Her eyes still on the floor.

'Your Majesty. My husband was killed today. I come to ask for blood payment from the killer.' She looked up directly at me, tears rolling over her cheeks and dripping off her jaw onto the floor. 'You killed my Leif! He wasn't even armed!' she pointed at me.

I felt sick. I hadn't wanted to kill him, the sword just slipped through his arm into his chest when I'd thrust. Now his widow was screaming at me for justice in front of the King.

The King turned to me. 'Did you use Jafnadr in the fight this afternoon?'

'Yes, your majesty.' I bit my lip. 'I killed him with Jafnadr.'

A gasp went round the room. The King turned back to the widow.

'You heard it from the Lady Yngvild's lips. Jafnadr killed your husband.' The King said.

She wailed, hugged herself and fell forward onto the floor.

I was confused. I'd just admitted killing a man, which seemed to shock many of those present, and it made me uncomfortable. Yet the sword was taking the blame, and that somehow increased the widow's grief so much that she collapsed.

A moment passed with everyone simply staring at the widow. Then she regained her composure enough and started to get back up. She was quite unsteady, and leaned forward to use the table for support. Fortunately it was a wide and heavy table. She pulled herself up with both hands opposite me, her breath was laboured and heaved with silent sobs. She leant there and muttered something else about Meniaxter. One of the King's Guard started to come over to escort her away.

'Stop your curse, woman.' Old Bjorn said, 'It won't work.'

She looked at him while carrying on with her muttering. She fumbled under her clothing. My amulet felt warm against my chest.

Old Bjorn stood.

The King's Guard leapt at her.

She threw a handful of dust at me.

I sneezed violently, closing my eyes.

I heard a thud as the King's Guard hit the widow, followed by splintering, clattering of metal against stone and the crash of breaking crockery.

I opened my eyes and the world sped back up again. The King's Guards were closing the doors, the two behind the King were hurrying him out of the hall by a back door. Old Bjorn and Lady Helga were on their feet. Noren was getting up too.

I pushed my chair back and brushed down my clothes. I couldn't tell if the dust had made it onto me. On the floor the King's Guard that had leapt onto the widow was getting back up. She did not.

FOUR

ᛗᛩᛋᛏᛗᚱᛁᛗᛋ
THE MYSTERIES

Lady Helga took Noren and I back to our quarters. Old Bjorn stayed behind to help question people.

'What just happened?' Noren said.

'Someone tried to kill Yngvild.' she said.

'Why? Was it revenge for Leif?' I said.

'No. It's more complicated than that.' she said.

'Please explain it to us.' Noren said.

'Maybe in the morning.' she said.

'I think we need to know tonight.' Noren said.

'It might be best to wait until Old Bjorn joins us, he'll be better able to explain.'

'Can you please start the explanation, and Old Bjorn can fill in any gaps?' said Noren.

Lady Helga kept on walking.

'You did promise to tell me about my heritage.' I said.

'Very well then. But only a bit tonight.' she said.

Linhildr was banking the fire in the room when we got there. The shutters were closed and the drapes on the bed were pulled to on three of the four sides. My clothes had been put away, and the mail had been polished while I was at dinner. Someone had also touched up some of the paint scratches on my shield.

'Linhildr, can you please leave us.' Lady Helga said.

Linhildr nodded, 'would you like anything brought up?' she said.

'No, thank you.' Lady Helga said.

Linhildr left the room, closing the door behind her.

Noren and I sat on the bench, and Lady Helga faced us from the sole chair in the room. Instinctively I cuddled into him. I needed all the familiarity that I could find tonight.

'So. What do you know about heroes?' Lady Helga said.

'They do interesting things and get sagas sung about their exploits?' I said.

'Heroes are born, not made.' said Noren. 'They're descended from the Nine.'

'That's fairly accurate, Noren. Although some heroes come from other gods than our Nine.' said Lady Helga.

'What's that got to do with us?' I said.

'I think Lady Helga is trying to tell you that you are one of those heroes, Yngvild.' said Noren.

'Not just Yngvild, Noren.'

'We're descended from the Gods?' I said.

'Yes. Your father was descended from Fafnir, the god of Justice. That's one of the reasons why you can wield Jafnadr, the sword of Justice.'

'There are other reasons?' Noren said.

'Yes. I'm a great granddaughter of Malfin. Jafnadr was blessed by Malfin, which is why the blade is dark.'

'Couldn't you have wielded Jafnadr?' Noren said.

'No. It can only be wielded by heroes with the blood of both Malfin and Fafnir in them.' she said.

'Who am I descended from?' Noren asked.

'On your father's side Meniaxter. On your mother's side Fafnir and Jorunn.'

'The widow called on Meniaxter to protect her.' I said.

'Well he does cover both war and death.' said Noren.

'I'd thought it was just because she was recently

bereaved,' I said. 'but she must have known she was going to attack me.'

'We'll probably never know for sure.' said Noren.

'What does this mean, and why would it lead to someone trying to kill Yngvild?' said Noren.

'Good question. I think Old Bjorn would be a better person to answer it.' said Lady Helga.

'Have a go, please.' I said, my mind was whirling.

'The first, and most obvious thing, is that you are both heroes. That means a lot is expected from you. People will want to make friends and influence you. Others will want you out of the way.'

'Why would they want us out of the way?'

'Heroes destabilise things. They achieve extraordinary things and defy the odds. For some people, that can be bad for business.'

'Enough to kill someone before they've done anything?'

'But you have done some extraordinary things already Yngvild.'

'Like what?'

'You used Jafnadr in combat, and you defied that curse to live.'

'How are those extraordinary?'

'Jafnadr can only be wielded by someone descended from both Malfin and Fafnir. You are the only person currently alive that can use it, as far as I know.' Lady Helga said. 'There's more to it though. Jafnadr is a legendary sword. It was forged for Fafnir by Frijdodr from star steel. Malfin blessed it and gave it to their granddaughter Jafnadr when she came of age. The blessings from both mean that it cannot injure an innocent. Yet it will cut through any armour as if it wasn't there on an evil-doer.'

'But the widow was correct, her husband wasn't armed. I hadn't intended to kill him.'

'The sword is sentient, it helps those able to wield

it, and hinders the unworthy. If your opponent has evil intent then Jafnadr will ensure they receive justice.'

'Is that why the King said Jafnadr killed him?' said Noren.

'Yes. It's seen as a divine judgement directly from Fafnir. There's no blood price when the gods decide you should die.'

'Is there more that I should know about Jafnadr?'

'I don't know the full extent of its abilities, but Oddmundr used to tell me that she was self-cleaning, and that sometimes she talked to him.'

'Oddmundr?' I said.

'Your father. The last wielder of Jafnadr. We spent a decade together, although I could never work out whether or not he was serious about the sword talking to him.'

'It does. It talks to you, I mean.'

'Jafnadr has talked to you?' Lady Helga said.

'Yes, although I thought it was Malfin because it was a female voice.'

'What did it say?' Noren said.

'She gave me some warnings, and she told me to kill Arald.' I said. 'she said that if I let him escape it would spell my doom.'

'That's what Old Bjorn said about him too.' said Noren.

'Do you think Jafnadr heard?' I said.

'As I understand it, Jafnadr has a way of understanding people's intentions and motivation that's similar to how the King's Justices tell the guilty from the innocent.' Lady Helga said.

'Should we do something about it now?' I said. 'The Mangandlese Ambassador petitioned for him to be released.'

'Don't worry, the process isn't that fast. Someone will look into all the petitions tomorrow and a King's

Justice will be asked to make decisions.' Lady Helga stifled a yawn. 'Time for bed.' She stood and made her way out of the room.

I yawned too, and felt a sudden wave of lethargy overtake me.

'Noren, bed.' I said.

~

I didn't sleep well. My dreams were riven by the faces of the man I killed, his widow, and Arald. Familiar people would turn round when I talked to them and they'd have the wrong face on. I'd turn to run and the widow would be screaming at me, before she was squashed like a bug.

Every now and then I'd almost wake up, and be comforted by Noren cradling me. When I did finally wake up I realised that we were both fully clothed on top of the bed. We must have been too tired to climb inside.

I left Noren to his slumber, he murmured something, I doubted that his dreams had been any better than mine.

I couldn't take the bodice off on my own, it was laced up the back, but I rummaged through the chests for some plainer clothes. I was careful to be quiet so as not to wake either Noren nor Linhildr, who was sleeping on the bench wrapped in a blanket. The silk looked fabulous, but not something that I could wear every day.

I found my clothes neatly folded in the chest that Jafnadr sat on. My shield hung on the wall above it, with the padded jacket next to it on a peg.

The mail was also in the chest. I took off the silk skirt, but kept on the silk hose. I thought I might try to keep the silk hose and the city shoes while I was here. They wouldn't be much use in the countryside, but they were very comfortable indoors. I pulled on my woollen skirt and put my jacket over the silk bodice to protect it.

The fire had been well banked up last night, but it would need attention soon if it wasn't to go out. I settled for opening the curtains, it would be too warm for the fire before long.

I was up early, the sun was up, but the shadows were still long. The window gave me a view of the fjord, and the park I'd seen on the way in. At a guess we were in a side building next to the main palace.

The road outside was paved with stone, and free of rubbish, unlike the streets we'd brought Arald up yesterday.

The air was fresher too. I could smell the flowers from the gardens. These weren't the wild flowers that grew on Straven, or even medicinal herbs. Someone had deliberately planted several beds with flowers, and co-ordinated them by colour. I needed to go take a look at them.

Linhildr woke while I was still contemplating the flowers.

'My lady. Did you sleep well?' she said.

'A few unpleasant dreams, but well enough.' I said. 'How about you?'

'Well, thank you.' she shook out the blanket and folded it. 'Would you like anything to eat or drink?'

'I think I'll be fine for a bit, but could you please help me out of this bodice?' I shrugged the jacket off my shoulders so that Linhildr could get to the lacing.

'Of course, I should have helped you last night.'

I took several deep breaths when the bodice was unlaced, I'd not breathed freely since it went on yesterday evening.

'Are you well my lady?'

'I'm much better now that I can breathe.'

'They take a little getting used to, and best not worn overnight, my lady.'

'Do you need me to help with anything?' I asked.

'No. No. No. My lady. It is my role to serve you.'

'Oh. At home in Straven I look after myself, and sometimes the little ones. Mainly the sheep though. I herd them up the hill for grass and heather, and collect their milk to make cheese. I also choose the ones we're going to eat, and slaughter them myself.'

'I'm sure those skills will come in useful for you when you leave here, my lady, but until then it's my job to look after you.' Linhildr opened the closet next to the fire.

There were several items of clothing hung in there, most of them red. 'Lady Helga prepared some less formal clothing for you, some of it might need adjusting for size.'

The closet had three shifts, all plain and the brightest white I'd seen. Two were linen, and had relatively modest lines, they came below the knee and covered my bosom. The third was silk, and went just below my hips. On top it was square cut, unlike the t-shape of the linen ones.

'You might like to wear that one when you want Noren to pay you more attention, my lady.'

'Noren's very preoccupied, I usually need to climb on top of him before he pays me that sort of attention.'

'There are many fish in the sea, my lady.'

There were also a couple of linen underskirts, with cartridge pleating to make them broader, and two identical woollen skirts made from a very finely woven twill. One of the skirts was green, and the other red.

There were matching hose, some in green and some in red, with spare pairs. For my top there was a red bodice in the same wool as the skirt, and two panels for behind the lacing, one in red, the other in green.

In the bottom of the closet were thick winter boots, which came to just below the knee. There were also another pair of shoes, similar to the ones I'd arrived in, but of a better quality. To round out the outfits there was also a set of man's clothing, in my size but not my usual red.

'Why is there men's clothing too?'

'Lady Helga thought that there might be times when you wouldn't necessarily want people to know who you were.'

Just for the fun of it I decided to try on the male clothes. They looked slightly too large when I held them up against my body.

'Before you put the tunic on, we need to do some other things first, my lady.' Linhildr pulled two scarves out of the closet, one thin silk one in black, and a thicker patterned woollen one.

'What are those for? It isn't cold outside.'

'You'll have noticed that men and women are different shapes, my lady?'

'Yes, some can be very pleasing on the eye.' I looked over at Noren's sleeping form, giggled and blushed.

Linhildr smiled. 'These scarves are for altering your shape a little. There are some other adjustments built into the clothes.'

Linhildr wound the silk scarf around my breasts and tied them so that they were separated and flattened a little. The other scarf went round my waist and was pinned with a brooch. I watched in the mirror as she worked.

'Now for your jacket.'

I put my arms into the sleeves of the black jacket. It wasn't a style worn in Straven, but several of the men I'd seen yesterday had been wearing similar ones. This one was slightly older and worn in places, with some concealed repairs.

Linhildr fastened all the buttons. In the mirror my shape had changed. It was nothing like Noren's, but I had wider shoulders than hips, and my waist looked much fatter.

'You need to do something about my hair.'

'There's a plan for that too. I'll need to take the braids out and redo them to look more like the men.'

Linhildr sat me in the chair and undid my braids. She then did them to be collar length like the warriors have. I had a mass of braid on top of my head.

'You need to keep the hat on, my lady.' Linhildr put a woollen hat on my head.

Old Bjorn opened the door. Took a look at me, at the bed and then at Linhildr. I saw her nod to me in the mirror.

'Hello, young man, I don't believe we've met?' Old Bjorn grinned.

'Well met, old man. What news?' I said.

'It's a good disguise, keep it on, and bring Jafnadr with you.'

'Won't Jafnadr attract the wrong sort of attention?'

'Not if you ask her to look inconspicuous.'

'Will that work?'

'Why don't you try it and see.'

Old Bjorn woke Noren up and told him we needed to go out very soon. I buckled Jafnadr round my waist, the padding helped the sword belt fit better.

I put my hand on the pommel. *'Can you try and look ordinary please?'*

'Ordinary! Why would you want an ordinary sword?'

'I'm trying to blend in.'

'I'll see what I can do.'

I couldn't tell any difference in the mirror, I'd just need to trust Jafnadr.

~

Old Bjorn hurried us out of the house. When Noren

complained about not having had breakfast Bjorn took us through the kitchen to grab something to eat on the go. I ended up with an apple, some cheese and some bread.

I'd put my helmet on over the large woollen hat, after detaching the face plate. I was now Old Bjorn's guard, as was Noren. My new name was Ingwald.

'Where are we going?' Noren said.

'We're following a lead from last night. Down in the docks.'

'Did the widow have an accomplice then?' I said.

'Yes. She was too scared to come in on her own, and the people that sent her didn't trust her enough to let her come unescorted. The chap was supposed to leave before she kicked off, but she needed more persuasion than expected.'

'What sort of persuasion?' I said.

'She had children, and a sister. They promised to help them if she did what they asked.'

'Won't they have cleared off by now?' Noren said.

'Not quite yet. They'll have known something was up when their folk failed to return. Some of the contact people will be hiding for a bit. But I've found out who organised it.' said Old Bjorn.

'Shouldn't we get some help?' I said.

'It will take too long to organise, and by then they will have slipped away. Also it's more complicated than you might expect.'

'Can the three of us deal with it safely?' Noren said.

'Yes. We have the element of surprise, and the people we will be visiting have some rules to keep to.'

We had almost crossed the park area towards the main port. Old Bjorn pointed out the alley we needed.

'We're going to go straight through. Don't stop for

anything, and try not to kill anyone.' Old Bjorn raised an eyebrow at me as he said the last part.

We passed into the alley and there were few people around at the inland end. I could see some down the far end. We turned left at the first junction, then right, then another two rights until we were back where we'd first turned off.

Old Bjorn took us into the passage on the left and then broke into a run. Noren and I chased him, and we ran back round to the left at the next two junctions. Old Bjorn slowed to a walk just before we reached that junction and calmly took a right.

'Do you hear anyone following us?' he said.

'No.' I turned round and looked behind us. 'I don't recognise anyone either.'

'Good. Never hurts to take precautions though. No rush to die.' he said.

'Not even when we're your age, Old Bjorn' Noren said, finishing the familiar rejoinder.

A fast but wary walk took us to the sea front. The people here came from all parts of the world. They were tall, short, dark, pale, lean, meaty and in all colours of hair and skin. Most of the ships were recognisably Skyssian, but I saw several that I recognised as Mangandlese and a few other types I couldn't place.

'This is the place.' Old Bjorn said.

We stopped.

'Are you sure? This is the local office of the Board of Trade.' Noren said.

'Absolutely sure. They've been rather naughty.' Old Bjorn said.

'It looks closed.' I said.

'I expect it is, they don't open to the merchants until later. Let's go in.' Old Bjorn marched up to the closed door and banged his fist on it. 'Open up!'

The door opened. 'We're closed now, come back in an hour.' said a clerk.

Before the clerk could close the door Old Bjorn had pushed him inside. Noren followed, I was close on his heels.

'King's business, don't go anywhere.' Old Bjorn said.

I closed the door behind me and put my hand on the pommel of Jafnadr.

'Who is in charge?' Old Bjorn said.

'No one, I'm in here on my own.' the clerk said.

'He's lying. There are two others here, upstairs.'

'Two more upstairs.' I said.

'You, with me.' Old Bjorn said looking at me. He then turned to Noren. 'Tie the prisoner so he doesn't escape. A King's Justice can get the truth from him.'

Old Bjorn lead the way up the stairs. We went slowly and quietly. I could hear some talking upstairs, a man and a woman.

'...a Justice will have the story out of them in no time. We need to be scarce before they're questioned.' a woman said.

We were almost at the top of the stairs. Old Bjorn motioned for me to stay quiet.

'Relax. There are at least two levels of cut-out that they'll need to interrogate before they come near us.' a man said.

'I'm worried they'll do it quickly because the King was there.' the woman said.

'They need to find out who the escort was tasked by, and then they need to catch him and find out about Gunnar. Gunnar is on a ship already.' he said.

'It can't sail for another two hours, and if they decide to search the outgoing ships...' she said.

'We do the searching when that happens. So Gunnar won't be found.'

Old Bjorn nodded to me and then stepped round the corner at the top of the stairs.

'I wouldn't rely on that.' Old Bjorn said as I followed him.

The man dropped the ledger he'd picked up and went for a sword in the rack behind him. I drew Jafnadr.

'Don't be foolish. I'm a King's Justice.'

'I'll come quietly' the woman said. 'Finnvald, put the sword down.'

Finnvald turned, the sword held point down. 'They will pin it all on us.' he said.

'Of course, but you're already in crown service, and it isn't a death matter.' she said.

'Good choice. In the name of the King I command you to drop the weapon.' Old Bjorn said.

The sword clunked on the floorboards.

'No danger. They're bound to crown service already. Guilty as anything, but no danger.'

I returned Jafnadr to her scabbard, but kept my hand on the pommel.

'Tell me what was going on.' Old Bjorn said.

'We were under orders to delay the new heroes from leaving Kronstadt.' the woman said.

'Who gave the orders?'

'I cannot say, even under compulsion.' she said.

'Truth. Even I cannot tell.'

'Did you order the curse?'

'No. The agent extemporised. We couldn't have ordered anything like that knowing the King might be present.' she said.

'What's in the ledger?'

'Nothing of importance.'

'Impressive. A lie that could fool a Justice. But pointless when we can look for ourselves.'

'Shall we have a look?' Old Bjorn said.

'No! No!' she shook her head vigourously while

speaking, 'That won't be necessary.'

'Interesting. Strong involuntary compulsion. Someone tried to tie you up tightly. There aren't many with that level of power.' Old Bjorn said. 'I think I know exactly who gave your orders.'

We took the ledger and the prisoners back through the city to the House of Justice. This time there was no ambush.

~

It was lunchtime before we got back to the house. I'd been right about it being a side building of the palace. I also got to walk through the park again and smell the flowers. The disguise worked. As long as I didn't talk much, no-one figured me for a woman.

The first thing we did was find Lady Helga. She was in her office attending to matters as Second Sea Lord.

'The B--. Sorry. Radulfr is up to his tricks again. He's trying to stop us going anywhere.' Old Bjorn said.

'Well we weren't planning on going anywhere for a bit anyway. So what's the problem.' Lady Helga said.

'I'd forgotten how blasted annoying he is.'

'He's annoying, but also predictable. He's still making the same old mistakes.'

'Did you sort out Arald?'

'No.'

'What do you mean no?'

'I didn't have to. Someone else got there first.'

'I was sure they'd want him back alive.'

'I think they probably did. He was poisoned with angelfish eggs. At the right dose it makes someone appear dead.' Lady Helga said.

'They got the dose wrong?' Old Bjorn said.

'I think so. I put the body under guard and have

arranged for a funeral tomorrow.'

'How sure are you that he's dead?'

'Not completely, that's why I put the body under guard.'

'Why would they fake his death when the Mangandlese Ambassador has petitioned to have him released?' Noren said.

'Hm. Good question, Noren.' Lady Helga said.

'There's more than one actor at play here.' Old Bjorn said. 'We've got the Mangandlese who were carrying him. There's the Cottalem connection too, I'm pretty sure that's who Arald is working for. They're usually quite subtle. Angelfish eggs would be right up their street.'

'What about the people we visited this morning?' I asked.

'They're involved too.' Old Bjorn said.

'One of the other petitions was a chap that wanted to take steel to Cottalem.' Noren said.

'That's no coincidence. There's trouble brewing in Cottalem.' Lady Helga said.

'What sort of trouble?' Noren said.

'War, death, destruction and slavery.' Old Bjorn said. 'There's been a power struggle and the new ruler is consolidating his position before having a go at expansion.'

'It's a terrible situation, which is bad for business. So the Board of Trade is stopping people taking arms to Cottalem.' Lady Helga said.

'How far away is Cottalem?' Noren said.

'Probably two thousand miles. Over two weeks by boat if the wind is favourable, or several weeks by land, once you're on the correct continent.' Lady Helga said.

'Why are they getting involved here then?' Noren said.

'Most of the world's trade runs through Skyssian hands at some point. We have more merchant ships than anyone else. If you want something a Skyssian can deliver it. We pride ourselves on that.' Lady Helga said.

'So why try to kill Yngvild?' Noren said.

'I'm not sure that they were specifically after Yngvild, she was just in the way. Also, it wasn't them that made the attempt.' Old Bjorn said.

I saw him exchange a look with Lady Helga. She shrugged slightly.

'Noren, the new leader of Cottalem is your father.' Old Bjorn said.

Noren's eyebrows rose and his eyes widened. 'My father?'

'Yes.' Old Bjorn said. 'Your father.'

'Wouldn't he be a Hero too?' Noren said.

'He is, but not all Heroes are good.' Lady Helga said. 'He started out fine, but he got arrogant about his abilities. He thought people should serve and worship him, rather than him serving them.'

'With power come responsibility. He only wants the power.' Old Bjorn said.

'Why haven't you told me this before?'

'I wanted you to grow up before I burdened you with the legacy of your heritage.' Old Bjorn said. 'You are your own man, and you don't have the flaws he does.'

'Thank you for telling me now. Does this mean that we're going to Cottalem to stop him?'

Lady Helga and Old Bjorn looked at each other.

'He's more perceptive than even I'd thought, Helga.'

'That's his mother's influence.' she said.

'Not yet, Noren. There are other things we need to do first.' Old Bjorn said.

'Like what?'

'You need some initiation in the mysteries and training to use your abilities. You also need equipment suitable for a hero.'

~

Noren needed initiated into the mysteries, but Old Bjorn reckoned that he needed protection from Jorunn rather than Malfin. Jorunn specialised in the Lost and Found. As a hero foundling Noren fit that perfectly, and he was already channelling those powers through his perceptive questions.

After a very informal dinner Noren and I had our usual alone time.

'You know that neither Old Bjorn nor Lady Helga can initiate me into Jorunn's mysteries.' he said.

'It had crossed my mind. I'm sure they know someone that can?'

'That's not how it works. I have a talent for this sort of thing. Jorunn deals with the Lost and Found.'

'Like us both. We were lost by our parents, and found by others.'

'Sort of. I think that I need to find someone to initiate me.'

'How are you going to do that?'

'I'm going to need to go out and look for what has been Lost.'

'Have you spoken to Old Bjorn about it?'

'Not yet. I thought I'd ask you to come with me first.'

'Do you have anywhere in mind to look?'

'My first thought was to go look in the city and see where the temples to Jorunn were. They say you can find anything that you want in Kronstadt...'

'You have some second thoughts?'

'I had a dream. The same dream more than once. It might be best to go find my mother, if she is still alive.'

'I noticed that they've not named either of your parents.'

'Me too. I think that's significant. Will you come with me to see Old Bjorn?'

I stood up and pulled at his hand. 'Let's go.'

'Now?'

'No time like the present. He'll be in his room or in Helga's study.'

'Let's start with the study, it's closer.'

The study was the largest collection of books and papers I'd ever seen, but up until I'd arrived here I'd thought Old Bjorn's seven books made him a scholar. The room had two walls filled with shelves of papers or books. A table sat in the middle, about Noren's height on the King side and about two thirds of that on the shorter sides. One of the walls had a window with a long bench underneath, just like my room, and the last wall had a fireplace and the door.

Old Bjorn stood over a large sheet of paper on the table, weighed down by some books and a candlestick. I recognised it as a navigation chart when I got closer, but I didn't recognise the sea area. He was tracing distances with dividers.

'Where is that?' I said.

'Oh, it's you. It's the sea route between here, Mangandlay and Cottalem. I'm trying to work out how long ago all this was set in train.'

'I don't think we need to worry about that right now.' said Noren.

'What do you think that we should be worrying about Noren?' Old Bjorn said.

'How to find my mother.'

'I don't think she will get involved.'

'I'm certain that she will help. She's the one I need to find to learn the mysteries of Jorunn.'

'There's merit to that. It might be worth visiting her. But she's been living as a recluse since before you were born. I'm not sure where she is.'

'If I'm right then I think I can find her. I'll need some help, will you come with me?'

'I'll help you get closer, but she might not want to see me. It might rekindle painful memories.'

'Painful memories?'

'I was around during a bad time in her life. I gave her some advice, which turned out to be wrong. It's partly why she lives as a recluse. But it's not my place to share that with you. It's up to her.'

'What can you tell me about her?'

'Her name is Alfarinn. She's descended from both Jorunn and Fafnir. It's an unusual combination, because Jorunn has an element of mischief, whereas Fafnir is about Justice and Equality. She was always good about finding the lost souls and setting them back on the right path.'

'Where did you last see her?'

'Here. In this very room. It was just before she disappeared into the forests. A devotee of Jorunn that wishes to be lost can disappear easily.' Old Bjorn said. 'About a year after I last saw her a priestess of Fafnir brought me Noren and asked that I looked after him.'

'Did the priestess say where Alfarinn was?'

'She didn't even tell me who your parents were. All I was told was that you were of divine blood and that Fafnir needed me to look after you. For years I thought you might be a demi-god directly descended from Fafnir.'

'What made you think that?'

'You, Noren. You have a charisma that draws people to love you. You learn rapidly, you're unusually tall and strong and even without initiation or training you can manifest divine abilities. That's more than most heroes manage after a decade of training and experience.'

'Wow! No wonder I love you so much Noren.' I said.

He blushed at that and squeezed my hand.

'I hadn't realised. I mean I knew I was stronger, taller and likeable. But I didn't realise that it was so unusual.'

'You wouldn't. It's normal for you, and we deliberately kept the pair of you away from civilisation. It was necessary.'

'Why?' I said.

'Because one day we'd need to defeat Noren's father, and there aren't many heroes powerful enough to do that. In fact there really aren't that many heroes. Not Skyssian ones at any rate.'

'How many do you think there are?'

'Skyssian Heroes?' Old Bjorn said. 'Maybe a couple of dozen still living. We last a while, but we don't breed new ones often. You two are probably the youngest, and the next ones to you are maybe twenty-five to thirty years older.'

'How old are you?' I asked.

'He's four or more generations older than us.' Noren said.

'It's politic not to ask old people their age. If they want you to know then they'll tell you.' Old Bjorn smiled at us.

'So how do we find your mother then?'

'She's in a round leaved forest. Somewhere warmer than here, but only a little. We'll need to get a ship, and then go overland.'

'The Board of Trade have proscribed us for travelling. So it might be tricky.' Old Bjorn said.

'We also need to have a better idea where the ship needs to go.' I said.

'Let me look at the chart.' Noren moved round the table and studied the chart. Kronstadt was near the top of the sheet. He looked at it for a moment and then closed his eyes. He waved his hands slowly over the map. After he'd covered it all he opened them again.

'What sort of trees grow here?' he pointed at a large island just South West of Kronstadt on the chart.

'That's Grunwald. It's the southern most part of Skyss. Some of the forests are deciduous.'

'Let's start there.'

'Fine. But you need new clothes and armour that fits. We also need to find a ship that will take us there.' Old Bjorn said.

'How soon can we leave?' Noren said.

'Two or three days.'

~

While Noren was getting fitted for clothes and mail Old Bjorn took me for some tuition in the mysteries of Malfin and Fafnir, both of which he knew something of. We used Lady Helga's study.

'The thing to remember is that almost anyone can call on any god for assistance. What determines if you get that assistance is how devoted you are to that god, and whether or not you have divine blood in you.' Old Bjorn said.

'Does being a hero make it work better?'

'Your divine blood gives you personally some of the abilities of the god that you are descended from. It gets weaker with each generation.'

'So my parents are more powerful than me?'

'Generally yes. But you get the average of your parents. So if one is a demi-god and the other a normal human than you'd have half the demi-god's powers, but way more than your other parent.'

'I see.'

'There's three kinds of abilities. There are rituals,

which anyone with belief can do.'

'Like the curse the widow tried to use?'

'Exactly like that. '

'What's the second type?' I said.

'Words of power. Some of the most devout followers can use these to cause effects. It needs a strong level of belief, or heroic levels of divine blood, to carry off.'

'How does that work?'

'Remember the geas I put on the raider captain?'

'Yes. You bound him into crown service.'

'That's a common example. The compulsion to act or speak that King's Justices use are also words of power. So is your amulet, we bound it to protect you, and it works because it can draw divine power from you, and from Malfin.'

'Is that why it sometimes feels cold or warm?'

'Yes. It's either drawing energy in to feed some kind of effect, or its absorbing energy to protect you from someone else's attempts to use an ability on you.'

'and the third type?'

'That's divine intervention. For the areas that you have divine blood then you can achieve almost anything that you can clearly imagine as an effect.'

'So if I wanted to know if you were telling the truth all I have to do is think about it?'

'That's not the best example, because King's Justices can do that, and they aren't all Heroes. What you and I can do though is more powerful than an ordinary King's Justice.'

'Like what?'

'Say you wished it was darker at night. You might consider some cloud covering the moon, or maybe a fire dying down. If you thought it the right way then it could happen. If you are powerful enough.'

'I could stop the light seeping under the door?'

'Maybe.'

'Can I try it?'

'Of course.'

I closed the shutters on the window, and the door. It was bright outside, so there was still just enough light to see by. I concentrated on it being dark in here.

Too dark to see my hand in front of my face.

Make it darker!

No apparent change.

I closed my eyes and concentrated on the dark.

Make it darker!

I opened my eyes, still concentrating on it being dark. It was pitch black.

'Well done. Now make it light again.'

I stood up, and realised that I really couldn't see at all.

'without opening the shutters or door.' Old Bjorn said.

I stopped thinking about it being dark.

That didn't work.

Make it light!

Nothing.

Silly me. No power over light, power over darkness.

Make it less dark!

The room slowly brightened.

'That was interesting' I said 'I had to say the right thing in my head to make it work.'

'You need to practise to get used to what you can do and to stretch your limits a bit.'

'What can Lady Helga do?'

'Her main ability is with Kari, she can take a ship out in any weather and the wind and the sea will usually be good for where she wants to go.'

'I thought that she was descended from Malfin?'

'She is, but as a great granddaughter. She's the granddaughter of Kari. So those abilities are much stronger. You will have them in some measure too.'

'But I thought I was mainly Malfin and Fafnir?'

'You are those more than Kari, you get Malfin from both parents, which makes it stronger.'

'Do I have any other divine blood in me?'

'Your lineage is as mixed as Noren's. As I told you yesterday, new heroes are rare. Most come from older heroes having children together.'

'So what have I got?'

'Let me find the book. Your family tree, and Noren's, are listed in The Book of Heroes.' Old Bjorn said. 'It's on the shelf here somewhere.'

'There's a book of heroes?'

'Of course. Everyone with at least one eighth divine blood has their lineage recorded.'

Old Bjorn pulled a large black bound and well worn ledger from the bottom of a stack of rolled paper on the lowest shelf.

'Here it is.'

He put the book onto the table, it thumped. The Book of Heroes was a thick volume hand bound with string. The covers were stiffened leather that had blackened with age. The leaves inside were irregular and the colours varied from almost white to a mustard yellow.

Old Bjorn opened the book.

'How old is the book?'

'Some of the pages are ancient, older than anyone can remember. The covers are about four hundred years old, that's when it became a book rather than a collection of papers.' Old Bjorn turned to the middle of the book.

'So people have been recording the line of heroes for a long time?'

'Yes. It's been going on for a while. New pages get

added every time we find out about a new hero.' Old Bjorn flicked through the pages looking for Noren.

'Couldn't someone remove pages if they wanted to hide their abilities?'

'There are several copies of the book. It would be difficult to do.' Old Bjorn said. 'Ah. Here we are. Noren, son of Alfarinn and Rojden.'

'I've never actually looked this up before. I knew them both well enough, but one doesn't pry more than is strictly necessary. Alfarinn is practically a demi-god. Both of her parents were, and she's older than I am. Rojden is the grandson of Meniaxter, and his mother was also a grandchild of Meniaxter, although with a completely different human lineage. It sort of explains why he was able to do what he did.' Old Bjorn said.

'What does that mean for Noren?' I said.

'Noren is his own man, he seems to have the closest affinity to Jorunn, so he takes more after his mother than his father. But I wouldn't want to cross him in a rage, he'd be truly terrible.'

'I can't imagine him in a rage. He's the most in control of his emotions and feelings that I've ever seen.'

'I agree, I don't think he has ever had a tantrum, not even as a small child. He's remarkable.'

~

The night before we were going to set off Linhildr told me that Lady Helga wanted to see me in her office.

'Yngvild, My daughter.' she said when I arrived at her office. 'sit down.'

I sat in the chair, and took the drink she offered me.

'You asked to see me?'

'I did. I wanted to tell you some things and give you a small gift before you leave.'

'You're not coming with us?'

'Nothing would make me happier right now than to come with you. But my duty lies here in Kronstadt. I'm the youngest Second Sea Lord in living memory, at First Sun of the new year I will become the First Sea Lord, and an Elector of Skyss.'

'So you're tied to your desk.'

'Apart from short journeys or official business I need to stay in the capital. But I can help you from here if you can get me messages.'

'It's not the same as having you with us. I've enjoyed my time here, and getting to know you.'

'When you come back I want you to stay with me again.'

'I'd like that.'

'I have another gift for you. I made it myself.' Lady Helga opened a drawer in her desk and took out a green velvet bag. She untied the drawstring and opened it up before tipping the contents onto the palm of her left hand.

'This ring is a duplicate of my own, in silver. When you need me touch it to your amulet and think of the message that you want me to have.'

I held out my left hand for Lady Helga to put the ring on my finger. She slipped it onto my middle finger. It was a silver band with waves embossed all the way round. In the centre was a slightly larger oval with a ship superimposed on the waves.

'Thank you. It's very you. With the waves and the ship.'

'It's also an amulet, from Kari. It might help you have a smoother voyage. You have some of her blood in your veins too.'

'I hadn't realised that. Although it makes sense when my mother is a Sea Lord.' I said. 'I also didn't know that you were a silversmith.'

'I'm not a silversmith, it's the last part of your divine heritage from me. I'm a great, great granddaughter of Frijdodr, which lets me channel a little of her creativity. I find it hard, so it may not work at all for you.'

'So from you I have a little of Frijdodr, some of Malfin and more of Kari?'

'Yes. You get some Malfin and some Fafnir from your father. You probably have more of Malfin than of anything else.'

'Can you tell me about him please?'

'About Oddmundr?'

'Yes. I'd like to know what he was like.'

'I first met him when I was about your age. A fresh young woman just learning about her abilities. The Board of Trade had assigned him as my mentor. He--'

'The Board of Trade? Why were they involved?'

'We were both special agents for the Board of Trade, with a roving brief to solve problems before they developed into something larger. The Board likes peace and stability for the most part.'

'Oddmundr was fairly tall, not quite as tall as Noren, but only a couple of inches shorter. He was a good bit older than me, and way more experienced in the ways of the world. That's why they assigned me to him. Between us we had a good range of abilities. I could get us into places faster than most sea transport, and I could delay others trying to follow us. He could winkle out truth and we could both hide ourselves well when we had to. We were an ideal team.

He was to me what Noren is to you. I loved him from the beginning and never looked that way at another man. We spent almost ten years together chasing down troublemakers and setting them back on the right path where we could.

He was always reluctant to wield Jafnadr. He'd do it when necessary, but he'd rather talk sense into people than hit them. It worked most of the time. Especially when people knew who he was. Jafnadr is famous, and not just in Skyss. People in other lands that worship other gods know about Jafnadr. They know you can't hope to stand against its wielder and live. Oddmundr traded on that, and stopped a lot of deaths. That's a big part of why I loved him. He cared about people, not just the big shots, but the little people too.'

'He should probably have been a devotee of Jorunn like Noren wants to be.' I said.

'He was. You can be a devotee of any of the gods, and Oddmundr chose Jorunn because it made sense for what we did, and because he cared about people.'

'What did my father look like?'

'The whole time I knew him he looked like he was in his early twenties, and he must have been at least forty the day I met him. His eyes changed colour with his abilities. When he was channelling Jorunn they were green, they went almost black when he used Malfin's abilities, and an unnatural purplely violet with Fafnir's abilities. Most of the rest of the time they were clear blue with little flecks of hazel round the iris.'

'Is that usual for heroes? Changing eye colours?' I asked.

'Not that I know of, although Oddmundr wasn't the only one with similar effects.'

'Noren said that the gods can control exactly what they look like, and that we might be able to change our appearances too.' I said.

'It's an interesting theory. I'd ask Old Bjorn, he'd know if anyone does.'

'How old is Old Bjorn?'

'I have no idea. Heroes age much more slowly than normal humans. We hit adulthood just as fast, but stay looking in our twenties for decades. How old do I look to you?'

'If I didn't know that you had to be at least twenty five years older than me, I'd say you were about four or five years older.'

'Old Bjorn has looked old for as long as I've known him. None of the people I met knew him as a young man.'

'What about Captain Ragnar of the Seagull. He said he'd worked with Ragnar as a boy before Ragnar had retired.'

'Not even Ragnar. He remembers Old Bjorn as an older middle aged man, with some white in his hair but still mostly fair.'

'Doesn't that help?'

'No. Ragnar is a hero too, and maybe in his sixties, or perhaps older. We last a long time.' Lady Helga looked wistfully at a picture on her wall. 'unless something bad happens.'

I saw her gaze move to the picture of a young man on the wall. He was wearing mail and a King's Justice surcoat.

'Is that Oddmundr?' I said.

'Yes. He sat for that portrait just before I gave birth. He'd just become a King's Justice, it took ages to happen formally because he could already do more than the normal ones because of his heritage.'

'So what happened to him?'

'He went out to deal with a problem that another hero had failed to resolve. Radulfr was a senior field agent in those days, and put too many restrictions on his teams. Oddmundr was sent in to provide independent oversight, and to fix whatever wasn't working. He thought it was a case of conflicting priorities and mistaken advice amongst friendlies. It turned out rather different.'

'How different was it?'

'The witnesses were confused. Radulfr had put a geas on them all to accept geasa from their superiors. This was stupid at best, but Radulfr told the inquiry that he'd thought that all of their seniors would be bound by the usual crown service geas that prevented from them acting against the interests of the crown. It turned out that assumption was false.'

'So no-one knows exactly what happened then?' I said.

'I'm not saying that, I think that Radulfr had a pretty good idea, and maybe the people that ran the inquiry did too. Also the other hero involved certainly knows exactly what happened. But none of them have been inclined to share.'

'What did happen?'

'My beautiful Oddmundr was stabbed in the back while asleep, and then they cut his head off.' Lady Helga wept.

I moved closer and hugged Lady Helga. My mother. I held her as tight as I could while she cried. It wasn't long.

'Even Heroes can't fight against that. He came home pickled in Brandy, and I was passed Jafnadr to hold, along with his other possessions, against the day that someone else would come along to wield it.'

I had a flash of inspiration. Jafnadr was sentient, and she had been there. She could share what happened. I wasn't going to ask now, nor did I want to raise my mother's hopes. But maybe I could find out what had happened to my father and ensure that Justice took its course, however long it might have been delayed...

FIVE

ᛋᛏᛟᚱᛗᛉ ᛋᛗᚠᛋ
STORMY SEAS

We packed all our gear and left Lady Helga's official residence just before it got dark. I left the silks and the larger skirts behind. I did take the male clothing and the green skirt to wear under my old one.

Kronstadt never quite seemed to sleep completely, even in late summer when the nights came back. There were still people moving around when we were leaving.

'They'll know we've left. But that's not the point. We need to confuse them about where we're going.' Old Bjorn said.

'That's no problem, because I don't think we know where we're going.' I said.

'I know where we need to go. I've dreamt it more than once.' Noren said.

'I have a plan. Follow me.' Old Bjorn said.

We walked due East across the front of the Palace, heading for the road inland to Heimdall. We made no effort to hide or disguise where we were going.

When we got to the road we turned North and followed it into the woods a mile or so from the city. Twilight came as we left the city, and I concentrated on being able to see clearly and also about how dark it was under the trees.

We disappeared to any watchers into the dark forest. About fifty yards in we turned East again and skirted along just inside the edge of the forest round the city. The gates of Kronstadt were still open, and we could see the fires the sentries had lit.

'See that guard tower, with the brazier on the roof?' Old Bjorn indicated with his hand.

'Yes.' we both said.

'There's a door in the corner of the tower against the wall. We can get back in there.' Old Bjorn said.

'Won't we be seen crossing the field?' Noren said.

'I'll keep it dark enough.' I said.

We set off in a straight line using the sentry's brazier as our navigation point. The ground was close cropped grass and was easy to walk over. I could see like it was daylight. Noren kept stumbling against me, and held my shoulder to keep on course.

As we approached the tower Noren kicked a stone which bounced and clattered loudly against the wall. I froze.

The sentry leaned over the wall. He looked straight at me. I could see his eyes trying to focus and his eyebrows squinting together as he stared at me.

The guard called out 'Who goes there?'

I stood frozen to the spot. None of us answered.

The guard stared.

He must have seen us.

A second guard came over and also peered over the edge.

'I heard something, there.' the guard pointed straight at us.

'I can't see anything.' the other guard said.

'Maybe we should throw a torch down?'

'You might set the grass on fire.'

'What if we go down and look?'

'You can go if you want, but we're supposed to stay here.'

They had heard, but hadn't seen us. I chanced moving carefully while the guards debated. Even though they looked straight at me they didn't raise the alarm.

Old Bjorn got to the door first. It was firmly shut.

He tried pulling the handle down further and leaning against the door. It wouldn't budge.

'I can't open it.' Old Bjorn whispered. 'Noren. I want you to think carefully about this door opening for you.'

Noren stepped up to the door and paused to look at it. Then he stretched out his right arm and pushed on the door. 'Open!'

It opened to his touch, and we went back into the city.

The inside of the tower was darker than outside, and I abandoned trying to make the area around us darker. We closed the door behind us and made our way out to the streets. Old Bjorn seemed to know the way well, and I held Noren's hand to guide him in the dark as I followed Old Bjorn. We took a zig-zag route through the city, sometimes through the middle of buildings, and sometimes in alleys. Eventually we arrived at a mostly empty warehouse on the dock front.

'Well met!' Old Bjorn said as a woman stepped into the warehouse from the front door.

'We need to hurry, the ship will be sailing on the morning tide.' she said. 'I've got the crew trimming the other cargo.'

'You haven't told them about us?' Noren said.

'That's what we agreed, not until we're at sea.' Old Bjorn said.

There were four large sea chests in the warehouse near the door. The woman opened the lids for us. 'Put your helmets and shields in the canvas bag, and then climb into a chest.' she said.

'What about me? I'll never fit.' Noren said.

The woman looked him up and down, and then looked at the chests. She grimaced.

'Take off your mail and sword and put it in the chest. You can be a new crew member.' Old Bjorn

said.

'Good idea. Let's do it.' she said.

I put my battle gear in the canvas bag, although I kept Jafnadr. My spare clothes went in the end of the chest, and Jafnadr down the long side. I lay down with my knees bent and fitted snugly into the long sea chest.

'Are you comfortable in there?' Noren said.

'Yes, be gentle though.'

'I'll carry you on myself.' Noren closed the lid.

~

It felt odd as Noren hoisted the sea chest onto his shoulders. The chest rolled, pitched and then rose back to straight and level. There was a smooth rise and fall as Noren strode. The air lightened perceptibly as we left the warehouse. It had become daylight while we were inside.

'Who's the guy with the sea chest?' a man asked.

'New guy, wants to work his passage back home. Looked useful, so I said yes.' the woman said.

'It's coming out of your share of the boat.'

'I'm fine with that.'

'That sea chest is special cargo for the owner. Let me show you were to put it.' the woman said.

Noren followed her and shortly afterwards I felt the sea chest being lowered very gently to the deck. The familiar rock of the waves let me know I was on board a ship.

'Don't move or get out until I get back.' Noren said.

A few minutes later I heard another sea chest being delivered, and a bump as it was pushed up against mine. This was followed by a clatter of shields and helmets as someone dumped the canvas sack with the battle gear in it nearby. I hoped nothing was dented or scraped. There were several pairs of feet from the noises, and the voices were all concerned with co-ordinating movement of cargo. None were familiar.

It seemed an age before Noren and the woman returned with the sea chest containing Old Bjorn. Noren opened the lid of my sea chest.

'Are you well?' he said.

'I am. Can you help me get out please?'

'Of course.' Noren put his hands round my waist and lifted me bodily from the sea chest.

'I think Old Bjorn might need some help too.' I said.

'You need to stay in here quietly until I come back.' said the woman. 'We'll be getting under way soon, and Noren needs to earn his keep.'

Old Bjorn nodded and smiled at her, before turning to me and putting a finger over his lips and pointing at me with a wink.

Noren and the woman left the cabin we'd been deposited in and closed the door behind them. Old Bjorn followed them to the door and latched it from the inside.

~

I fell asleep holding Jafnadr. I'd asked her to show me what happened to my father Oddmundr. She gave me a vivid dream.

It was winter. There was snow outside and everyone that I could see was dressed in warm thick clothing. I couldn't feel the cold, even though I was in my summer clothes. I couldn't recognise where we were, but it was not typically Skyssian, although it had to be quite far North.

'We're in Trollheim. On the other side of the mainland from Skyss.' Jafnadr said.

I knew it was her because of the voice. She'd joined me in the dream. She looked just like me, except with skin as dark as charcoal and white hair.

'I thought only Trolls lived in Trollheim.'

'There are people here too.'

'Don't trolls eat people?'

'Stories. Trolls are a sort of living rock, people aren't food to them.'

'My mother is known as Trollslayer.'

'Sometimes people and trolls fight. Especially when diplomacy goes wrong, or someone stitches up the trolls for killing a human.'

'So what are we here to see?'

'You wanted to know what happened to your father, Oddmundr.' Jafnadr said. 'Watch!'

We were out in the street, with buildings down both sides. It was twilight, either a not quite day in mid-winter, or near the end of a short day. People were moving about, but purposefully. No-one loiters outside in the depths of winter. A man came towards us, he was clad in furs and wore Jafnadr on his belt.

'There he is.' I said.

'Follow him inside.' Jafnadr said.

We went into the building I'd been standing outside. There was a lobby inside the outside door. Oddmundr closed the outer door before opening the inner one. Inside it was well lit by a fire and by candles. There were several people waiting.

'Well met!' Oddmundr raised his gloved hand in greeting to the others.

'Oddmundr! It's a pleasure. We've been looking forward to your arrival.' A tall, fair haired man stepped towards Oddmundr and swept him up in a hug.

'Rojden! One day you're going to kill someone with that hug!' Oddmundr said. 'It must be tough if you're here too.'

'Radulfr is worried that a full scale war with the trolls might break out. It seems a troll killed Magnleif.'

'Helga's tits! That's serious. You get the name of

the troll?'

'Alfarinn did, I understand she's on her way to Kronstadt with the message.' Rojden said.

'That's a bare faced lie. Rojden killed Magnleif because he wouldn't join Rojden's faction. Rojden framed a troll because he wanted to start a war.' Jafnadr said.

'Drink?' Rojden offered a horn of steaming mulled beer to Oddmundr that one of his crew had passed to him.

'Thank you.' Oddmundr took the horn and raised it. 'Your health!'

'Our health, indeed' said Rojden.

Oddmundr took a deep drink and emptied the horn in one. He brushed his mouth with the back of his glove. 'Interesting mix of spices in that, is it a Trollheim speciality?'

'Not really, it was a poison.' said Jafnadr.

'Is that what killed him?' I asked.

'No, but it stopped him from being able to defend himself, and me being able to warn him.'

'So how did he die?'

~

Old Bjorn woke me up before Jafnadr could show me any more. I was curled into a narrow bunk in a cabin onboard a ship to Grunwald again. Noren and the woman had returned to the cabin.

'I think some introductions are in order.' Old Bjorn said. 'Everyone, meet Bergliot, one of the co-owners of the Thunderbird.'

'Pleased to set you Bergliot. I'm Noren.' Noren raised his hand in greeting.

'...and I'm Ingwald, excuse the disguise. I needed to hide.' I pitched my voice as deep as I could. I doubt I fooled her, but by the time I was in my male clothing it would be enough to fool the crew. So long as I didn't talk to them much.

'Well met. I'm going to tell my co-owner about you, in the most general terms. But you need to keep the Board of Trade agent happy. I'm leaving that to you to sort out.' Bergliot said. 'You will find her finishing the cargo inventory in the hold, she will want to check this cargo soon.'

'Thanks. We'll sort that in a moment.' Old Bjorn said.

Bergliot left the cabin.

'I'd better get changed then.' I said.

'Noren, you and I should go and see the Board of Trade agent.'

As soon as they left I started changing into my male persona. Just as I was putting the doublet on there was a knock at the door.

'One moment, I'm changing.' I said.

I hastily shoved the discarded skirts under the blanket on the lower bunk as flat as I could make them.

Once they were hidden I opened the door, still barefoot. A woman stood waiting outside, she was slightly shorter than me and a few years older by the look of her. She'd filled out in places I hadn't. Her dress was mostly Skyssian blue.

'Well met. I'm Birgitta Freyasdottir, working for the Board of Trade. I understand that you came aboard just before The Thunderbird left Kronstadt?'

'Yes, that's correct.'

'Where are you going to?'

'We're on our way home.'

'Knarvik in Grunwald?'

'It's on the way. We can go overland from there.'

'How many in your party?'

'Just me and my seneschal. He just went to find you, I suppose you came here by a different way than he went.'

'He must have. Now, what are your names?'

'I'm Ingwald Oddmundrsson. My seneschal is Arne Leifsson. We're both from Brevik, a small fishing village along the coast from Knarvik.'

Birgitta took a small book out of a fold in her skirt when I started talking and wrote down the details.

'So, Ingwald, why did you join the ship at the last minute?'

'It was an early departure and I overslept. I don't sleep well on board ships and wanted to get a good night's sleep before I came on board.'

I willed her to believe me. There was more talking than I'd hoped for. My voice was my main weakness in passing for a man.

'So long as you weren't running out on a woman!'

'No, nothing of the sort. I don't have a woman in my life.'

'I'm a little surprised that a handsome young man such as yourself doesn't have a train of heartbroken maidens behind you.'

'If only...'

'Well Ingwald, in future please report to the Board of Trade agent as you come on board. It makes both our lives easier.'

'I will. Don't worry, I don't want to cause anyone trouble.'

'Enjoy your journey,' Birgitta winked at me over her shoulder as she left the cabin, 'look me up next time you're in Kronstadt.'

I hadn't thought my disguise was quite that good. But I was pleased it had worked.

Old Bjorn returned to the cabin a short while later.

'I've not been able to find the Board of Trade agent. I did hear that she was a stickler for the rules. She might not be easy to persuade.' he said.

'Don't worry, she came in just after you left. I charmed her.'

'You charmed her?' Old Bjorn raised an eyebrow.

'Yes. I told her that you and I were travelling home via Knarvik. That you were my seneschal, Arne Leifsson. I'm Ingwald Oddmundrsson.'

'Of course.' he said. 'and she was happy with that?'

'Happier than I had expected, she started flirting with me.' I said. 'It was quite a shock!'

'It would be.' he said. 'What were you thinking at the time?'

'Thinking?'

'Yes. What were you thinking?'

'I was hoping she'd see me as a man and not as a woman.'

Old Bjorn laughed.

'What's so funny?'

'You did charm her. Well done!'

'You mean she bought it because of my abilities?'

~

Noren reckoned that we wanted to go to the southern most tip of Grunwald, which was just forest. It was a long way on foot from Knarvik. So we set about persuading Bjorn to ask for us to be dropped off by boat. He was the one with the relationship with the owners of the Thunderbird.

While Noren was at that I tried an alternative tack. I went up on deck and found a place in the prow of the ship. We were sailing slightly west of south, with the Eastern coast of Grunwald off our starboard, a long smudge on the horizon. Thunderbird was quartering the south westerly wind, and we had full sail up. Although we were out in open water the sea was relatively calm.

I touched the ring my mother had given me and thought about storms over the horizon between us and Knarvik. Something a little nasty looking that would perhaps make us take shelter in a bay.

I spent most of the morning staring at the clouds on the horizon and willing them to turn into a storm. By lunchtime it looked like the cloud in the distance seemed to darken as it came to us. The waves had risen and the ship was starting to roll over them rather than just cutting through. I thought the sails slackened a little too.

Shouts from the ship's officers trimmed the sails and the ship tacked slightly West of our current course. The wind was veering.

I concentrated more on a storm front coming in. The longer I concentrated the easier it became as I could see what I'd visualised before me.

We tacked again, this time more noticeably towards the coast. It was working. Sailors began reefing sail.

The storm was coming in faster than I had expected, it seemed to be gaining speed. I didn't want it to overtake us, just divert us. So I imagined it slowing down and maintaining station to herd us into the coast.

'Excuse me, I think you should go below before that storm hits.' a sailor said.

'I will, but I'd like to watch it a little longer.' I said. Behind her I could see the crew were tying down hatches and deck cargo.

The storm didn't seem to be losing much momentum. The sea had risen even more, and the ship was climbing hills diagonally as each wave passed us. With each wave the hull creaked as the wood warped and returned to its shape. I thought about the storm slackening and passing well behind us.

The coast was closer. It had grown from a smudge into a visible line of low green hills.

'Hold tight, we're about to come about!' an officer shouted.

I braced myself in the prow and thought more

about the storm abating and blowing astern of us. The Thunderbird pitched and pivoted sharply starboard with some disturbing creaks. We were heading straight towards land. The waves were now coming from behind us, as was the wind.

More sail went on to gather speed to let us run ahead of the storm. The coast became clearer. I could see the green resolve into trees.

Flat calm. Flat calm. Flat calm.

I went astern from my place in the prow so that I could still see the storm front. Most of the crew seemed to be on watch, either lashed into the rigging or helping to keep lines trimmed on the deck. The pitching and yawing had subsided now that we were running directly ahead of the storm onto the land.

The storm front was only a few miles away. We seemed to be keeping pace with it. On the stern I found Old Bjorn with Bergliot, the Thunderbird's steersman, and the other co-owner who was the captain.

'There's a sheltered bay just North of the course we're on, and rocks to the South.' Old Bjorn said. 'We should put in there until it blows over.'

'I've never seen one like this come on so fast in the summer!' said the steersman, adjusting the rudder to take us slightly to the North.

I willed the storm to abate and let us get to safety.

'Yes, it's unusual. Didn't your lookout spot any odd weather earlier?'

'He did, but I thought we'd be able to make it round the point before turning away from it.' Bergliot said. 'It seemed to accelerate after we spotted it.'

'It happens sometimes. Best we pray to Kari for our salvation.'

With that a loud splintering sound rent the air. The main mast tore free of its mounting and sagged. The rigging kept it from falling, but several sailors lashed to it dangled in free air, kicking and flailing for holds to get them to safety.

'Bring the sails in!' Shouted the captain.

'Oars! Get the oars out!' Bergliot shouted.

Now the storm was catching us up. Losing the mast robbed us of the speed we'd needed.

Above the sailors on the rigging hauled the sails up and lashed them to the masts. Those on the main mast simply cut the sail loose and climbed down before the rigging gave way.

Sailors on the deck tied off the lines they were trimming and went below.

Make it calm! Make it calm!

The storm front would be on us in minutes. The ship was pitching with the waves again. We'd sat atop them when the sail was up. Now they were washing against the stern and water was being thrown over the gunwales before washing back over the side.

Old Bjorn grabbed me and passed a rope through my belt. He passed it through his own and then tied both ends round a substantial looking railing.

'Hold tight, it's going to get very rough!' he shouted.

I could barely hear him, the storm had got loud. Waves were crashing into the ship, which was creaking in response, and the wind shrieked, flapping the main sail. Looking back the steersman had been joined by another sailor. They were both tied onto the ship, and leaning hard on the rudder to keep the ship on course.

The ship lurched suddenly, and I came off the deck, before slamming back into it. While I was in the air I saw the oars come out of the water. It wasn't as fast as the sail had been, but we were moving. The time between each wave crashing got slightly longer. Rain started falling onto the deck, big heaving drops, easily distinguishable from the spray by the size and regularity of their impacts.

The Thunderbird got closer to the shore, although it was hard to make out the detail through the mist and rain. The wind and waves made it hard to hear anything else. I just kept on willing it to be calm. Old Bjorn shook me to attract my attention.

He gestured rather than spoke, waving his hand to the right, and then flattening the palm down. I couldn't quite work out what he was trying to tell me. The ship leant slightly to the right as it turned, and then it yawed alarmingly left, a large wave crashed over the side of the ship, submerging me and Old Bjorn. It took all my effort to hold onto the railing, I was feet down still in contact with the deck. We weren't going to make it.

The wave washed down the other side of the ship and I scrambled to brace my feet onto the railing. I was going to need to cut myself free if the ship was going down.

Then the ship righted itself. The oars sped up, and the Thunderbird leapt into the lee of a rocky headland, the next wave hitting only the stern and skewing our course slightly. In front of us the sea was calm. The headland sheltered us from both the wind and the waves.

I breathed a sigh of relief.

~

The Thunderbird beached in the middle of a semi-circular beach surrounded by cliffs, with a river cut through them. It needed repairs before it could get anywhere safely.

Some of the crew set about searching for some fresh timber to help brace the ship during repairs. Others unloaded some provisions and made a makeshift shelter. I recovered my kit from the cabin, and along with Old Bjorn we climbed down onto the beach. Noren was already down there helping the sailors secure the Thunderbird to the beach so that she wouldn't float off at high tide. He came over to join us when they were done.

'It's going to take the ship's carpenter several days to fix the Thunderbird, and even then she'll need an overhaul in a shipyard.' Old Bjorn said.

'Best we walk from here. It isn't far.' Noren said.

'I can't come with you.' Old Bjorn said.

'Why not?' I said.

'Alfarinn won't want to see me,' Old Bjorn said. 'And it's best to respect her wishes.'

'I'll miss you.' I said, hugging him.

'You'll be fine. Best get some provisions and start off immediately.' He said.

'I've already got some ship's biscuits, cheese and dried meat. I think we can probably find some fresh on the way.' Noren said.

'Farewell then.' Old Bjorn raised his hand.

'See you back in Kronstadt, at Lady Helga's.'

'Until then. Remember. No rush to die!' Old Bjorn turned away from us and climbed back into the Thunderbird.

Noren and I gathered up our kit and walked up the beach to the gap in the cliffs made by the river. The sun had come back out and we were both steaming gently as we walked. The storm had finally stopped roaring and I could smell some wild flowers as well as the sea. Birds sang in the trees. It was such a contrast to earlier. It felt like home, Noren and I walking along the beach to spend some time together, with fragrant flowers and singing birds. I felt empty inside, I'd lost it all. Would Straven still be there to go back to, and if it was, would it ever be the same again?

Noren took my hand. 'We'll have those times again, when we've found out who we are, and stopped Rojden from causing trouble in Cottalem.'

'If we stop him.'

'We will. I've seen what you can do. When I'm properly initiated I'll be able to do similar things too. Between us we will defeat Rojden.'

'I hope so.'

'That storm was you, wasn't it?'

'I hadn't expected it to be so hard to control.'

'I was surprised that we made it. That last wave should have kept the ship down.'

'It took me by surprise too, I was just concentrating on us making it to safety and the storm stopping.'

'Well it has stopped now.'

'A bit too late.'

'How did you make it happen?'

'I spent most of the morning thinking about a storm coming in from over the horizon, and forcing us to head for land.'

'You just imagined it up?'

'For about three hours.'

'No wonder it took a life of its own.'

Once we were off the beach there started to be trees. They were quite different from the ones that I was used to. Instead of green needles for leaves these had far fewer rounder leaves. They came in all sorts of varieties, some were like spear heads, others irregular waves, some were almost round. The trees were mostly bushier than the ones on Straven, they didn't have the conical shape of the pine trees. Most of them had straight trunks for nine or eight feet above the ground before their branches spread out.

'Deer.'

'Where?' I said.

'Nearby, the trees grow like this where there are deer.' Noren said.

'We might eat well at some point then.'

'We can look later. Let's get some distance in.'

'After we've changed. I'm soaked to the skin. I was

on deck when that last wave came over.'

'I'm nearly dry again, I was on the larboard oars, we didn't really get wet.'

I peeled off my sodden clothes and wrang the water out of them. Noren purposefully turned his back when I got down to my shift, but I wouldn't have minded if he'd looked. I put my other shift, skirts and bodice on, they were mostly dry having been in the battened down cabin during the storm. I put the battle gear on top, it was slightly incongruous with the skirts, but it was easier to carry it that way. Remembering what Jafnadr had said in the dream we'd shared about my father's fate I made a point of resting my bare hand on the pommel as we walked. It also helped to keep the sword from catching in my skirts. No rush to die, as Old Bjorn often said.

SIX

ᛟᚾ ᛏᛟ ᛒᛖᚱᛖᛏᚢᚨ
ON TO BERETHA

Night came on us sooner than I had expected. We'd been going South through the forest since mid-afternoon, perhaps four hours. It was relatively easy going, the trees were spread out, with very little growing on the ground, mainly ankle height blue flowers in bunches between bare loam. The deer and other wildlife seemed to have eaten all the other vegetation.

'I think we're being watched.' Noren said.

'Jafnadr isn't telling me there's any danger.'

'Maybe there isn't yet.'

'How sure are you?'

'I've been aware there are fewer animal noises, and sometimes I hear other noises off to our right rear.'

'We could change direction to look for shelter for the night.'

'Or we could break and run for a bit.'

'I vote for turning. Easier to do and solves the worry faster.'

We walked round the next large tree to the right and both jogged back to where Noren thought the follower might be. Our rush onto them was effective. A young woman broke cover and ran away from us. She had been shadowing our progress. Noren caught her by the shoulder and she stopped running.

'Hey there, be careful!' she shook her shoulder free from Noren's hand.

'Don't worry, we mean you no harm. We just

wanted to know why you were following us?' Noren said.

'Strangers aren't welcome here.' she said.

'Do you live here?' I asked.

'What business is it of yours where I live?'

'It became my business when you started spying on us.' I said.

'Leave now!' her voice became unusually deep.

Leaving seemed like a sensible option. The locals clearly weren't too friendly.

'Nice try.' Noren said. 'We're not going anywhere until we've done what we came for.'

'Who are you to defy us?'

'I'm Noren the foundling, son of Alfarinn. I'm in search of my mother. My friend is Yngvild the Fierce, Helgasdottir. Who might you be?'

'You claim to be the son of Alfarinn?'

'It is what I'm told. I seek her for certainty, and to request that she initiate me in the mysteries of Jorunn.'

'No man is allowed in the presence of Alfarinn.'

'How do you know this?' I said. 'Do you know where we can find her household?'

'I cannot tell you that until you pass the tests set by Alfarinn to prove you worthy.'

'Can you set us on the path of the tests, I am sure we can prove our worth.' Noren said.

'The first test is to work out what the tests are.'

I looked at Noren, taking my eyes off the girl, and when I looked back she had gone.

It was fully dark, but there was no cloud and the moon was up. I could see like daylight, but Noren kept crashing into the lower branches. Not a problem for me.

'Noren, why don't you sit down against the tree trunk and scrape a bare patch of earth so that we can light a small fire.'

I dropped my shield and pack on the windward side of Noren and then gathered some fallen sticks. It took three or four trips to get enough for a small fire to warm us up. I was lucky to find a dead branch that had fallen off a nearby tree.

'Might be a good idea to find some stones too.' Noren said.

I handed him a bundle of smaller twigs to use as kindling and went off to grab some stones from the stream we'd followed.

While Noren got the fire going I arranged our shields to give us a little shelter from the wind. I propped them both up with some long sticks and then draped my still damp clothes over them to dry overnight.

Noren broke some of the ship's biscuits and cut some cheese for us to eat.

'What do you think the tests are?' I asked as I settled down next to Noren.

'They will be something to show we respect Alfarinn and pose her no threat.'

'Might be worth stashing our weapons and armour somewhere safe then.'

'You probably ought to keep Jafnadr with you.'

'Maybe, but not wearing mail should show we trust that we don't need it.'

'Yes. We should do that. Also maybe we shouldn't hunt anything. Just stick to the bread and cheese until it runs out.'

'I was also thinking that the girl said Alfarinn hadn't allowed a man to enter her presence for years.'

'That might be one of the tests. Need to think about it some more.'

'What about bringing Alfarinn a present of some kind?'

'Possibly. What do you recall of Alfarinn?'

'She's the granddaughter of both Alfarinn and Jorunn.'

'So she believes in Justice and Mischief, and in the Lost and Found.'

'Is there an injustice Alfarinn has suffered?'

'That would be a test.' Noren said. 'I think I'll sleep on it though.'

'Good idea.'

I checked that the fire wasn't going to spread and banked it up with earth on the side furthest from us before I cuddled up against Noren. The loam floor was soft, and I quickly fell asleep.

We stayed in place the following morning. Noren wanted some time to think more on the tests that were mentioned, and he thought it might be useful for me to ask Jafnadr what she knew about Alfarinn. Once we'd stretched our legs and eaten some breakfast I settled against the large tree we'd slept under and laid Jafnadr across my lap.

'Jafnadr, I'd like to talk to you about Alfarinn.' I thought.

'What I know about Alfarinn is old news.' she replied.

'Old news?'

'You need to understand my limitations. I know what my wielders know, and I perceive the world through their senses.'

'So you only know what I know?' I was a little puzzled, Jafnadr had seemed more aware when I'd spoken with her before.

'Not only what you know, what every single person who has wielded me knows.' Jafnadr said. *'and when I am fully awake I can sense what those near me know, even if they do not touch me.'*

'When do you sleep?'

'I sleep when I do not have someone to wield me.'

'You mean every time I let go you fall asleep?'

'No. When my wielder dies, or gives up carrying me, then I become dormant. It takes a little while, a few weeks, and then I lose consciousness until someone else picks me up.'

'Is that what you mean about only having old news about Alfarinn?'

'Yes. You know almost nothing about her, and my last source of news was before you were born.'

'I think I understand. Please tell me what you can, it might help Noren meet her.'

'Alfarinn is one of the oldest heroes still living. She has lived nomadically for centuries. She is usually accompanied by a group of her daughters, the last I knew there were four of them. Mostly they have had mortal fathers, and Alfarinn is only ever known to have borne girls.'

'So Noren would be an exception?'

'Her only recorded son if what you have been told is true.'

'Could it be wrong?'

'Of course. We only have the word of the woman who delivered Noren to Old Bjorn that his mother was Alfarinn, and that was revealed much later as she had been under a compulsion not to tell.'

'Old Bjorn forgot to mention that.'

'Old Bjorn forgets to mention lots of things.'

'I blame his advanced age.'

'Alfarinn has a reputation for being flighty, and hard to pin down. She is also a woman of her word, and when she promises something then she always delivers. She takes a very dim view of people that do not honour their word, and even dimmer view of those that betray others.'

'So she'd see someone who betrayed her as a

personal injustice?'

'*Definitely. There were rumours that she'd gone into isolation a couple of months before Oddmundr was killed. She was reported to have been furious at just such a betrayal.*'

'*Old Bjorn mentioned that he'd given her some advice that turned out to be wrong. Do you have any idea what that might have been?*'

'*I was there when he gave it.*'

'*What was it?*'

'*Rojden's one of the good guys, you can trust him.*'

'*So does she think that Old Bjorn betrayed her?*'

'*I can't be certain until I get close to her, or someone who knows for sure why she has hidden herself away all these years.*'

~

Noren shook me gently out of my chat with Jafnadr.

'It's time for us to move on.' he said.

'Have you worked out where to?'

'I think so.'

'Will we be coming back here?'

'Best to take all our gear with us, but carry the mail.'

'We still need to look unthreatening?'

'Yes. Also we need to take a gift to Alfarinn at the place where I was born. That's where she'll see me again.'

We gathered up all our gear while we talked. It didn't take long. I was the only one with a complete change of clothes. We used some string to tie the mail over the outside of our shields. Now I understood why Old Bjorn had insisted on extra straps and rings around the inside of the shield.

When I'd been making it with him I'd complained that it just added weight. Now it was coming in very useful. The mail jangled with each step, it was pleasing.

It was another dry late summer morning. The sun dappled the forest floor through the leaves. In places there were tangles of brambles. Many of these were turning from green to red and then to an almost black. We stopped near one of the bushes to gather some for breakfast.

'Where were you born?'

'Somewhere warmer than here, and with trees.'

'That narrows it down.'

'It's like coming here. I'll know it when I see it.'

'We didn't find her here though'

'Didn't we?' Noren said. 'Where did the girl come from then?'

'One of her daughters I expect.'

'Alfarinn sent her.'

'I forgot, I haven't shared what Jafnadr told me. She lives nomadically with her daughters and their daughters. She hasn't seen a man since before you were born.'

'What else did Jafnadr tell you?'

I told Noren everything that I knew about his mother, and what had been reported by others as we walked through the forest. I was watching him more than our surroundings, so I was slightly surprised when Noren put his hand on my midriff and pushed me behind him.

'Quiet, Yngvild. Bear.' he said.

I looked out round Noren. In the middle distance a large brown furred bear was advancing through the forest.

'I don't think it's seen us.' I kept my voice low so that the sound didn't carry.

'Let's back off and go round.'

'North or South?' We'd been travelling almost due West, hoping to make Knarvik for another ship.

'North, we'll need to go that way when we hit the

coast.'

I turned round slowly so that my mail didn't jangle. As I did I became aware of another bear to our North. It was about half the distance away as the first bear. I tugged on Noren's sleeve. 'Another bear.'

He turned away from me and did a slow full circle.

'There are six bears.' he said.

'That isn't natural.'

'No. It's a test.'

I pulled the bow from where it was slung over my shoulder.

Noren put his hand on my shoulder. 'No. Let me deal with it. It's my test.'

He dropped his shield, sword, rolled blanket and food bag. He turned to face the Northern Bear, which was the closest, and stood looking at it. I watched, glancing over my shoulders every now and then to check none of the other bears were coming closer. Every time I looked back Noren seemed bigger.

The Northern Bear saw us and started to come towards us.

It's walk turned into a determined lope. The other bears had seen us too, their faces fixed in our direction, but no other bear moved.

Noren was waving his arms to attract the bear.

It was heading straight for me though.

I stood stock still and prepared to crouch and turn my back on it if it lunged so that the mail covered shield on my back would take the force of the blow.

The bear was running dead at me. If I had shot an arrow into its roaring maw and it would have come clean out of its behind.

I dropped the shield onto the ground in front of me and braced. My amulet an angry bee. Jafnadr!

Too late.

The bear leapt. Huge claws like daggers reaching

for me through treacle.

As I dropped and turned I saw Noren leap at the bear. He was huge and fast.

I curled up under the shield and dreaded the impact. I touched Jafnadr's pommel.

'You are safe, for now.'

I glanced round the shield, dreading what I'd see.

Noren was sat on top of the bear, pinning it's front legs to the ground with his hands, and preventing it from escaping by locking his thighs round it's middle. The bear wasn't taking it lightly and struggled and thrashed.

'Turn back into your own form, sister.' Noren said. *'You're no more bear than I am.'*

The bear shrieked and wriggled, but as she did so the form gradually changed back into a woman.

I looked around, the other bears were gone. There was just us and this strange shape shifting woman.

'I bear you no harm.' Noren said.

I stifled a giggle. Had he really intended that? The woman also laughed.

'This isn't a laughing matter.' he said.

'Well you shouldn't use such awful puns then.' she said.

Noren relaxed and got up.

'I believe we are siblings.' Noren offered the woman his hand to get up from the forest floor.

She took his hand and levered herself up from the ground.

'We are. You've passed the first test, but the remaining ones will be more perilous and less obvious.'

'Is there any advice or help that you can offer me?'

She laughed some more.

'Nice try brother, but you need to do this on your own.' she looked at me. 'Who are you?'

'I'm Yngvild Helgasdottir. Noren is my intended life

partner.'

'Good for you, girl. Just make sure he's worth it before you jump in too deep.'

'He's definitely worth it. All I need is for him to realise that.' I said.

'Ooh! You've got a fancy sword, girl. Know how to use it?'

'She's already used it.' Noren said.

'Respect, girl. That's what you demand from the world. Don't take no attitude from anyone. And learn to be a bear...'

'I'll bear that in mind.'

She chuckled. 'Time I was elsewhere, see you in the sun.'

The woman turned and loped off into the forest.

'That was strange.' I said.

'Very. But it gives us some clues. We're on the right track.'

'Where do we go when we get to Knarvik?'

'Somewhere south. She said she'd see us in the sun.'

'That could mean west.'

'If I might butt in, Alfinna was here long enough for me to get her name and some information. They've just moved from here and they're going south. I didn't get a place name though, just a familiar winter home.'

I thanked Jafnadr.

'South sounds good. See what other clues you get when we reach the port.'

We carried on walking.

'Did you really mean what you said to her?' Noren said.

'What do you think?'

'Do I have to answer that?'

'Only if you want it to be true.'

~

We hit Knarvik early the following morning. There was a major flaw in our planning. We had neither money nor goods to barter. We had packed the bare minimum, and up until we abandoned the Thunderbird, Old Bjorn had handled everything.

'What have we got left to eat?'

'Enough for some bread, cheese and blackberries for lunch. After that we're down to five ship's biscuits and a small bag of seal jerky.'

'Not sure I feel that hungry, yet.' I said.

Knarvik was bigger than Portree, and not the sort of place that would take in two hungry young people and feed them. In Straven we routinely fed visitors, but then we weren't exactly over run.

The port had a T shaped jetty and a harbour wall. A couple of big ships were moored at the end of the jetty and some smaller ones were loading or unloading against the shore end.

'Let's go ask at the Board of Trade if they know what ships have left recently going South.' Noren pointed at a blue painted hut where the arms of the T joined.

'That's a crazy idea, but I can't think of anything better.'

'Jafnadr, try to look inconspicuous, please.'

We walked along the sea front to the hut. Sure enough it was the Board of Trade. Noren went in first and I followed.

'Excuse me please. My mother and sisters sailed south recently, and I wanted to pass them a message.' Noren said.

The official looked up, he had grey hairs starting to appear in the light brown of his beard.

'Unless you are on official business I can't tell you anything.' he said.

'I wouldn't ask you to do something wrong. But I need to tell my mother and sisters about the impending death of my father.' Noren said.

'Well that puts a different light on it. How many people are in the party?'

'I have a lot of sisters, and some of them had their daughters with them. I'm not sure exactly how many were travelling, but you'd have noticed them. They're all beautiful and there were no men or boys with them.'

'Hang on, I think Gorm mentioned a party like that.'

'—was it about two or three days ago?'

'Gorm! Man down here needs your help.' the agent turned and yelled up the stairs behind the counter. 'One moment, he'll remember.'

Another man came down the stairs, two at a time, and crashed against the wall at the bottom. A younger man, no older than us, beardless and wearing rumpled blue clothes.

'Gorm, tell these people about the party of ladies you mentioned the other day.'

'Yes, boss.' Gorm said. 'Loads of kids, all girls, and some high born lady that stayed in her chair. One of her daughters, name of Alfinna, did all the paperwork.'

'Can you tell me what ship they got please?' Noren said.

'It was the Nordic, bound for Caratis.'

'Thank you, are there any other ships due to go that way we could get a message on?'

'The Albany at the end of the dock is going to Beretha, which is about a day's sail short. They'd be able to pass the message on via the local office there. Shouldn't be more than three or four days behind them.'

'Thanks. You've been very helpful.'

Noren and I hurried out of the office and down the jetty.

'That was very smooth' I said.

'I just sort of knew that he'd help if I gave him a good reason.'

'Impending death of your father?'

'Well, it's likely someone will try to kill him soon. He's causing too much trouble to be left alone.'

The Albany was a long sleek vessel with three square rigged masts. It was maybe half as long again as the Thunderbird but not quite as big as some of the ships I'd seen docked at Kronstadt. She wasn't fitted with oars, just sails. I guess she was too big for oars to be any use. She was tied up against the end of the jetty, with a temporary bridge set between the ship and the jetty.

Several people were moving carts down the jetty to the ship. Others were moving the contents of the carts into the cargo hold of the Albany. A beam was being used to lift and swing cargo from the jetty into the ship through a large hole in the middle of the main deck. The Albany was taller than the jetty was and there was a steep slope up the bridge.

A sailor stopped us as we approached the ship.

'Well met! Can I help you?' she said.

'I understand you are going to Beretha.' Noren said.

'That's right, sailing as soon as we've got the cargo aboard.'

'We're looking for passage to Caratis, and wondered if you could take us with you?'

'I'll need to check with the captain, it's a good ten day journey, we charge 10 siller a day per passenger. Up front.'

'Do you have any crew vacancies, we're both off the western isles fishing boats.'

'I'm pretty sure we've got a full complement.'

'Any chance you can ask the captain, please?'

The sailor shrugged and walked off up the bridge

and onto the ship.

'What are we going to do if they say no?' I said.

'We'll have to find a way of earning some money to feed ourselves and then get another ship.'

'What if Alfarinn keeps on moving and we lose the trail?'

'We'll have to find it again somehow.'

'Look! It's the captain.'

A well dressed man with lace on his coat came down the bridge and approached us. He wouldn't have looked out of place at the dinner we'd had with the King. Although he did look out of place on the jetty. He strode over to us, I bowed slightly when he closed, as did Noren.

'Well met, good captain!' Noren said.

'Well met, young man.' he said. 'I understand you want to work your passage?'

'Yes. We both grew up in the western isles and were on the boat crew. We know how to sail, row, steer and navigate.' Noren said.

'and use arms?' the captain said.

'Yes. They call me Yngvild the Fierce because I stand well in the line and hit back hard.' I said.

'I see.' the captain looked me up and down, and had a good look at my sword, like he was trying to see something that wasn't quite clearly in focus.

'Do you have any places for us?' Noren said.

'We've got a full complement of sailors. Can you show me how good you are with your weapons?'

I unslung my bow and bent it to fit the string.

'Captain, I am second to none with a bow. Name your mark and I will put an arrow in it.' I took an arrow from the quiver and knocked it.

The captain had a good look around.

'You see the weather vane on the end of the harbour wall?' he pointed out a flag like weather vane over the harbour from us, about two to three hundred yards away.

'I see it. Which part would you like me to shoot?'

'I was going to suggest seeing if you could get an arrow to go that far.' the captain said.

I raised my bow and pulled back the arrow in one smooth action, just like I'd been taught. I focused on hitting the target and let the arrow loose.

It wiggled away from me and I watched it shoot towards the weather vane. It made contact with the middle of the vane and sent it spinning around the staff. The arrow continued straight over the harbour wall and ended up in the sea beyond.

'Was that good enough?' I said.

'Passable. You can join the security team.' the captain smiled.

'What about him?'

'He can join too.'

'Are you expecting trouble?' I asked.

'It pays to be ready just in case.' the captain said. 'Go on board and report to Arne the Armsman. He'll sort you out.'

As we walked up the bridge onto the ship Noren turned to me and said 'No storms or shipwrecks. I want to get there smoothly and in one piece.'

~

The voyage to Beretha was remarkable only by its smoothness. We did the ten day trip in nine days due to some exceptionally favourable winds. Each day we did raider drills, just in case. On two occasions we saw what could have been hostile sails, but both times we outpaced them easily.

The speed of the trip resulted in a bonus for the crew, including us. We left the company at Beretha as soon as the cargo was unloaded and the crew paid. We'd added 22 siller to our purses. 1 each for the days we'd been on crew and a bonus of 4 because some of the perishable cargo was worth a lot more than expected.

Beretha was a fairly major port, slightly smaller than Kronstadt, but not by much. It straddled a very wide estuary of a major river and faced North, and was just off the Great West Road. It was a good deal warmer, even though the nights were noticeably longer than Knarvik. We were sweating in our woollen clothes under the weight of all our gear. The port was busy, people were coming and going, stalls on the ends of the pier were piled with all sort of foods and spices, many of which I'd never seen before.

'Let's find somewhere to stay for the night, and then we can get a ship lined up to take us to Caratis.' Noren said.

'Fine by me. I'm famished, can we get some food?'

'You want place to stay? I got top place to stay.' A boy tugged at my arm. 'Come with, come with. Top place.'

'How far?' I asked.

'Top place, come with.' He kept on tugging my arm.

I put my hand on Jafnadr, but she was silent.

'Why not, we've got nothing to lose.' I said.

'Right, take us.' Noren said.

We followed the boy, who looked about ten or eleven winters, through some narrow streets and down an alley full of refuse that stank of rotten food and excrement. The houses were wood and plaster, with red ceramic tiles on the roofs. The windows were all shuttered, and a number of them seem to be missing slats.

'I'm not sure it's going to be the best place.'

'As long as it's cheap, clean, and safe.' I said.

'You don't ask for much.'

The boy lead us up a flight of wooden stairs to a

landing with two doors at the top. 'Top place, you like.' He said, before opening the left hand door.

Inside a young woman sat on the bed. She stood as the door opened.

'Two? Why have you brought two?' she hit the boy with the side of her hand on the top of his head. 'You like to watch, miss?' she said, looking at me.

I think the boy made a mistake' I said 'we only wanted a bed for the night.'

'He's no use. I can get you a room though.'

'Will it be clean, and how much for the night?' I said.

'Very clean, my older sister runs a guest house, not all sailors want company when they get off the ship.'

'Does your sister do food?'

'For two of you, a room to share and dinner will be one siller, tell her Tanni sent you.' She said, then turned to the boy. 'Take them to Yanni's and tell her one siller for two, with dinner.'

'Thank you.' I said.

We followed the boy back down the stairs and round the corner to another house. This time we went in the front door from the street rather than up the back stairs. The fronts of the houses were in better repair than the backs. This house was recently painted, and there was a defined line on either side of it. It also had Yanni's Guest House painted above the door.

The boy took us in and passed the message on. We got shown a clean room only slightly larger than the bed that filled it. There was a small table on the side of the bed nearest the door, the other side of the bed was pressed against the wall. On the table was a jug of water and a basin.

'Dinner is downstairs, in the common room. Drinks extra. We stop serving when we run out of food.' Yanni told us as she showed us to the room. She took the siller from us before leaving.

We left our gear under the bed and then went down to eat. I took off my bodice and one of my skirts before we went down. It was too hot to keep them on.

~

The next day we made our way back to the docks to look for a ship to take us to Caratis. The local office of the Skyssian Board of Trade was open.

'Well met!' said the agent as we entered.

'Well met!' Noren said. 'We're looking for a ship to Caratis.'

'You'll be lucky, the locals have banned ships to Caratis.' The agent said.

'When did this happen?'

'About a week ago. There's been some sabre rattling, people are worried that Cottalem is going to invade here. So no trade.'

'That's bad for business.'

'Isn't it just. We're expecting some people to come and help us broker a deal, but no sign of their ship just yet.'

'We came incognito' I said. 'We're heroes.'

Noren looked at me with his eyebrows raised.

'Jafnadr, show yourself to him.' I thought.

'Oh! So I see. Did you need any more briefing?'

'It's always best to be briefed by the local agent, you know the place better than we do.' I said.

Behind him Noren was shaking his head at me and waving his hands for me to stop. I ignored him. *'Jafnadr, if you can give me any clues about what he's expecting that would be fantastic.'*

'Would you care to explain what you hope to achieve?' Jafnadr replied.

'I want to gain entry to Caratis, and if we can help solve the problems here, so much the better.'

'He's expecting two Board of Trade agents, but hasn't been told who they are. They're special agents from the department of resolutions. Rojden used to run that before he went off the path.'

'We're from resolutions, Radulfr sent us personally to resolve the situation. Anything you share that's helpful will be appreciated.' I said. 'But remember, this is a secret operation, and nothing is to be entered into your logs or reported. We'll handle the reporting back home.'

'I understand. I'm Erik.' He said.

'Best you don't know our names, makes it harder for anyone to get anything from you if they take you. We're expecting two more colleagues to join us.'

~

Erik briefed us on the local situation. Beretha was the main city in the Kingdom of Salicia, which was bordered to the West and South by the Kingdom of Cottalem. We already knew that Cottalem had been trying to start a war, which was why the Board of Trade had embargoed selling iron and coal to them.

The King of Salicia was an old man, and the succession wasn't certain. He'd had two sons and a daughter. Both of the sons had died in the last few years, although the elder had two young daughters. The daughter was married to a Skyssian, and the Board of Trade thought he might be a good candidate for King. The locals had a couple of other candidates in mind, including a nephew of the King and another major noble.

The previous King of Cottalem had been married to the sister of the current King of Salicia, and so the new King of Cottalem was claiming that he ought to inherit Salicia when his uncle died. This was muddied by allegations that the Salicians had been implicated in the killing of one of the princes.

The local Board of Trade agents had been busy

working out who the key protagonists were in stirring up the war. They'd narrowed it down to a couple of key people that we needed to visit and persuade them to talk it down. If we couldn't persuade them to do that then other methods were authorised to resolve the situation.

'So we're hired killers now.' Noren said.

'Not if they see sense.' I said. 'I'm not going to kill anyone just because someone else has told me to.'

'*Good girl*' Jafnadr said.

'So who is our first target then?'

'Which do you prefer, the Earl of Beretha, or the King's nephew?' I said.

'Well the nephew has a genuine claim, so the Earl needs persuading first.'

'Have you had any ideas on how we go about it?'

'Walk up to the front door of the Earl's house, ask for an audience, and then tell him to talk it down or he doesn't have a Kingdom, or an Earldom.' Noren said.

'That sounds obvious, but how do we make it work?'

'Well we get a paper from the local agents, and we tell him its an official visit, which it is.'

'What if he's busy, or away or something?'

'Well we either make an appointment and go back later, or we find out where he's gone and follow him. Eventually we'll catch up with him.'

'And when we do see him, how are we going to persuade him?'

'I thought you might be able to charm him, just like you dealt with the Board of Trade agent on the Thunderbird.'

'I can't think of anything better, so it's worth a try.' I said.

We put all our battle gear on before going downstairs from the upper floor of the Board of

Trade office that we had been offered. Erik gave us the paperwork we asked him for.

'*Jafnadr, is there any way you can hide our battle gear in the same way that you make yourself look inconspicuous?*'

'*You don't need me to do it. You should both be able to do that yourself just by concentrating on it. People see you as you want to be seen.*'

'Noren, remember you've mentioned that we ought to be able to change what we look like?' I said.

'Of course, that's how I dealt with the bear in the forest.'

'I thought I'd imagined it that you'd got larger.'

'Thanks.'

'Well, Jafnadr has just suggested that we could look unarmed if we wanted to.'

'Interesting. Did she offer any suggestions on how to do that?'

'We concentrate on how we want people to see us.'

~

It was a short walk to the large imposing residence of the Earl of Beretha, it was by far the biggest building we'd seen since we arrived, although not on the scale of the King's Palace in Kronstadt. The sand coloured stone was clean like it had been freshly cut. The whole front was covered in decorations, including gilded lilies on the tops of the facade, and a range of painted animals carved in relief in the stone. The house was set back a little from the street, and surrounded by a black iron fence with gold painted spikes on top.

The main gate was open, but two guards stood on either side of the gate posts, and a third was questioning those that arrived and checking them for weapons. A fourth could be seen inside a wooden hut just behind one of the gate posts.

'Good afternoon. What is your business?' the guard

asked.

'We're here on Skyssian official business to see the Earl.' I said.

'Do you have paperwork?'

'I do.' I pulled the credentials Erik had given me out from my skirt pocket and handed them to the guard.

The guard spent a moment examining them and then handed them back to me. 'Everything is in order. Please go in the main door.'

'That was easier than I expected.' I said.

'They didn't search us.' Noren said.

'The concealment must be working.'

'I hope that's what it is.'

'Jafnadr would warn me if it was a trap'

'Did Jafnadr warn you about the bears?'

'Oh.'

'Don't rely on being warned ahead of the trap springing. Look for the signs yourself.'

I looked about, just in case. We were on the steps leading up to the door. I checked that Jafnadr was loose in the scabbard.

Noren lead through the door, and I followed closely.

The entrance hall was empty of people. Noren stopped a couple of paces in. His left hand drifting near his pommel. I let my hand stay in contact with Jafnadr.

'We've been expecting you.' a man said from above us.

I turned to look at where the voice was coming from. A man stood on the stairs above us, hands on the rail looking down.

'Come on up, the Earl will see you soon.' he said.

We walked round to the bottom of the stairs and met the man as he came down. He was wearing a silk suit in burgundy, his fingers adorned with several gold rings set with jewels. His face was clean shaven, and his black hair cut short.

'Good day, I'm the Earl's private secretary, if you follow me I can take you to the private audience chamber.' he said.

The entrance hall was truly impressive, every inch of wall and ceiling was painted, gilded, carved or decorated in some way. Various scenes of battles on both land and sea, fairs, and a collection of family groups adorned the walls. Someone had built this room especially to impress visitors. It worked on me.

The wide staircase was made of a smooth, shiny white stone with a patterned carpet laid up the centre. It was wide enough for Noren and I to walk abreast on the carpet without touching.

At the top of the stairs we turned into a wood panelled corridor with more portraits of men on the wall. At the end the Earl's private secretary showed us into another opulently decorated room. Two gilt and red velvet high-backed benches formed part of a square with a stone fireplace and a more ornate chair. Behind the single chair was a door into another room. The walls were painted with scenes of countryside and men hunting animals.

'Please, take a seat. Help yourself to the refreshments.' the private secretary indicated a selection of jars and pottery on a tray on the low table in the middle of the square. There were several plates with a variety of foods on them.

'Thank you.' Noren said. 'Will the Earl be long?'

'Not long. He's just finishing up another issue and he'll be with you then.' the private secretary left us via the other door.

'What do you think?' I asked Noren.

'I think we should help ourselves to some refreshments and wait patiently.'

'Good idea.' I stepped into the square and took a look at the selection. There were small plates, cups, jugs with various liquids in them, I recognised none of them.

'Maybe we should just sit down, I don't know what any of these drinks are.'

Noren stopped examining the picture that faced what had to be the Earl's chair and came over. He looked at the various jugs, and sniffed a couple.

'I think a couple of them are wine, but I'm not sure.'

'Best to leave it alone then.'

The other door opened and the Earl came in, followed by his private secretary. The Earl was dressed in black silk, with black lace striped diagonally across it. He strode in and sat down in his chair. The private secretary sat on the closest corner of the bench to the Earl.

'Good day.' he said.

'Well met, your grace.' I said, bowing slightly.

'Please, sit.'

Noren and I sat down on the bench opposite the Earl.

'I'm Lady Yngvild Helgasdottir, and this is Noren Alfarinnsson. We're here on behalf of the Skyssian Board of Trade.'

'I've been expecting someone to turn up. You Skyssians poke your noses in everywhere, even when it doesn't concern you.' The Earl smiled at us.

'We like peace and prosperity, and things that threaten that concern us all.' I said.

'So what are you doing about our neighbours threatening to invade Salicia?'

'Exactly what you would expect. We've stopped selling them anything that might help them wage war, and some of my colleagues will without doubt be speaking to their King.'

'I am honoured that you have taken the time to tell me this.' The Earl said. 'I shall sleep easier in my bed tonight.'

'There is something that we think you could do to help prevent a war.'

'Here it comes. Skyssians sticking their noses in.'

'I believe our suggestion is mutually beneficial for the people of both Salicia and Skyss. Neither of us will prosper if Cottalem invades here.'

'While we might both benefit, I am sure that Skyss will benefit more than the people of Salicia.'

'You haven't heard what we're suggesting yet.'

'Unless you're suggesting that I am your preferred candidate to succeed our dear beloved King, and I do hope that succession is a long way off, then there isn't much I'm prepared to do that will help you.'

'I wasn't going to comment on the succession here in Salicia, although I did hope that you could help prevent a war by talking it down. You are one of the most influential nobles in Salicia, people listen to what you say.'

'The reality is, that the threat to invade is driven by the erroneous belief that Cottalem's King is the rightful heir to Salicia. That's the reason that we can't be reconciled easily. You'd be far better using your efforts to persuade them not to start a war.'

'I think others are doing exactly that. We've been sent here to resolve things at this end.'

'A war is not something I seek, and I'm already on record saying that. However, if you were to back me as your preferred candidate to succeed then I might be able to be more active in helping you.'

'I'd be happy to put that to Kronstadt, we can see that you are highly influential, but I can't see how you can claim to succeed to the current King.'

'That's because you don't understand the history. My claim to the throne is from the previous house that ruled Salicia. My great grandfather was usurped as King by the grandfather of the current King. His house took over by main force, my grandfather was lucky to escape alive. So I do have a legitimate claim, and many in Salicia know this. With the support of Skyss I could make it real.'

'That's very interesting, your grace. I'll be sure to report it back to Kronstadt. It may be enough to influence their thinking.'

'Thank you for your time, your grace.' Noren said. 'It has been most enlightening.'

'I shall look forward to hearing what your bosses in Kronstadt think of your report.'

~

As the Earl's private secretary walked us out of the audience with the Earl of Beretha I interrogated Jafnadr for her impressions of the meeting.

'What did you make of the Earl?' I thought.

'For a nobleman he was easy to read. He cares most about his family's position, and his primary objective is restoring them to the throne of Salicia. He'll support anyone that will help with this, and stand against anyone that threatens it.'

'That's what I got too, I didn't think he would try to help stop the war though.'

'He seemed genuine in not wanting a war, but the threat of war is definitely in his interest, as it keeps others in Salicia doubting the claim of the King of Cottalem.'

'That would explain why he wasn't too keen on talking it down.'

As soon as we were outside the gates of the Earl's house Noren spoke. 'I don't see how we could persuade someone like the Earl. He has a strong power base, feels his family was cheated out of the throne, and is totally convinced that he's right.'

'I agree. Our other alternative seems more dangerous and unhelpful than simply leaving it well alone.'

'There's no way I will be involved in killing the

Earl. It just won't help.'

'So what do we do then?'

'What we really need is to get to Cottalem to catch up with my mother. So we should work on the Earl's suggestion to carry on the persuasion there.'

'You think the Board of Trade will get us through?'

'We'll need to speak to the King's nephew first. I reckon though that if we said the best way to head it off would be to buy off the King of Cottalem they might just send us there to do it.'

'Only if there isn't already another resolutions team in there already.'

'Doesn't matter if there is or not. All we need to do is persuade the team here to help us get to Caratis. Then we can go find my mother.'

'Noren! If we can stop a war then we need to do that.'

'That's not the reason that we came here, Yngvild, and you know it. We've only got involved in this because you saw a chance of getting us through the closed border.'

'I'm sorry, Noren, I care about peace too. A war would inconvenience your mother and sisters as much as anyone else, especially as they seem to winter in this area.'

Noren stopped walking. We were on our way back to the Board of Trade residence a couple of streets back from the port. The street that we were in seemed to empty suddenly around us. My hand flew to the pommel of Jafnadr, as soon as I made contact she spoke to me

'Yngvild, it's about to get interesting. I can sense it.'

'So has Noren. Any advice?'

'Run fast, pick an alley on the right, and stay in it all the way to the sea front.'

'Noren, that alley, follow me.' I said, and then broke into a fast run immediately. I had to let Jafnadr go to get a decent speed up, but thought that would be enough to follow her advice until it seemed safe enough to stop.

Shouts came from behind us, and footsteps running in pursuit. Someone cried 'Thief!' and it was taken up from all around. A group gathered in front of us to block our way. They'd heard the cries to stop a thief and seen Noren and I running and made their own conclusions. In most circumstances this would have been exactly the right thing for them to do. However, for us it was completely wrong.

I stopped running ten feet before I got to the group.

'I'm not the thief they're crying after' I said. I could hear Noren coming to a halt right behind me.

'So why's you runnin' then?' asked the front man.

'Someone was threatening to rob us at sword point, so we ran away from him.'

'Did you start the hullabaloo?'

'Not us, must have been someone else that saw the men that tried to rob us.' I willed them to believe us and get out of the way.

'Did you see the ones that did do it?'

'Only very briefly, as soon as I saw they were coming for us I started running right away.'

'Best you keeps goin' then' the men all stood aside so that we could carry on running.

We were almost at the bottom of the alley where it opened onto the main street, when three men with shields and swords drawn stepped in to block it. I whirled to a halt while drawing Jafnadr from her scabbard. Noren drew up beside me.

'This is your only chance, surrender now or I will kill you.' said Noren.

'Come on if you think you can.' The middle ambusher said.

'Put your weapons down now.' I said.

'You don't frighten us.' the man said.

'Right then, this is the last time you threaten us.' I said. '*How guilty are these people?*'

'*I wouldn't have any qualms about them, they're Rojden's men.*' Jafnadr replied.

'Noren, we only need one alive for questioning.' I said loudly, hoping it would intimidate the men facing us.

I thought about how Old Bjorn and Arne had trained us. Usually we'd had shield and spear. You held firm while others shot arrows into the enemy. They'd either run or charge. If they ran then you'd won. If they charged you tried to take it on the shield and stab them with your spear.

We didn't have any arrows, nor shields to take the blows. There were three of them, and the alley was so narrow that they blocked it.

'*You need to get a move on, they're waiting for reinforcements.*' Jafnadr said. '*Remember that I can cut through anything.*'

'Noren. Remember Arne's advice about the best way to fight?' I hoped Noren would understand that I wanted us to fight two deep.

'Of course.' Noren stepped back and to the left.

I slid sideways as fast as I could to be in front of Noren. Then went straight into attack before the men had time to envelope us.

I could feel Noren leaning over my head and shoulders and sweeping a slashing blow at the enemy's heads. They did the predictable thing of ducking back under their shields.

I thrust my sword through the middle of the shield of the left-most enemy, and pushed the shield back with my other hand too. He fell backwards.

Noren cut into the middle enemy and pushed him physically by the shield into the third enemy, pinning both against the wall.

I pulled up Jafnadr. 'Drop them or die!'

'Quarter! Quarter!' the closer enemy yelled, his sword hitting the ground point first. There was real fear in his eyes that hadn't been there before we launched ourselves at their shield wall.

I looked at the other one, he was still struggling to move and had a determined malice on his face. I brought Jafnadr up to his eye-line, blood still dripping off the blade. 'Drop it!'

He froze. Noren lifted his colleague with one hand and threw him over his shoulder. 'I've got he prisoner we wanted, see you at the office.' Noren continued down the alleyway at a jog.

I gestured to my prisoner to follow. He looked like he was thinking about it.

'Here come his friends, kill him or leave him.' said Jafnadr.

I smashed Jafnadr's hand-guard into his face, breaking his nose and covering him with blood. I must have hit him harder than I thought, because he bounced the back of his head off the wall.

I ran after Noren and his prisoner.

~

We'd taken prisoners before, and I'd even watched Old Bjorn interrogate them, but I'd never actually interrogated anyone myself. Jafnadr made it a little easier, because he could lift some things straight out of people's heads. However I wanted to be able to get my own interpretations and hear it directly if I could. Somehow I didn't know how far to trust other people's views of the world.

The Board of Trade safe house had its own guards, and it was a sturdy property that would withstand being entered for long enough for the local authorities to intervene. So long as they weren't the people that wanted us out.

Noren sat the prisoner in a chair in an otherwise

empty room. He'd soiled himself when Noren pushed him up against his erstwhile comrade, and he'd realised that his other comrade was no longer with him. We'd removed his soiled clothing and allowed him to clean himself up as best he could with a bucket of water and a cloth. We didn't have any spare clothing for him though, so he was clad in a jerkin with a towel wrapped round his nether regions.

'What's going to happen to me? Are you going to kill me?'

'We're not going to kill you. In fact we might let you go if you answer the questions well.' I said.

'I don't want you to let me go, they'll kill me if they think I've told you anything, but they'll torture me first to find out what.'

'Well, I'll have my friends put you on a ship to somewhere else if you like.'

'That would be good.'

'Well if you help me, I'll make sure you're looked after.'

I gave him a moment to let that sink in.

'So, tell us your name and who you were working for.'

'My name is Adan, I was employed by the Duke Xaime as part of his outer guard.'

'Outer guard?'

'Duke Xaime has a personal bodyguard that protect his person. The outer guard do other things, and prevent threats to his person from becoming real.'

'So why did you and your comrades attack us?'

'We were told to detain you for questioning, it was a standing instruction from our commander to stop Skyssian agents that we didn't recognise.'

'Why did you have instructions to stop Skyssians that you didn't recognise?'

'The boss said Skyssians always poke their noses in

where they shouldn't.'

'Does your boss have a name?'

'I told you, Duke Xaime.'

'That's not helpful. I meant the one that gave you the instructions.'

'The commander of the guard is called Rojden, he made the standing instructions. The guy that told us to do it today was Llucas, he's the sergeant in charge of my section.'

'What can you tell us about Rojden?'

'He's a foreigner, but fiercely dedicated to ensuring Duke Xaime is the one that succeeds to the throne.'

'Is he here, in Beretha?'

'No. He hardly ever comes here in person.'

'When was the last time you saw him?'

'I've never seen him.'

'How do you know about him then?'

'Sergeant Llucas sometimes mentions him. Says he's very scary, but also the cleverest general he's ever served under.'

'Has Sergeant Llucas met Rojden?'

'I think so.'

'When was the last time Sergeant Llucas went to a briefing where Rojden might have been present?'

'He hasn't been away since I've been with the outer guard.'

'How long have you been with the outer guard?'

'Since the spring. I spent a few weeks at a training place after we did the spring plantings and the I decided to be a guard.'

'Best choice you ever made. I'm going to send you to Kronstadt.'

I didn't think I could get anything else useful from him, so I stopped the questions. Noren and I went into another room.

'So, what do you think, Noren?'

'He's small fry. He thinks his guard commander is

Rojden, but he hasn't seen him. So it could be our guy. It could just as easily be a decoy, a trap or someone else with the same name.'

'So what?'

'We'd be foolish to take on all of Duke Xaime's guard just to try and chat with someone that might know something.'

'So we ignore this part of the scheme too?'

'Not ignore, just skip it for later. I don't feel that we are ready to face Rojden yet.'

'We might be able to take him by surprise, if we do something quickly.'

'I doubt that. We've already left two of his men down on the street, and they had friends coming. So the word we're here is already out. Being the river is the right thing now.'

'A boat for Caratis then?'

'Either that or an overland trip. We need to speak to Erik and give him some despatches for Kronstadt.'

'as well as a prisoner.'

~

'Well met, Erik!' I said.

'Well met! I see you have a new friend.' Erik said.

'Yes. He's a former employee of Duke Xaime, and he needs passage on the next ship to Kronstadt, along with our despatches. Can you arrange that?'

'Of course I can.'

'He might also need some clean clothes. We've done our best, but he'd be harder to spot in something else.'

'Sveinn, take this man upstairs and see what you can find for him to wear. He wants to be on the Seagull as soon as you can arrange it.'

'Erik, is that the King's Ship Seagull?' said Noren.

'It is.'

'In that case we might want to speak to the

captain.' I said.

'Do you want to escort your friend to the Seagull yourself?' Erik said.

'That might be easiest.' I said.

We waited while Sveinn found Adan some fresh clothes. Adan came back down the stairs almost unrecognisable in Skyssian Board of Trade messenger overalls with his dark hair bundled inside a blue woollen hat. His colouring wasn't quite pale enough, but it worked. We walked him out of the office and down the jetty. The familiar line of the Seagull was moored a short distance from the Board of Trade office. We attracted no special attention from the guard, who I recognised from the ambush in Kronstadt. He'd watched us emerge from the Board of Trade's office and walk straight to the ship. On the bridge from the dock to the deck we were spotted by Lieutenant Snorri.

'Well met!' a smile shone from him.

'Snorri!' I felt the warmth in my cheeks.

'How did you two end up here?' Snorri said.

'It's a long story, I'll tell you another time. Is Captain Ragnar around?' I said.

'He's in his cabin.'

'Do you think he'd mind if we disturbed him?' I said.

'Yngvild, I doubt he'd ever mind if a woman half as beautiful as you disturbed him.'

I blushed again at the compliment. 'We've got some despatches, and also Adan here needs to go to my mother.'

'Let me look after Adan, you take the despatches to the captain.' Snorri bowed and then ushered Adan towards the cabin in the bow where Arald had been lodged.

I knocked on the door of the captain's cabin.

'Enter!' Ragnar said.

I opened the door and Noren followed me in.

'Well met, Captain Ragnar!'

'Well met! Yngvild the Fierce, and Noren the Dwarf. Well, I never expected to see you two here.'

'We're just passing through, but we thought that you might be able to do us a favour. I understand that you are bound for Kronstadt?'

'Yes, back on the message run. Nothing exciting. What can I do for you, dear lady?'

'We've just delivered a prisoner to Snorri. He needs to go to my mother, the details are in this despatch here. It might be best to hide him when you move him to her. The other despatch is for the Board of Trade about the local situation here, but it needn't go to them until Adan, the prisoner, is safely delivered to Lady Helga.'

'Of course I'll do that. Where are you off to next then?'

'We're trying to get to Caratis, to find Noren's mother.'

'I've been told that the port of Caratis is closed to traffic to and from Salicia. There's a blockade by the Cottalem navy just to the East of Caratis.'

'We'll have to go overland then.'

'I might be able to save you some time. If you are up for it?'

'What have you got in mind?'

'Well, we're quite good at sailing at night, and we could row out to where we could drop you off by boat later tonight. The Cottalem Navy go back to port before it gets dark and sail out again at sunrise.'

'I'd be up for that.' I said.

'Faster than walking' said Noren.

'Excellent, let's get ready to sail.'

SEVEN

ᛋᛗᚠ ᛒᚢ ᚩᛁᚷᚾᛏ
BY SEA, BY NIGHT

While the Seagull left port and used what was left of daylight to minimise their rowing, Noren and I were fed and then ordered to get some sleep. Snorri promised to wake us before we were needed. I'd not realised how much I'd missed Snorri until I saw him again. He paid me compliments, looked genuinely interested in what I had been doing and was generally helpful.

'You could learn from Snorri, Noren.' I said.

'You mean you'd like me to be nicer to you, rather than completely honest.' Noren said.

'You're still doing it wrong Noren.'

'Doing what wrong?'

'Wooing the woman that loves you.'

'I'll give that some thought.'

I fell asleep, and was woken an instant later by Snorri gently shaking my shoulder.

'Wake up, dear Yngvild.' he said.

'Mm. Just got to sleep.'

'Not at all, it's been several hours. You must have been tired.'

'Oh. M'wake now. Thank you.' I tried to get out of the hammock gracefully, but that's probably impossible.

Snorri caught me in his arms. He smelt nice. Manly. His body was solid and muscular, much like Noren's, only a bit more me sized. I stood and enjoyed the contact for a moment longer than I probably should have.

'Sorry. Thanks for catching me. Not quite awake enough yet.' I said.

'You're welcome. There's some food if you want an early breakfast.' Snorri said.

'Where is Noren?'

'He said he had a weird dream and couldn't get back to sleep. He's on deck already.'

I put my shoes back on and gathered my gear. Snorri helped a little and then showed me to the galley for some food. I told him the heavily edited highlights of our time apart.

Up above the Seagull had brought its mainsail down and the pennants it usually flew as identification. The running lights it used at night to avoid collision had been doused, as had cabin lights. I realised that I could see in the dark without specifically thinking about it.

The coast was ahead of us, and we were coming in slowly under oar power. The paddling was measured and smooth. In the bow a helmsman was casting a weight ahead of the ship to test the depth.

'As soon as it starts to shallow we'll put you in a boat to go ashore.' Snorri said.

'How far do you think?'

'Probably half an hour, hard to be certain when it's dark like this.'

I looked at the headland. I could see some horsed figures silhouetted on it. They were about the size of my fingernail when I held it up. We were maybe half a mile offshore.

'I think we're about half a mile offshore. I can just about make out some horses on the headland.' I said.

'Maybe time for the boat then.'

Snorri took me to find Noren at the stern. He was speaking with Captain Ragnar and the steersman.

'Time to put the boat out, captain.' Snorri said.

'It was a pleasure seeing you both again. I hope we catch up again soon.' Captain Ragnar said.

'Do you make this run regularly?' I said.

'About once a month. There's a set of ships that tour in sequence.'

'We might see you in a month then!' I said.

'Fare well until then.'

Snorri took us both over to the rail at the rear. A boat with our gear in it had already been lowered. Five sailors in darkened clothes and with blackened faces and hands were sat in the boat, four on oars and one as coxswain. I climbed down and sat at the front.

Noting the spare oars in the bottom I said 'Shall we take an oar too?'

'That won't be necessary my lady, but thank you.' the coxswain said.

I turned to face the way we were going and Noren climbed down and sat beside me.

The sea was as flat as it gets. The sailors rowed steadily for shore. As we approached I could see movement on the coast road. Given how late it was, I wondered what was going on.

'How will you find the Seagull again ' I said.

'When we're out a bit I'll light my hooded lamp and point it out to sea. They'll flash me if I go off course.'

'We're nearly there.'

The boat ran aground on the sand. Noren got out and it floated off again. I passed him our gear, which he slung around his body, including my shield and gear. As I paused to say thank you and goodbye to the sailors Noren picked me up too.

'No point you getting wet either, Yngvild.'

I waved over his shoulder as the Seagull's boat pulled backwards into the sea.

Noren put me down above the high tide mark.

'Nice to know you listen sometimes.' I pulled his

face down so that I could kiss him.

'I suppose we'd better get moving inland a bit before it gets daylight.' Noren said.

'You know how to spoil a moment.'

I reclaimed my gear and we walked away from the beach.

Noren put his hand on my shoulder so that I could guide him in the dark. I willed us to be hidden by the night. No point in risking discovery by those horsemen or their friends. Whoever they might be.

Ten minutes walk brought us to a small copse on a higher bit of ground. I could see a coast road ahead of that, and there seemed to be frequent traffic, even though it was just before dawn. Mostly individual riders.

'Noren, I think we should rest in the copse until after sunrise. Then we can come out and join any other travellers we see.'

'Shouldn't we push inland a bit further? This is quite close to the coast.'

'We could, but there are horsemen riding around a lot.'

'I still think that we should push on.' Noren said.

'I'm not so sure, I've seen a lot of horse riders go past while we've been coming in.'

'How about we go through the wood, and we can stop on the edge nearest the road to check the coast is clear before crossing?' Noren said.

'Fine, but if we see more riders then we hole up in the middle of the copse until after sunrise.'

'Agreed.'

We carried on. I aimed for the part of the copse that was furthest from the road. Cloud rolled over as we got there and blotted out the starlight. I could still see well, but Noren's night vision completely disappeared. We slowed down so that he could avoid making any noise.

I stared at the trees looking for signs of life. The only movement was the wind gently moving the tops of the trees.

Every step we took I strained for signs of people, on the road and in the trees. Finally we got to the point where I could see the individual trees three or four layers in from the edge. I found an animal track that seemed to lead into the wood and got Noren onto it. From there progress was smoother and less likely to involve holes in the ground or noise. The track took us into the heart of the copse, it wasn't very large, but big enough that in the middle there was no sign of anything that wasn't in the copse.

The cloud blew away, and things got brighter. As they did I became aware of some straight lines in the copse. As we progressed through to the other side I became more certain something wasn't quite right.

I stopped. Noren pressed up against me.

'What?' his lips brushed my ears, as he breathed quietly into my ear.

I indicated a few times around us where I could make out the straight lines of shelters. Noren felt tenser. I touched Jafnadr's pommel. *'Jafnadr!'*

'You appear to be surrounded and significantly outnumbered, although most of them are asleep.' Jafnadr said.

'Backwards or forwards?'

'Hard to be sure. You seem to be closer to the front than the rear. However there are rather a lot of people here. It feels like a whole regiment.'

'A regiment?!'

'Move quietly and purposefully out the front and you just might get away with it.'

I pulled on Noren's hand and started moving again. The light was starting to improve. I could feel the night starting to end. I willed us hidden and pulled Noren after me as fast as I dared.

Ahead and slightly to the right a man loomed out of the forest. He crashed out of his shelter towards us. Then started to pee against the tree. It was loud. Another man stumbled into a branch and started cursing the tree.

The troops bivouacked here were starting to rouse, I moved faster.

'Halt!' a soldier said.

I stopped and looked towards the voice.

'Best to talk your way out of this one.' Jafnadr said.

The soldier looked at us. 'Where have you come from?'

'We're just looking for somewhere quiet to sleep' I said.

'Juan! Jose! Pedro! We've got visitors.' The soldier said. 'You aren't supposed to be here, I'll need you to come see my officer.'

More soldiers came out from behind the trees to escort us to their officer.

'Don't worry, we'll come very quietly.' Noren said.

~

The soldiers took us to a large square tent just off the edge of the road outside the copse. Once we were out in the daylight they realised that we were armed.

'Hands up! Hands up!' a soldier shouted.

'Archers!' shouted another. More soldiers came running as Noren and I stood with our hands above our heads and spears pointed at our throats.

'Stand perfectly still, or we'll shoot you.' An archer knocked an arrow and pointed it at me. A comrade of his did the same and pointed it at Noren.

The shouting brought another soldier. He looked older than most of the others, and his equipment looked better than the others too. The panic in the others faded.

'Didn't any of you idiots think to disarm them?' he said.

'Sorry Sergeant Leon.' Another soldier said.

'Don't be sorry son, just get on and bloody do it.' Sergeant Leon said.

'You.' He pointed at me, 'Take off your shield and lay it on the ground.'

I pulled the shield over my head and put it on the ground.

'Now take off your belt with the sword and dagger and put them on the shield. Only touch the end of the belt.'

I complied, taking off each belt in turn. Then he got me to take off my other bags and the mail and my padded jerkin.

'Right. I want you to take ten paces from the shield and lie face down on the ground.'

Once he'd got me away they repeated the process with Noren. We both ended up with nothing but our clothes and shoes. None of our other possessions were with us, although I did have some papers in my skirt pocket.

It was first light, and the troops all seemed to be up for the day. While we awaited the attention of the regimental officer several riders came past. They left messages with a clerk and rode off, except for one who spent several minutes staring at us.

'I never got time to tell you about my dream.' Noren said.

'Tell me now.'

'We went looking for my mother, and she wasn't there because of the men. These look like the men she was hiding from. In my dream they were Rojden's men.'

'No talking!' A soldier rushed over and made us

stand further apart.

'No talking!' he repeated for emphasis.

The rider that had been watching us dismounted and went into the tent. A moment later a soldier came out and dragged Noren back into the tent.

~

I sat on the green grass and watched the sun rise. It was warm on my face. The birds sung in the tree tops, in contrast to the noises and cursing of soldiery getting their breakfasts and breaking camp.

I watched a pair of larks swooping and zooming around above the trees. Behind me I could hear horses and men passing by on the road, and the occasional cart rattling past.

A shriek rent the air from the centre of the wood. It sounded like someone who'd never done it before was slaughtering an animal.

~

The soldier came for me. I went into the tent voluntarily. Noren was nowhere to be seen, but the tent was sub-divided into rooms. The light diffuse through the canvas roof. The part I was in was carpeted, and a table and two chairs lined the right of the walkway in from the tent flap. I was facing the table. The rider sat in one of the chairs, and an officer, judging by the quality of his clothes, sat in the other.

I turned to face them, aware of a soldier behind me in each of the corners of the space.

'Name.' The rider spoke.

'Yngvild'

'Where are you from Yngvild?'

'Skyss'

'How did you get here?'

'By boat mostly. We walked the last bit.'

'What are you doing here?'

'I came with my betrothed to find his mother and sisters.'

Silence.

I looked at him, waiting for the next question.

He looked back at me.

What else did he expect me to say?

Where was Noren? I strained to listen. The tent muffled noise, but I could clearly hear the soldiers outside. They seemed to be packing shelters into the carts I'd heard.

More silence.

'Do not lie to us, Yngvild Helgasdottir. We know who you are.' the rider said.

I looked at them both. The officer's eyes were hooded, the rider had a gleam in his eyes, like catching Noren and I was the best thing that had happened in a while.

'These are your possessions?' the rider stood and walked round the side of the table to where my shield lay on the ground.

Everything seemed to be there, although someone had looked through it because they were layered differently from how I'd taken them off.

'They're mine.' I said.

'Why were you armed?'

'The world is a dangerous place, I've needed to fight off attackers.'

'Exactly how often have you needed to defend yourself?'

'Since I left home there have been three separate times where I have been directly threatened, not including today.'

'It isn't normal in Cottalem for people to go about armed.'

'Everyone I've see in Cottalem appears to be armed.' I said.

The officer chuckled. Rider shot him a dirty look. The officer tried to put a serious face on.

'Why are you in Cottalem?' Rider said.

'I'm here with my betrothed to find his mother and sisters.'

'So why do you have papers saying that you are a Board of Trade agent?' Rider picked up a copy of the introductory letter that Erik had written for the Earl of Beretha and waved it in my face.

'I did some freelance work on the way here because we'd run out of money.'

'You are a Skyssian spy, and so is your friend!' Rider went red in the face as he screamed his accusation at me.

'Take her away.'

A guard pulled my hands together behind my back, and the other bound them with some thin rope. Then they put a bag over my head. I was carried bodily out of the tent and thrown over a horse, it certainly smelt like one, and was large enough. I fought against the urge to struggle. If I was going to get out of this I needed to remain calm.

I could hear orders being given to take us both to their HQ. I also heard Rider tell them to follow him.

I've no idea how far we went, or even if we went directly there. I was hungry again before we arrived at the HQ. If it was the HQ. I was hauled off the horse and roughly pushed to the ground. There were at least two of them, but neither spoke. When I tried to sit up I was rapidly pushed back down. I lay and listened for clues.

I could smell fresh horse dung. It was a strong smell. There was no hint of the sea. There was a tinge of wood smoke from a fire, but I couldn't smell any cooking over the horse dung.

There were sounds of horses and harnesses. I could hear a blacksmith, some distance away and muffled. Horses neighed and there was at least one dog.

Two sets of feet came to me, one on each side. I felt them as much as heard them. I got grabbed by the elbows and dragged backwards without any attempt to put me on my feet. My shoes started to come off, so I brought my knees up. They dropped me without warning, the shock winded me.

As I was getting my breath back one of the people kicked me viciously in the side. I cried out with pain. '*My pain is your pain*' I thought.

I got kicked again, and it felt like I'd been stabbed. There was a loud crunch and I was sure he'd broken my ribs. I coughed and tasted the salt of blood. The one that kicked me cried out. I curled up with my arms over my ribs, I also kept my knees bunched up.

I wasn't kicked or hit again. I was left for a short while. My pain subsided.

Someone came back later and set me on my feet. They also took the hood off when I'd gone a few paces into a building. I felt two stone stairs and then a wooden floor. We were in some sort of hall, wooden benches all faced the same way. A raised Dias at the other end had a stone sacrificial table on it.

The man walked me to the end of the hall with the table and sat me on the front bench facing it. All the time he stayed behind me, and when I tried to turn he pushed me back round.

'What happens next?' My mouth was dry, my voice croaked.

There was no answer.

I looked at the sacrificial stone table in front of me. It was a single large roughly hewn block. About five feet long on top, at least three feet off the dais and a similar width. The top looked like it had been polished flat. It was slightly above my eyeline when I was sitting in the front bench. The two front corners had rounded edges, and I could see channels cut into the top corners. The channels had fresh blood in them. The blood dripped into shaped buckets hanging at each corner of the table. There was a lot of blood.

What had they sacrificed earlier this morning. Was that the shriek that I'd heard?

Who had they sacrificed?

Was it a person?

I am sure that this is the message they want me to absorb. To give me fear.

Were they going to sacrifice me to appease their gods, or even to ask for victory for their army?

Another set of footsteps came up the hall. I tried to turn, but was again gently pushed back to face the front.

I glanced sideways as far as I could. Someone was sat on the bench over the passage from mine. I couldn't tell who it was. I didn't risk speaking.

Where was Noren?

If they've harmed him I'll die.

No.

No. I won't die.

They'll die. Jafnadr and I will wreak justice on them.

The sun from the windows set high in the hall had moved across the floor and disappeared. That meant that it was sometime around noon.

I'll never watch the sun set cuddled into Noren, or feel the warmth of his body against mine. His hard muscular form, with his special scent.

Hunger gnawed at my insides. I hadn't eaten anything since I was on the Seagull, which was late last night.

Noren might have been killed. That could be the shrieking I heard, when they cut his throat.

The ropes binding me chafed my wrists, I wished they were looser. I twisted them, but the hands behind me stilled my wrists.

Am I going to be tomorrow's blood sacrifice? Is that what they want from me?

My head hurt, I could feel it throbbing, and my mouth was dryer than I'd ever known it to be. On the plus side, my body had stopped hurting from where I'd been kicked and thrown about.

How much blood is in a person? Was it all in those buckets, or had they taken some away?

I wasn't tired, but I closed my eyes because it helped me take stock of the situation and think about it more clearly. I listed what I knew for certain.

I was held prisoner by an army that thought that I was a spy.

They'd roughed me up a bit, but not done any real damage to me. Clearly they still wanted something from me.

The papers that they found were genuine and showed us both to be Skyssian Board of Trade agents, even if that was based on my deception of Erik they couldn't know that.

Skyss likes to avoid wars breaking out because they are bad for trade. Once a war starts we back whoever can finish it fastest.

Killing Board of Trade agents isn't going to get backing from Skyss. Delaying them to stop them preventing the war, or getting in the way of your hammer blow? That made sense.

So I'm probably not going to be killed out of hand. Or be tomorrow's blood sacrifice.

Noren is probably alive and nearby. I haven't lost him, not yet.

That made me happy. But I wasn't going to sit and wait now. I needed to drink and eat. We'd been held since before breakfast, and now it was after lunchtime.

The sun had started to heat up this hall, and the air was dry. The runnels of blood that had been on the sacrificial stone table had dried while I'd sat and watched it.

'You're not going to kill us. It would be too dangerous for your leader' my voice cracked. I licked my lips, my tongue felt swollen and sticky.

The silence continued.

'You want Skyss to end the war when your victory is certain. You need our help for that.' I said. 'Killing us brings Skyss in on the other side.'

'Clever girl. It only took you four hours to work it out. Many never get it.' The man behind me said.

I shook my hands behind my back, and the bindings fell off. I turned quickly, but he made no attempt to keep me facing the front. As I turned I saw that it was Noren sat over from me. He carried on looking straight ahead when I whirled round.

'If you give your parole not to escape you can stay as our guests for a week or two, and then we'll let you report back in to the Board of Trade.' He said.

'What did you kill this morning?' I said.

'Nothing.'

'The blood on the table?'

'I didn't kill anything, but someone else must have.

We found it like this just after we crossed the border.'

'Are we back in Salicia?'

'Oh yes. Their King died in his bed last night, and we marched to help our King secure his claim to the throne of Salicia. We're joining the Crowns. It will be very good for business when the war is over.' He said.

I looked at him. He was in his mid-thirties, and had intelligence behind his eyes. I was sure he had already read me before he brought me in here. His face was clean shaven, as was the custom here, I guess it was too hot for beards. His fair hair was cut short too, unlike the Skyssian men who wore long hair and beards and usually plaited and decorated them with ribbons. Something about him seemed familiar, his eyes were a bit like a younger version of Old Bjorn's.

He smiled at me.

I smiled back. 'I would be delighted to give my parole, if you promise to feed and look after us both well.'

He laughed. 'I will treat you as my long lost children!'

'If you lost them that doesn't bode well for our treatment.'

He laughed even harder.

'I like you, Yngvild. No-one has made me laugh like that in an age.' He said when he'd recovered his composure.

'Noren, I think you can move now.' I said.

'Ah, I might need to release him from the geas I placed on him.'

'You put a geas on Noren?'

'It seemed prudent. He's too large and strong to rely on binding his hands.' He said. 'You two are proper Heroes, I can tell. You need special treatment.'

Noren stood up, pulling his hands free from the bindings.

'I'm fine, Yngvild. It didn't hurt. But it was boring.'

EIGHT

ROJDEN

Being with an army on the march was a new experience. The largest group of fighters I'd seen was when the crew of the Seagull had joined up with the Straven community to stand against the raider ship. There had been about sixty of us stood together, plus some more sailors crewing the ship.

When we got outside with the man it became clear that he was one of the key figures in their army command. His clothes were unadorned, and hadn't offered that clue. The officers that we'd seen earlier had finer versions of what the soldiers had been wearing, with silver or gold lace on them. They'd stood out as being more important. Apart from the rider, he'd looked plain too, but the officer had treated him as a superior.

'I'll need to leave you two in the charge of Major Duerte. I've got to catch up with some army business that I've neglected while watching over you two.' He pointed out Major Duerte, a dark haired man with a swarthy skin tone. He was slim and fit, dressed in a tight-fitting blue tunic covered in silver lace that looped across his chest and stomach around two rows of silver buttons that almost formed a V from his waist to shoulders. He had tightly fitted pine green trews on, with brown leather reinforcing the seat and inner thighs. The trews had a line of silver lace either side of the seams. This was all set off with a silver embroidered waist belt with a curved sword in a shiny metal scabbard. On his head he wore a conical helmet with a brim, cheek pieces and a wide neck flap. The cheek pieces were tied up just behind a white horse hair tuft on the top of the helmet.

'Major Duerte, at your service. My lady.' He bowed to me. 'My lord.' He bowed to Noren.

'Major, my belly thinks my throat has been cut, I haven't eaten since before dawn. Can we please get some food?' I said.

'Certainly. Come with me.'

I noticed as we followed Major Duerte that he walked with a wide stance, and that he was slightly bow legged. Too much sitting on horses did that to you I supposed.

We were in a small village, with maybe a dozen buildings. The large hall was in the centre, and there were some houses scattered around it. There were also two large barns. We went into one of them, our captor had gone into the other ahead of us. The yard outside our barn had several horse soldiers in it, all of whom jumped up when they saw us and stood stiffly staring to their front until Major Duerte waved them to carry on. Also in the yard were two tents like the one I'd been taken into when we were first taken prisoner. One of these had the front pinned open and there were several men inside preparing vegetables. A strange looking cart with a chimney on it stood outside, and another man was feeding wood into a door on the side of the cart.

'That's our field kitchen' Major Duerte said when he saw me look at it. 'It's more efficient than just building an open fire, and harder for the enemy to spot because the fire is inside the cart.'

'Doesn't it just end up setting the cart on fire?'

'The fire is inside a clay and brick container, the cart is just for moving it about easily.'

The door to the barn was open to let the light in. Inside were tables with benches on either side of them. Each of the tables was covered in a white tablecloth and had place settings with knives and spoons already laid out. A soldier in a spotless white apron came over when he saw us.

'Sir!' he said, standing stock still in front of the Major.

'We need some luncheon. See to it.' The Major said.

'Yes, sir!' the soldier dashed off out of the door to the field kitchen.

'Take a seat, he'll be back with some food shortly.'

We sat at one end of the table, Noren at the head, me on his left and Major Duerte opposite me on the other side of the table. The soldier returned with a board with some cut bread, a very fine looking white. He was closely followed by another soldier in an identical white apron who bore a tray with three steaming plates of food. There were a variety of vegetables, I recognised carrots, peas, beans, but not some of the others. Half of the plate was filled with a succulent looking white meat that I thought might be chicken. A third soldier brought a sauce jug, which the Major took control of. As soon as each had delivered their offerings, the soldiers left silently.

'You should try the chasseur sauce, it is exquisite and brings out the flavours in the chicken very well.' He said, offering to pour some on my plate.

'Thank you.'

He poured for me and Noren before serving himself.

I felt much better when I had some food inside me, and the Major had been right about the taste being exquisite. It was one of the best meals that I'd ever eaten, rivalling even our festival dishes from back home. I'd certainly never tasted anything so lightly balanced with sweetness, savoury and a tongue tingling spicy heat.

'That was lovely, I feel ready for anything now.' I

said.

'That's excellent, my lady, because we need to mount up and follow the army.' Major Duerte said.

'Mount up?'

'Of course, we're a cavalry army for the most part.' He said.

'I've never been on a horse.'

'Ah. Well we'll need to show you the basics then. Riding is so much more civilised than walking.'

We went out into the yard, the soldiers were still there, but the field kitchen was packing up. Several horses with tall saddles were now in the yard, including a white one with a silver trimmed green saddle cloth. A line of soldiers held the reins of horses, two or three each. The other soldiers were fixing saddles or bags onto some of the horses towards the rear. The soldiers had the same pine green trews and blue tunics, although theirs were looser fitting and lacked the silver lace. Their helmets, belts and scabbards were plainer too.

'Corporal of Horse!' Major Duerte called.

An older man, maybe about thirty, with a moustache appeared from behind the white horse. His uniform fitted reasonably well and he had diagonal white lacing on his sleeves. His helmet and scabbard both gleamed in the sunlight.

'Major.' The Corporal said.

'We have two guests that need some basic instruction in riding. Can you assign them a trooper each to look after them.'

'I'll get Jerre and Javier on it, they're both excellent riders.'

'Good show. Carry on, Corporal of Horse.'

The Corporal of Horse turned to find the troopers.

'We'll sort you two out with a horse and the Corporal will teach you the basics, he's plenty experienced at that, all the new troopers spend time with him.' Major Duerte said.

We walked out of the yard, troopers Jerre and Javier leading two horses each, and the Corporal of Horse accompanied us. Once we were away from the other horses in a patch of common grazing the Corporal of Horse stopped us.

'Right. This will do. Take a horse each, and lead them round. It'll help you see how they work, and help the horse know you. Jerre, you help the lady. Javier, you have the young gentleman.'

Jerre passed me the reins of one of his horses, it was a tall dark brown beast with white splashed on its face between the eyes. It was taller than I was at the shoulder.

'She's called Whiteface, she's a mare, a girl horse' Jerre said.

I took the reins 'Thank you.' and started to walk away from Whiteface. She didn't move. 'Come on.' I said.

Whiteface started walking with me. She blew hot steamy breath into my ear.

'She likes you.' Jerre said. 'You'll be fine.'

We walked round in a circle for a few minutes, the Corporal stood in the middle and watched us. He reminded me of the way that Arne taught us kids the battle drills when we were little. Mostly he told us what he wanted to happen and then watched us do it. We got repeated nuggets of encouragement and advice.

'Show the horse who is in charge.' The Corporal said. 'Look after the horse, and the horse will look after you.'

'Right that's enough for introductions. Time to show you how to mount.' The Corporal said. 'Watch how Jerre does it. First he checks the saddle is secure. No point getting on if the first thing that happens is you fall off!'

'Once you're happy that the saddle is secure, you

put your left hand on the Horn at the front, and your right on the Cantle at the back.' Jerre demonstrated as the Corporal called it out. 'Then put your left foot in the stirrup and push yourself up and over into the seat.'

Jerre vaulted effortlessly into position, but he was half a foot taller than me.

'Your turn now.' The Corporal said.

I reached up as high as I could and grabbed the horn and the cantle as demonstrated by Jerre. They were both high above my head, but reachable. The stirrup was almost at waist height, but I managed to get my foot into it. I bent my right knee and pushed up while pulling with both arms. I just about made it onto the seat, but my skirts got in the way, so it wasn't that comfortable. I stood with both feet in stirrups and re-arranged to be more comfortable.

'That's good. You need to be mindful of your balance on horseback. The main thing is not to fall off. Use your thighs and knees to grip the saddle. Get the reins in your hands and make sure the horse knows you are in charge.'

'How do I make sure the horse knows that I am in charge?' Noren asked.

'Keep control of what it does. Tell it the direction by moving its head with the reins. Encourage it to speed up or slow down as you wish.' The Corporal said.

We spent ten minutes practising walking in the circle and then stopping. We also had a couple of dismounts and mounts to make sure we could get on and off safely. Thankfully neither of us fell off.

'Good, you'll manage today I think.' The Corporal said. 'The troopers will shadow you and help show you how to look after your horses when we get to our destination.'

We rode back at a walk to the rest of the troop, who mounted when they saw us. Noren and I tagged along near the rear of the troop, where I spotted one of the pack horses carrying our shields.

The day was spent riding at a walking pace, with short stops every hour to let the horses graze. The saddle was high both in front and behind, so I found it easy to stay in it even when the horse was bouncing around. When I asked, Jerre said the cavalry saddles were designed for you to fight from. So they were hard to accidentally fall out of.

The cavalry troop escorting us didn't seem to be in a rush. Towards sunset we approached a city on a river, ringed by a wall. The gates were open, and guards on the wall waved to us as we got nearer. Two different pennants flew over the main gate, and also from the top of the largest tower that we could see as we approached.

~

We left the troop outside the walls, Major Duerte, Noren and I carried on into the city accompanied by the pack horse with our gear, Troopers Jerre and Javier and five others. The Major lead, with the rest of us in pairs, me with Jerre, and Noren with Javier. We went to the main citadel in the heart of the city. The gates there were also open, with more cavalry troopers in the same uniforms as our escort. In the courtyard inside there some piles of sawdust in seemingly random places, discarded armour and weapons in the corner told their own story. Along with a couple of splintered long spears and a dead horse.

'Looks like we fought for this.' Major Duerte said.

We dismounted and passed the reins to our partner troopers. Major Duerte ushered us to follow him into the Tower.

The main door into the tower was splintered off its hinges, and was propped up next to the doorway. More sawdust in the corridor and gouges in the wooden panelling testified to the forced entrance into the tower. There were still several arrows embedded in the ceiling of the corridor, too high for anyone to reach without a ladder.

Another officer came down the corridor towards us. He had less lace, but it was gold rather than silver.

'Major Duerte! His Grace is expecting you upstairs, two levels up, second door on the right. Guards'll show you the way.' The officer said.

'Thank you. On my way, Colonel.'

We took the stairs, on the first level a guard halted us.

'Major Duerte and guests, His Grace is expecting us.'

'Pass, sir.' The guard stood out of the way.

On the second level the guard wasn't one of the familiar cavalry troopers. He was clad from head to foot in steel plate armour. It bore some dents and bashes. He must have been one of the assault troops that had forced their way in here earlier today.

On seeing us the guard stood aside and pointed us down a passage. The passage contained three more guards, one outside each room, and all in full armour plate. We went through the door that was opened for us into a room lit by high level windows and with hanging tapestries on all four walls. The wall to the left also had a fireplace, the tapestry came short above it. The centre contained a table with six chairs set round it. One of these was occupied by the man we'd met earlier. He was still dressed in the same clothes, as we'd seen him in before lunch.

'Come in, sit down. Eat.'

The table was set for six, and there were several dishes on the table, including some of the same vegetables I'd had at lunchtime. I still didn't know what they were, but I'd loved eating them. There was also some chicken, I recognised the whiteness and the texture of the flesh, and lamb or beef, and some fish.

We sat down and dug in.

'Who are the other two place settings for?' I said.

'The table takes six, so the servants set it for six. Just in case.' Our captor said.

'You're not expecting anyone else?'

'Not expecting them, but ready should they arrive.'

'You are a prudent sort of man, aren't you?' I said.

'Very much so, it's the best way to live.'

'No rush to die. Eh?'

'You know, I used to have a very old great uncle who said that a lot.'

'My adopted dad said it a lot too, and he is unspeakably old.'

'That would be Old Bjorn, wouldn't it?'

'How do you know Old Bjorn?'

'Old Bjorn is a legend. Anyone that studies the Skyssian Heroes like I have knows of Old Bjorn.'

'I've never heard the legends.'

'Well you wouldn't, not if you lived with him. He doesn't like people telling the stories.'

'He's modest, I think, he never talked about his past, before he came to live quietly on Straven.'

'Secretive, and devious, more like. Old Bjorn is the oldest living Hero, bar none. The legend says that he is over a thousand years old and was one of the founding fathers of Kronstadt.'

'But the city is nearly eight hundred years old.'

'Exactly. He's ancient. As old as modern civilisation itself.'

'What else does the legend say about him?'

'Old Bjorn acts with the best of intentions, but often what he does backfires. He tells people what they need to hear so that they will do the things that Old Bjorn needs to have done. He keep secrets because he can't bear the scrutiny he would get if people knew what he was up to. People have died, or had their lives wrecked, because of the secrets that he has kept or the mistakes made.'

'How do you know all of this?'

'There are many tales from legend, when you have time you should have someone tell you them, or find a written copy somewhere. The saga of the Seacrest is a good one to illustrate the point. But there are others, and I've seen some of them personally.'

'I know the Seacrest, that's the one where the captain doesn't tell the crew where they are going or why, and then they end up being eaten by a sea monster instead of killing it?' Noren said. 'The captain goes back later on his own to avenge the death of his crew.'

'Yes, that's the one. The crew die because the captain wasn't straight with them about what they had set out to do. None of them were prepared for the sea monster and it took them by surprise.'

'I didn't know it was about Old Bjorn.' Noren said.

'In his youth, long before Kronstadt was founded. He still makes the same mistakes though. How much did he teach you about the mysteries or your heritage?'

'Nothing in my case.' Noren said.

'I got a little, but only when we decided to leave the island.' I said.

'I don't want to turn you against Old Bjorn. His heart is in the right place, but he's just not reliable enough, and he makes mistakes. Some of his advice has been awful. I think its probably his advanced age.'

'Lady Helga said something similar.' I said.

'She's a very smart woman, she'll go far. I expect that she'll be King of Skyss within a decade. Definitely the smartest one in her generation.'

'You think my mother will be the King of Skyss?'

'She's your mother? Ah, that explains your talent. It also means that Noren is probably my son.'

'You're Rojden!' I said.

'Yes, that's me. Don't believe all the stories you've been told. I don't kill people indiscriminately. Quite the opposite.'

'You killed my father!'

'I didn't kill him, but I was there when he died. It was a tragic waste, and completely unnecessary. I killed the man that stabbed him to death.'

'I thought the man that killed him was working for you?'

'He was a double agent.'

'Who else was he working for?'

'Old Bjorn. He didn't trust me, and spread lots of lies. I had to leave Skyss because of it. I couldn't trust anyone.'

I was confused. He seemed sincere, but so had Old Bjorn and Lady Helga. But the stories were all different.

'Oh. I don't know how to make sense of all this.'

'Take your time. I mean you no harm, and I doubt Old Bjorn does either. There's plenty of time for you to figure out what you think happened and who you believe.'

'Noren, you knew who he was?'

'Yes, Yngvild. I did. He asked me not to tell you anything until you worked it out for yourself. He said it would show that you could think clearly, and if you could think clearly than you would be able to come to your own conclusions and not rely on what others had told you.'

I couldn't quite believe it.

How much of what I had grown up with was based on secrets and lies. I knew Old Bjorn had kept secrets from us. I'd found out some of them, and he'd bound me to keep his secrets.

Did that binding affect how I thought about things? Was it stopping me from seeing lies?

How did Jafnadr come into this? Could I trust what the sword told me, were the dreams true. Did the man that passed the poison do it on the orders of Old Bjorn, or Rojden, or someone else entirely?

'I think I need some time alone to think about all of this.' I said. 'Is there a bed somewhere I could lie down?'

'Of course, Yngvild. If you go through that door there' Rojden pointed 'then a servant will show you where you are sleeping.'

'Thank you.' I pushed the chair back and stood up.

'Sleep well, dear Yngvild.' Rojden said.

'Good night!' Noren said.

Major Duerte also stood and accompanied me to the door, opening it for me. Outside a female servant stood waiting. She bobbed down as I came into the corridor.

'My lady, if you please.' She said.

Major Duerte closed the door behind me.

We went down the passage to a set of back stairs, which we took up to a higher level. There were no guards on these stairs. We went past the next level, a passage branched off the side of the stairs. At the top there were three doors around a tiny landing. We went left, into a carpeted room. A fire provided light, and a lot of warmth, more than was really needed given it was only early autumn. A very large bed stood in the middle of the room, with hangings on the top and sides to keep the heat in. They were open on the side nearest the door, but closed on the other sides. The room also had a very large shuttered window on the side opposite the door. Under the window was a small table with drawers in it and a mirror on the table top.

'My lady, if you need me call me Eva.' Eva shut the door behind her, and drew a bar across the inside.

'Are you worried Eva?' I said.

'There are a lot of strange soldiers in the city, my

lady. It pays to be ready to defend one's honour.' Eva said.

'I don't think we have anything to worry about.'

'Better safe than sorry, my lady.'

I stood for a moment looking at the fire. While I did Eva started to loosen the ties on my clothes and helped me to take them off. I lifted my feet off the floor one at a time when she took my shoes and hose off. Once I was down to my shift I shrugged it over my head and climbed into the bed and fell asleep almost immediately.

~

I woke the next morning to the sun streaming in the windows. They were glazed to keep the wind out. Something I'd only seen in the Palace at Kronstadt and the Earl's house in Beretha, and the one solitary window in Old Bjorn's secret room back on Straven.

The view from the window was spectacular. We were on one of the highest points in the city. Over the rooftops I could see forests and fields below. The river snaked away through the fields, boats moored on the river. Several barges formed a bridge a mile or so outside the city walls and were being used by the army to cross. I could see groups of cavalry going downstream, and there were foot soldiers getting into barges just downstream of the makeshift bridge. More cavalry fanned out on the far side of the bridge to form a screen.

On the table were some pastries, and a glass of milk. My fancy shift was laid over the back of the chair, and my silk hose draped over them. Eva had clearly found my pack and thought I should wear the nicer items today. As I put the hose on I noticed a red silk dress hanging on the outside of the bed. It seemed people wanted me to look like Lady Yngvild, and not like Yngvild the Fierce. I ignored it and put on my linen underskirt before sitting down to eat the pastries while admiring the view out of the window.

Last night's claims by Rojden put a different perspective on my life. He still fitted into the devious and ambitious reputation I'd been given for him. He was leading an army to take over another state, and he played mind games with me. He'd also told me a lot of stories designed to undermine my confidence in Old Bjorn. True, there was something in it. Old Bjorn hadn't told us all the things it might have been useful for us to know. But it couldn't just completely invalidate everything I knew. Could it?

I need Noren to talk to. But Rojden has done something strange to him. Can't risk speaking freely with Noren, while he's under Rojden's influence.

Eva came into the room, breaking my train of thought.

'You're awake, my lady, you should have called for me.' She said.

'I was enjoying the peace, Eva, and the breakfast. Thank you for laying it out.'

'No need to thank me, my lady, it's what I'm here for.'

'I see a lot of movement out there, is there any news?'

'None they've shared with me, my lady. Perhaps you might get dressed and go downstairs to ask?'

'An excellent suggestion.'

Eva bustled over to where the red dress was hanging and twitched it off the hanger with a practised flick of her wrists. I stood and moved closer to her. Eva turned to face me and threw the dress over my head. She then tugged it here and there until it fell into place.

It was shorter than my underskirt by several inches. It also had a lower neckline than my shift. Eva looked at me appraisingly.

'Your underskirt needs to come off, the shift will do, but you'll want another one for tomorrow.' she

said.

I fumbled through the dress to undo the waist button on my underskirt. When I got it undone I wriggled my hips while Eva tugged the hem to make it fall to the floor. Eva rearranged the shift so that the embroidered pattern showed well. Then she laced me into the dress.

'Not too tight, I'd like to be able to breathe' I said as Eva pulled it tight around my waist.

'Just getting your shape, my lady.'

Laced up I couldn't bend over to put my shoes on. Eva came back from a side room with some matching red silk slippers.

'Let me, my lady. I think these would better suit your dress.'

Eva kicked my scuffed and worn shoes out the way so that she could help me on with the slippers.

Downstairs I found Noren having breakfast with Rojden. Rojden was working his way through a pile of despatches.

'Good morning!' I smiled brightly at them.

'It just got better.' said Rojden.

Noren stared open mouthed. 'You look fantastic, Yngvild.'

That was the response I wanted, but I hadn't expected.

'Has anything interesting happened while I was asleep?' It clearly had.

'That depends on how you define interesting.' Rojden said.

'Has the war stopped yet?'

'Well, there are moves afoot to end it.'

'I saw some of the army going downstream.'

'Well, that's where you might be able to help prevent unnecessary bloodshed.'

'What do you want us to do?'

'I understand that you met the Earl of Beretha.'

'That's correct.'

'and you also ran into Duke Xaime's guards.'

'Someone claimed that you were the commander of the Duke's guard.'

'mmm, yes. They could have seen it that way. I helped the Duke to choose his personal guards.'

'Isn't there a conflict of interest there?'

'I don't believe that the Duke is in a position to complain.'

'Did his bodyguard kill him?'

'Oh no. Far from it. Many of them died trying to protect him.'

'What happened?'

Rojden made a show of digging into his pile of papers.

'According to the report the Earl sent some men to get the Duke's oath of fealty, or to arrest him. The Earl's guard outnumbered the Duke's. There was some bitter fighting, and the Duke had a most unfortunate accident.'

'What's your source for this?'

'Some survivors reached our lines and reported what happened. The Earl has proclaimed himself King of Salicia and has called for the army to support him against the invasion from Cottalem.'

'What about the old King's daughter?'

'She's here, she fled from the Earl's men, they killed her husband and most of her household.'

'So the Earl is the only one standing against you?'

'Yes. That's where you come in. I know you saw him a few days ago. I need you to go back to him and tell him that Skyss cannot support him.'

'What terms can you offer him?'

'He can keep his title and lands if he acknowledges the new King.'

'That's generous.'

'He's done us a favour by killing the other

candidates. Makes us look humane.'

'What if he says no?'

'Cottalem is much larger than Salicia. Our army will defeat his. Also the Salician army will be split, the King's daughter has recognised the new King. Xaime's former guards have also denounced the Earl of Beretha.'

'Are we free to go when we've delivered your message and reported back to you?'

'You can go when negotiations are complete.'

'When do we start?'

'Tomorrow. Today we have a coronation.'

~

The Coronation was a rapid affair driven by political expediency. The King was proclaimed and anointed. Those nobles of Salicia present, which included the old King's daughter, made their obeisance and swore an oath of allegiance.

Once that was done a series of proclamations were made. The country was called on to bear loyalty to the new King. The militia were called out to restore order and work with the friendly forces of Cottalem.

The Earl of Beretha sent his own emphatic message. A courier delivered the heads of several Cottalemnese merchants.

~

The following morning I dressed in my travelling clothes and went for breakfast with Rojden and Noren. Noren was late.

'Good morning, dear Yngvild' Rojden said.

'Morning. Is Noren not down yet?'

'I'm sure he'll be along in time to see you off.'

'Isn't he coming with me?'

'No, he's staying here with me.'

'Oh. I thought we were going together.'

'I've got other plans for Noren. But I understand that you lead all the dealings with the Earl when you visited.'

I didn't answer, and focused on getting some food. This wasn't what I'd agreed to.

'You're annoyed at me.' Rojden said.

I just looked at him and wished he'd change his mind.

'Do this job for me and you and Noren will get some time together.'

'Do you have any other surprises in store for me?'

'Well I was going to send you with Major Duerte and a troop of cavalry as an escort.'

'Why so many?'

'They need the reinforcements to help close down Beretha. You may as well ride with them on the way there.'

I finished off the rest of my breakfast in silence. I was too angry to talk. There was no sign of Noren, so nothing to lift my mood.

At the stables Trooper Jerre was waiting, he smiled when he saw me.

'I've got you Whiteface again. You seemed to work well together.' he said.

'Thank you.'

'We're all saddled up and ready to ride.'

'I need my battle gear.'

'You have battle gear?' Jerre looked puzzled.

'Of course, doesn't everyone?'

Jerre shook his head. 'No. Only soldiers have battle gear. You aren't a soldier, my lady'

'Where I come from we all have it, just in case the raiders come.'

'I don't think we've got any spare, we'd need to see the Q M about it.'

'I don't want your battle gear, I want my own back. It was on the pack horse that followed us in.'

'Oh. Maybe we should ask the Corporal then. He might know.'

Jerre pulled my forearm to indicate that I should follow as he turned to leave the stables.

Outside the troopers were mostly holding horses and checking straps and harnesses. A couple were mounted already. A short muscular trooper bustled around checking on the others. His uniform fitted really closely on his body, but the sleeves were rumpled and the trousers folded up. A single line of white trim round his cuffs marked him out as a little more special than the other troopers.

'Corporal! The lady wants her battle gear back. Says she's not going anywhere without it.' Jerre said.

It was a little farther than I'd expected, but I certainly agreed with the sentiment.

The Corporal turned from checking readiness and came over.

'I was told to give you it back at Beretha.' he said.

'I want to make sure it's all ready before I need it. I didn't get a chance to clean it or stow it properly before it was taken away.' *Let me have my battle gear* I thought at him.

'No harm in you checking it over. It's on the pack horse there' the Corporal pointed out the pack horse.

Jerre helped me unstrap the shield, which was fine. One of the pouches held my mail, which had gone slightly rusty, and another my padded jacket. I put both on.

I took a moment to handle Jafnadr, pretending to check how clean she was.

'I hadn't forgotten you, they just wouldn't let me keep you.' I thought.

'Don't worry. I understand, I've had my own eyes and ears looking out for you.' Jafnadr replied.

'We'll talk properly later.' I slid Jafnadr back into her scabbard and put it on over my mail. I also took my quiver and bow. They were good, someone had

lightly oiled the bow.

I decided to leave the shield on the pack horse. I wasn't sure how I would carry or use it on horseback. One day in the saddle wasn't enough to turn me into a mounted warrior.

No-one sees my armour I thought.

'I'm good now. Thank you Jerre.' I smiled at him.

'At your service, my lady' Jerre bowed.

I beamed at him, I was beginning to think Jerre liked me. Maybe there was some advantage to being a woman with an all male army?

We mounted up and rode out. No-one commented on my being armed. Once out of the castle we broke into a trot. I almost fell off, but Jerre rode close and steadied my arm. I got used to it, and the troop made a good pace up the Great North Road, the countryside swept past. We overtook marching men moving North towards Beretha. Off to the flanks of our route we saw cavalry patrols. Ordinary people worked in the fields bringing their harvests in, chopping wood, tending animals and the thousands of other things people do to scrape a living from the land. Only a few watched us pass. I guess the novelty of an army passing fades fast.

We stopped briefly for lunch and to rest the horses in a random pasture. We ate bread, cheese and ham from the pack horse. We drank water from bottles and Jerre refilled ours from a stream. The horses got oats from a bag attached to their harnesses. They also got an opportunity to drink from the stream.

After lunch we carried on towards Beretha. A pillar of smoke dominated the horizon.

'That doesn't look good for someone.' I said.

'I'm guessing their house is on fire.' Jerre said.

When we crested the hill I got a good look down into Beretha. The city mostly sat on the Eastern side of the river against the sea. Some of it had spread across to the left bank, over a wooden swing bridge that opened to let ships pass up and down the river. That was what was burning.

Around the city a series of makeshift barriers had been thrown up to prevent cavalry charging in. Many people with spades and shovels seemed to be digging earthworks, protected by small groups of archers. It looked like the entire population was out in the surrounding fields.

Closer to us a similar process was happening. The army of Cottalem was digging itself in to encircle the city. A row of barges were lashed across the river a mile upstream of the burning bridge.

We were approaching from the South on the right bank. Our path took us past the bridge of boats. Some sentries directed us to the back of a hill half a mile south east of the city. We found a village of tents, including a working field kitchen. I wondered if it was the same one that had fed me a few days ago.

Major Duerte came over as I dismounted.

'My lady Yngvild, my orders are to escort you to the city, to render you any assistance that you require and to return with you. What do you need?'

'I'll need someone to get me past the sentries, on your side. After that I can manage fine on my own.'

'Corporal, you and Jerre can accompany us. Dismiss the others to their duties.'

'Yes, sir.'

'I think we should eat first.' I said.

'I'll arrange that, my lady.' the Corporal said.

Jerre busied himself looking after our horses, taking their saddles off, feeding and watering them.

From here I would walk into Beretha.

~

Major Duerte took me up to where the infantry were digging their siege lines. I'd left my shield behind, but brought everything else with me. The infantry were digging themselves a long continuous ditch to stand guard in and shelter from arrows and other missiles that might get sent their way. The spoil heap was planted broadly behind their ditch, helping to screen off approaching friendly troops.

We were shown to a wooden hut protected by a screen of earth dug from the ditch. The infantry officer that met us seemed uncomfortable with Major Duerte.

'We need to wait until it gets fully dark, then I'll go across.' I said.

'It won't be long now. The infantry chap said to follow the ditch northwards. It will take us all the way to the front.' Major Duerte said.

'I still need to find a way in. I don't expect that the defenders will leave anywhere unguarded.'

'I think it might be time to go up to the front.' the Corporal was standing in the doorway watching the sun settle on the horizon.

'Let's go. That way I can have a look before we set off across the open.'

The ditch was level with the ground about 50 yards south of the hut. It gradually sloped down until the lip was about knee height. It was a little wider than any of us, but not enough to walk two abreast. The Corporal lead, I was next, followed by Jerre and Major Duerte in the rear.

There were piles of wood dumped on the side every ten yards or so. It wasn't completely straight, there were a couple of gentle turns as we approached the front. After the second turn the ditch went sharply down and the lip was above my head. The wood here had started to be used to reinforce the sides, but not all the way to the top.

It was only about 50 yards until we came to a join with another ditch going East to West. A couple of infantry soldiers sat on a step in their ditch, spades leant against the wall. Neither was armoured, or armed. It was still twilight, not that I could see the sun from inside the ditch.

'Come to 'elp 'ave ya?' an infantryman said.

'None o yer lip, lads. Got an officer and a lady with me' the Corporal said.

The infantry jumped up, grabbing their spades. One of them rushed off to my left. The other, who hadn't spoken yet, stood frozen.

'Right lad, where can the lady get a good view of the city?' the Corporal said.

He couldn't have missed it, but the infantryman didn't seem able to answer for a moment. 'Best go that way' he said, pointing in the direction that his erstwhile friend had gone.

The main ditch was a little wider. At the bottom it was the same, but it had a series of wide steps that let you see over the lip. It also wasn't straight. Every 30 yards or so there were two consecutive corners to twist the line one way or the other.

Each of the bays had a dozen or so infantry in them, all with spades. Bows, shields, swords and short pole-arms also rested within easy reach. In the third bay we were met by an infantry officer.

'I understand you've got an officer with you?' he said.

'Yes, sir. He's at the back.'

I climbed onto the step and risked a peek over the lip while Major Duerte pushed towards the other officer. Only the very top of the sun was visible against the horizon. The shadows would be gone soon. In front of the ditch was a series of sharpened wooden stakes. All the ones nearby pointed towards Beretha, but I expected that I'd find plenty pointing the other way when I got closer. There was no sign of movement out front.

'What have you got planned?' Major Duerte said.

'More digging when it gets dark. This section is

good, but we're not joined up on either flank with the other sections.'

'How many are going out?'

'Everyone is either digging or part of the covering force.'

'That's going to make a lot of noise.'

'We expect them to do the same at this stage.'

'We need to get someone into the city. Can you give us some time?'

'We've all got jobs to do, Major. I need to secure my flanks.'

'Don't worry about it.' I said. 'I think it'll be easier for me to slip through if there's a distraction.'

Major Duerte looked up at me. 'You have a plan?' he said.

'Now that I can see the city, yes.' I said. 'Let's stay here until it's fully dark.'

'Then what?'

'We slide onto the top and crawl forwards until we are in front of our stakes. After that we look for a Berethan work party, sneak around behind them and then walk into the city.'

'That's going to get us caught. We're bound to be challenged by a sentry.'

'You're not coming that far with me. I'll be going into the city on my own.'

'My orders are to—'

'—render me every assistance and to ensure I make it into Beretha.' I finished the sentence for Major Duerte. 'They don't say that you have to come all the way with me. You can come as far as the point where I stand up and walk into the city. After that you'll be a hindrance.'

The Major looked aghast, and his mouth flapped silently.

'But.'

'No buts. You do it my way, or I leave you here

now.'

'If that's how you want it, my lady.'

'It is.'

It didn't take long to get dark. I slipped over the top of the ditch first, Jerre and the Corporal started climbing either side of me moments after I did. The ground undulated and I crawled into a dip so that we could assemble. While I waited for them I thought about being hidden in the dark. This was different from when we'd doubled back into Kronstadt. There were a lot more people around for one thing. For another crawling was very slow and hard work.

The sound of wooden mallets banging against wood carried over the ground. It seemed to be coming from more than one direction. There was also some clinking of mail from my left, and slightly closer to the city. I guessed that was the covering force.

Jerre and the Corporal caught up, both had borrowed iron bound clubs from the infantry. I couldn't see the Major.

'Where's the Major?' I whispered.

Both of them looked round and then shook their heads.

I put my hand on Jafnadr. *'Any idea where Major Duerte is?'* I thought.

'Not his kind of thing, crawling about in the dark. He's a cavalry officer.' Jafnadr told me.

I shrugged my shoulders and then stood up. Looking back towards the ditch I still couldn't see the Major. I did a full circle, but could only make out the sharpened stakes between us and the city, and a group of archers about 100 yards away. Further in the distance was Beretha and its defenders.

I waved at the men to stand up and follow me. They both seemed to understand. We walked carefully through the stakes. I kept my eyes on a brazier on part of Beretha's walls. Walls that no longer marked the outer limits of the city, a couple of streets of houses had grown up outside them.

We were just over a bowshot from the outer ring of Beretha's new ditch. Although I could see very well in the dark I moved slowly and carefully to avoid making any noise. My companions were quiet too. I kept my hand on Jafnadr's pommel.

'You will tell me if we are about to walk into someone?' I thought.

'If I know they are there then I'll let you know.'

I picked a route through the stakes and walked slowly towards the brazier I'd seen earlier. It wasn't cold, so I couldn't quite understand why they'd lit it. Cloud rolled over, making the night darker, which suited me.

I stopped in another fold in the ground. We were probably half way to the city. The noises of digging and building were as loud from in front as behind. Jerre and the Corporal caught up, we were in touching distance because it was so dark. I took one in each hand and pulled them in closer to keep sound to a minimum.

'This is far enough. I'll go ahead alone.' I whispered into their ears. The Corporal nodded, but Jerre shook his head.

'Let me come with you' he gripped my arm like he didn't want to let go.

'I think the trooper may have feelings for you.' Jafnadr suggested.

'Is he spying on me for anyone?'

'Not that I can tell.'

'Corporal, go back to the Major and tell him Trooper Jerre has come with me.'

The Corporal nodded and then turned away and started back to the ditch.

I looked at Jerre and nodded towards the city.

I grabbed his left wrist with my right hand and steered him after me. My left hand stayed on Jafnadr.

We moved as fast as we could in silence. The noises of digging, hammering and cursing the darkness drowned out any sounds we might make.

A Berethan work party was hammering stakes into the ground right on our chosen path. We stopped, and I scanned around for their guards. They weren't immediately obvious, but they had to be somewhere close. I gestured to Jerre to come round to the right with me.

I went very slowly, looking for the guards that I knew had to be out there somewhere.

We swept round in a curve, keeping the group I could see and hear at a steady distance. The clouds parted from the moon and gave me a glimpse of a group of soldiers sat on a small hillock behind the stakes. Their raised bows silhouetted by the moonlight. They were off to my left, and we were between them and the city!

I shook Jerre's arm to point them out. He was already looking straight at them.

Darker around us. I concentrated hard on making us harder to see. The cloud covered the moon.

This was the crucial point. Once we were safely past the guard force we could walk into the city.

I carried on my wide curve, this time keeping the archers away from us, but getting back on the direct path for the brazier.

Lumps of earth started to appear to our front. The bank wasn't yet continuous, and there were people working on joining up the ditches.

I stopped and turned to Jerre, I pulled his head down slightly and whispered in his ear 'Jerre, I need you to be my prisoner.'

He handed me his club.

I tucked it into my belt and drew Jafnadr.

'Put your hands up and walk straight toward that brazier. I'll be right behind you with my sword.'

Jerre started walking, his hands resting on top of

his head.

'Still!' a sentry said.

Jerre stopped, still with his hands up.

'I'm bringing in a prisoner.' I said.

Let us pass I thought at the sentry.

'How many are you?'

'Just me and my prisoner.'

'Pass quickly.'

'Good luck.'

Jerre carried on, jumping over the ditch so that we could walk in the open direct to the city. Another sentry stood at the brazier. I realised that it had been lit as a navigation point. The other streets I could see had been blocked up with makeshift barricades. Windows and doors of the buildings on the edge of the city had also been barred or boarded up.

A sentry stopped us at the entrance, others were being brought in too. We joined a short queue waiting for the barrier to open.

No-one checked us at the barrier, I hurried Jerre down the street. It looked different from before. Most of the ground level windows had been boarded over. Upper level ones had been opened up, and from a few I could see archers standing watch. The first few side alleys had also been blocked with carts and piles of refuse.

Further in was a second block, this one guarded by spearmen with shields. Most of them were resting against the walls of the houses, but a handful were watching the people coming in.

'I'm bringing in a prisoner' I said before the guard had a chance to ask.

'Take him to the Market Square. Third on the left, and then second right.'

'Thanks.' I prodded Jerre in the back with the basket of Jafnadr.

Inside the second barricade the city looked more normal, although quieter than I'd seen it in daytime. I expected a shout from behind for us to stop. But it never came.

Once we were round the corner I put Jafnadr away.

'We need to get to the docks Jerre.'

'You are leaving?'

'No, but we need help getting in to see the Earl.'

'You have friends at the docks?'

'Every Skyssian has a friend in the Board of Trade. And they're always at the docks, every hour of the day and night.'

'That explains a lot.'

We took the next right to avoid walking through the Market Square. I also gave Jerre back his club, which he tucked into his belt. The streets were largely deserted, everyone was either in bed or helping to bolster the defences.

As we crossed Bridge Street, the main East-West thoroughfare, I spotted a glint in the middle of the road. I stopped midway to look more closely. It was a two siller coin, bent out of shape by the passage of a large wheel which had brightened it.

'Finding that's good luck, my lady.' Jerre said when he saw what I'd picked up.

'Maybe it's a sign from Jorunn.'

'Jorunn?'

'God of the Lost and Found, and the little people.'

'We call him Tiago, it's good to have the Gods on your side.'

I tucked the coin safely into a pouch. Maybe it would be a good start for Noren's amulet.

It was a quick walk to the docks, where we found the Board of Trade offices still with lights on in its downstairs windows.

'Good evening and well met!' I said as I opened the door.

'You're back! Where have you been?' Erik looked up from the report he was writing. A smile spreading across his face as he recognised me.

~

The guard at the gate had doubled and looked more alert, but we were met by the Earl's Private Secretary. He hadn't shaved, and looked like he hadn't slept either.

I spent less time waiting than the first time I went to see the Earl. He was already in the audience chamber when we arrived.

'Good day, Lady Yngvild, such a pleasure to see you again.' The Earl was also somewhat crumpled and less polished than before.

'Well met, Your Grace.' I bowed slightly. 'This is Jerre, one of my messengers.'

Jerre gave the Earl a deep bow from his waist before stepping back against the door we'd just came in.

I sat in front of the Earl.

'I passed your message on to my superiors in Kronstadt, along with a favourable recommendation.' I said.

'Thank you, Lady Yngvild, it is good to know that one has been listened to.'

'It was the least that I could do. However the speed of events have been much faster than my despatches.'

'Indeed they have. I don't think anyone expected our King to die quite so suddenly.'

'I have it on good authority that you reacted very promptly when the news reached here.'

'Not as promptly as the King of Cottalem, his army occupied the Citadel before daylight broke. But you know that too, because you were in the Citadel yourself.'

'Yes. I was in the Citadel later that day.'

'So what message do you have for me from the conqueror of Salicia?'

'My mission remains the same as it was before. To seek peace and prosperity for us all.'

The Earl laughed.

'Hah! Naivety does not suit you Lady Yngvild. Nor skulduggery. Be open, it makes it easier on us all.'

'I was taken prisoner and tortured by a man called Rojden. He holds my friend Noren still. I've come here under duress to give you his message.'

'Are you acting under a geas?'

'No, he hasn't done that to me, but I believe he has to Noren.'

'I've heard of Rojden. He was the captain of Duke Xaime's Guards. We didn't see him though.'

'That's because he was also working for the King of Cottalem as a senior advisor. The Duke of Xaime's Guards were supposed to kill you and the other claimants to the throne before betraying the Duke to Rojden.'

'Well they did most of that. There's just me and the King of Cottalem left now.' the Earl said. 'What is his message?'

'Rojden offers you life, liberty and property if you acknowledge his King.'

'It's a tempting offer, but I'm not sure how much I trust them to honour their word.'

'What guarantees would you want to ask for?'

'I worry most about becoming inconvenient alive. There isn't any surety that Rojden or his King can offer to that.'

'Nothing pays you back for being dead?'

'Exactly! You have the makings of a good negotiator, my lady.'

'So how do we keep you alive?'

'There are two ways that I can think of. One is to

make me King and I ally myself to Rojden's grand design.'

'—it may be too late for that. I was made to attend a coronation in the Citadel before I left.'

'He doesn't leave much to chance, does he?'

'I don't think he's comfortable with chance. Rojden likes to make his own luck.'

'Well my other option is to find some enemies of Rojden and stand firm with them against him.'

'While I empathise with that, I'm not sure that it will keep you alive.'

'Not if I stay here, no. Even I can see that the army of Cottalem masses outside. By this time tomorrow they'll outnumber us, and in a week we'll be cut off without hope of anything but starvation and disease. Time and numbers are against us.'

'Where would you go?'

'Skyss if you can arrange it. I understand that you are no friend of Rojden.'

'Many of us aren't, but he does still have friends in Skyss, not all of whom are obvious.'

'Can you lodge me with reliable people?'

'I can point out some people that I know are reliable, but I can't convey you myself until I've freed my friend.'

'I can get there under my own sail I believe, if you give me your recommendations.'

'I will gladly give you a letter of recommendation for my mother.'

'Can your mother protect me from Rojden?'

'Come new year she will be the First Sea Lord. If she can't protect you then no-one else can.'

The Earl turned and spoke to his private secretary 'Some writing paper and ink please, Allan.'

Allan turned to the cabinet in the corner next to where he sat and produced the necessary writing paper, pen and ink. He set them on the table in front of me.

I wrote. The Earl watched silently. All that could be heard in the room was the scratching of the pen on the paper.

'Thank you, Lady Yngvild. I will keep this letter safe.'

'What do you wish me to say in reply to Rojden?'

'Tell him it was hard work, but that you persuaded me to see the futility of standing against him. I have faith in him honouring his word and that I seek to protect the ordinary man more than my reputation or position. I will not stand against my lawfully anointed King, and will gladly uphold his laws.'

'In short, you are his most humble and obedient servant?'

'You are gifted.' the Earl smiled.

'What about ending the siege?'

'Please leave that to me. I will seek clarification that the army of Cottalem is not here in conquest and stands under the orders of the rightful King of Salicia. Once their commander confirms this then there is no siege, it was all a misunderstanding and we all acted out of absolute loyalty to our King.'

'If it is fine with you I may informally suggest to their Commander that approach?'

'So long as he understands that it is your suggestion rather than mine.'

'I will.'

'It has been a pleasure, Lady Yngvild. I do hope that we meet again in happier times.'

'Me too. Fare well, your grace.'

Jerre and I left the room, escorted by Allan. He took us back out to the guard, and handed us over to an officer to be taken out of the city under a flag of truce. We walked back out the way that we'd come in. The last hundred yards between the barricades was still and empty in daylight. The brazier had gone out and all the soldiers were out of sight inside the houses. Just before we passed the final barricade the officer stopped us.

'If you don't mind, my lady, we need to blindfold you.'

'But we've already seen your defences.'

'That's not why we're blindfolding you. It makes you look more like you belong to the Cottalemnese when we go over.'

'In that case let's do it.'

The officer nodded to a guard at a nearby doorway. A drummer and another officer came out. The officer had two scarves with him, which they used to blindfold Jerre and I. While they were doing that the drummer played a tune, which he repeated after a short pause.

The officers led us out across the open area. The drummer kept repeating his tune. I heard the same tune being played to our front, presumably the Cottalemnese playing in response.

Half way across the open area we halted and the officers removed our blindfolds. A couple of Cottalemnese approached with their own flag of truce. We met at the midpoint, my escort stopped and waited for them to approach.

'Do you wish to parley?' asked the Cottalemnese officer.

'We're on our way back from a parley' I said. 'can you take me back to your commander.'

He looked unsure about this.

'Sir, I'm the escort for the Lady Yngvild, from the Horse Guards. Major Duerte is in command of our detachment.' Jerre said.

'Thank you, trooper.' the officer said, then turned to my escort from the Earl. 'We'll take them from here. Thank you for your co-operation.'

Both drummers sounded in unison, and then we parted and walked into the lines of the Cottalemnese army.

~

At the HQ I passed on the news to the local commander, and then asked for horses to get us back to the Citadel and Rojden. Major Duerte appeared in the HQ when I was almost done reporting. He was keen to return with me to the Citadel and facilitated us getting away.

NINE

ᚠᚱᛖᛖᛁᛜᚷ ᛟᚢᚱᛖᛜ

FREEING NOREN

Once we were mounted and leaving Beretha I took the opportunity to converse with Jafnadr.

'Do you think Rojden will keep his end of the bargain?' I asked Jafnadr.

'Rojden has always been a closed book to me. I don't know how he thinks.'

'You don't know how he thinks?'

'That's the key to understanding what people might do.'

'What about Jerre?'

'He's easy.'

'How do I persuade him to help me?'

We ran out of daylight twenty miles short of the Citadel. So we stopped in a wayside inn for the night. It had already been taken over by the army as a way station for couriers to change horses. Major Duerte booked us in and grooms took our horses. Jerre helped them while I went inside to eat.

Because it had been an inn there weren't separate facilities for officers and troopers to eat like I'd seen at our tented rest stops and the lines outside Beretha. So Jerre came in and joined us as the Major and I were finishing our food. The Major left to get some sleep, cautioning me that we would be up early to continue our journey.

I stayed to talk over Jerre to my side.

'How are the horses?' I asked.

'They're in good shape. The lads here know how to look after them.'

'How early can we start again?'

'It'll be first light in about nine hours. We could easily start then?'

'Couldn't we start sooner?'

'Maybe, but it's safer in the daylight, and the horses need some rest. The Citadel will be locked up for the night.'

'What if we timed it to arrive at the Citadel as they opened the gates?'

'We could. If you wanted.'

'Can we leave the Major behind?'

'If that's what you want.'

'It would be for the best. We won't need him when we get back.'

'I'll tell the lads not to wake him.'

'Do you need to sleep?'

'I'll get some in the stable.'

I didn't go to sleep, instead I kept watch over Jerre and the Major by turns. I took some time to reflect while they both slept. The Major had a room to himself, on which I hung a do not disturb sign. Jerre slept on some hay in the stables.

I thought of the bargain I'd agreed with Rojden. Noren's freedom in exchange for ending the war. I couldn't quite see Rojden just handing Noren over. I'd been useful to him, and Noren was my leverage. What could I do if he refused?

'Jafnadr, could I defeat Rojden?'

'Not in a fair fight. He's far more experienced and skilled than you.'

'Is there another way that I could defeat him that might work?'

'Maybe if you got him out to sea, or perhaps while he was asleep.'

'Thank you for the vote of confidence. Is there

anyone that could defeat him?'

'Probably not anyone acting alone. But there are several that could possibly do so.'

'Do I know any of them?'

'Several, but if they'd really wanted Rojden done away with they'd have acted before now.'

'Good point. What should I do if he attacks me?'

'If he wanted you dead he's already had several chances.'

'I still don't trust him.'

'That makes at least two of us.'

I didn't have any means of telling the time, but the inn hadn't closed down as I'd expected it to. There were sentries and some of the army grooms were awake. I went over and asked if they could saddle our horses and prep them for leaving. I willed them to obey, and then felt a little bad about it. They seemed glad enough for something to do that helped them stay awake.

My next thought was to give Jerre and the horses the same sort of night vision that I had. We could go faster safely if we could all see in the dark. I hadn't done this before, so I wasn't sure that I could, nor how to achieve it. My previous attempts had just been about focusing on how I could see in the dark. I'd squinted harder, but that wasn't going to work with the horses, although it might with Jerre.

The only thing I could think of was to try something and see what happened. I'd kicked up a storm by focusing on changing the weather on the horizon. Maybe if I focused on changing Jerre so that he could see in the dark that might work?

I knelt on the straw beside the sleeping Jerre. Dark stubble poked out of his chin and cheeks, I gently ran my fingers over it. His eyelids fluttered as I touched him.

Keeping in contact with his skin I imagined his

eyes widening to work better in the dark. Giving him the same night vision that I had. I spent a few minutes concentrating on that, until I started thinking about other things. I bent over and whispered in his ear.

'Jerre, time to wake up.' I shook him gently.

Jerre stirred and opened his eyes. 'Gods forgive me, it's morning already.'

'Not yet Jerre, but it's time we left.'

Jerre rolled off the hay and stood up, 'But it's bright, must be a good moon up.'

It seemed that my efforts had worked. Now I needed to repeat it with the horses. I left Jerre to sort himself out while I went round to where the grooms had taken our horses.

I started with Whiteface, the horse I'd been riding. With the groom still holding the reins I stroked her neck and face. She was calm, until I focused on her seeing darkness. Her ears flattened back, her nostrils flared and she whinnied. I kept on stroking until she calmed down. Jerre came out, and looked puzzled by the cloud cover and lack of moon.

'Thank you' I said to the grooms 'we can take it from here.'

The pair of them nodded at us and handed over the reins before sloping off back into the stable. Jerre took a moment to loop the pack horse and the spare for Major Duerte into a chain from his saddle.

'It's me Jerre. I made your eyesight better.'

'You can do that?' His eyes widened.

'I can. Just sorting the horses out.'

Jerre's horse looked alarmed when I worked the magic on him too, but it recovered quickly. The other two I left, they would just follow Jerre's horse.

We mounted as soon as Jerre had finished securing the spare horses to his.

With our improved vision we were able to reach the edge of the woods outside the Citadel before the gates opened. We had time to feed the horses and have a cold breakfast of bread, cheese and water before they started to open the gates. I made Jerre wait a few minutes after they opened the gates before we mounted and rode at a walk through the wood to the road and then into the city.

We went straight to where the inner keep was. I wanted to report to Rojden before anyone else could get a message through. A guard stopped us as we tried to enter.

As I was trying to persuade the guard to let me in someone I recognised intervened.

'Let her pass, Rojden is expecting her.' he said.

I couldn't quite place him. He hadn't been here when I left, but I'd seen him before.

'Sir, I was told not to admit anyone I didn't recognise.' the guard said.

'You recognise me, don't you?'

'Yes, sir.'

'Well then. This is Yngvild Helgasdottir. Take a good look at her and remember how she looks.'

The guard looked at me closely, like he was inspecting me for fleas.

'Now, let her pass, Rojden wants to see her.'

While waiting for the exchange to finish I tried to place the man. His clothes were different, but the stance and face were familiar. He wasn't a sailor, nor a horseman. I touched my fingertips lightly on Jafnadr and was reminded.

'Arald! How did you get here?' I asked.

'Yngvild, sometimes it is best not to know the answers to questions.' Arald said.

He put his hand on my left elbow and guided me past the guard and into the Citadel proper.

'Rojden has been hoping that you would arrive soon with good news. You do have good news?'

'Of course. The war is over.'

'Good, good.'

Arald steered me into our breakfast room from a few days ago. Rojden sat at the table, Noren was absent. Food lay over the table, along with a stack of papers and a pot of ink.

'Well met, Yngvild.' Rojden stood and stepped forward to embrace me.

'Well met, Rojden.' I stepped into his embrace.

'Please, sit. Eat if you are hungry.' Rojden said.

Arald made a farewell and left us as Rojden and I sat at the table.

'What news do you bring?' he said.

'The war is over. The Earl of Beretha agreed to your terms.'

Rojden smiled, and visibly relaxed. 'That's a relief. One tries not to fight wars if one can possibly avoid them.' he said.

I realised that I hadn't eaten enough breakfast earlier and surveyed what was on the table. 'Is Noren around?'

'Somewhere. I'll bet Arald has already gone to tell him that you've arrived.' Rojden said. 'Tell me, was the Earl easy to persuade?'

'He didn't give in instantly. He needed some guarantees, but he could see that dying gloriously wasn't as good as living to old age.'

'What guarantees did he want?'

'He wanted recognition of his titles and lands, and a promise that he wouldn't be killed, now or later.'

'You gave him that?'

'It was mostly what you'd offered. I got him safe passage with the Skyssian Board of Trade too.'

Rojden looked at me and raised an eyebrow. 'You facilitated his escape?'

'It was what he wanted to call off the defence of Beretha. I figured you'd be happy with that.'

'I am. You negotiate well. I might hire you again.'

'Thank you. About Noren. I'd like us to carry on with our travels.'

'If you and he insist, but I could use good people like you.'

'I'd very much to spend some time alone with Noren. If he's changed his mind then we might take you up on your kind offer.'

'You are both free to go if you wish. With my blessings, and thanks for ending the war so rapidly.' Rojden said. 'But first, finish your breakfast.'

It was almost an hour later that Noren finally appeared. I was worried that Major Duerte would appear and scupper my plan to get Noren away. Even taking his horse wouldn't slow the Major much, he'd be able to requisition a spare mount from someone.

~

We turned left out of the gate. Instead of following the Great North Road towards Beretha and the sea we went westward along the Great West Road, towards the hills and Salicia.

'My lady, are you sure this is the way you mean to go?' Jerre said.

'Yes. We've got to meet some people in the foothills of the Sierra Cobre.'

Noren stayed silent, a glazed look on his eyes. He hadn't put up much of a fight when I'd led him to the stables and put him on the horse. Jerre had been hard at work while I'd breakfasted with Rojden. Four more horses had been saddled, a spare for each of us and another for Noren. The spare horses had bags of fodder strapped behind the saddles. Jerre had left Major Duerte's mount behind in the stables, it hadn't liked being with us.

The countryside was mostly fields, full of crops not far from harvest, with hamlets every couple of miles.

Some farmers were already collecting in their bounty. We rode at a canter without stopping, swapping horses shortly after noon. Only when we were over the second valley did we give the horses a rest with fodder and water before carrying on. We skirted the towns along the way, the fewer people that saw us the better.

Jerre talked about his boyhood. He'd grown up in a large town, the youngest child of an innkeeper. He'd spent most of his youth in the stables helping the grooms. When his father died he'd joined the Horse Guards as a trooper. His brother, fifteen years his elder, had thrown him out of the inn so that he had room for his own children. Jerre wasn't bitter about this, it was all matter of fact. If it hadn't happened he wouldn't have been a Horse Guard, and he wouldn't be here now on the greatest adventure of his life.

Noren said nothing. He sat stock still on the horse while we moved. He didn't even blink when I stared him in the eyes. Usually I won our staring contests.

He only got off the horse when I physically coaxed him and told him what to do. That scared me. I'd never seen anyone act like this before.

Eventually we reached the edge of the forest that lead to the Sierra Cobre. The farms got further apart, and less of the ground was cultivated. There was still a clear roadway, wide enough to let two carts pass in opposite directions, and clear of trees either side for a bowshot.

'Let's find somewhere to camp a little off the main way.' I said.

Jerre nodded. 'Next time we see a stream we could follow it upstream a bit. It'll give us water for the horses.'

It didn't take long for a stream to appear, although it was no more than a shallow trickle. We turned upstream and followed it until the roadway was out of sight and we found a clearing.

'We'll need to use more of the fodder, there isn't enough grass for the horses to eat here.' Jerre dismounted and set about unsaddling the horses.

'How much did you bring?'

'There should be enough for three days if they only eat fodder, but if we find good grass it might last twice as long.'

Noren still hadn't spoken. I nudged him and spoke gently to give him instructions about getting off the horse. I had to push his right foot out of the stirrup and over the back of the horse before running round to support him getting off the other side. It was a wonder he didn't crush me.

I led Noren to a fallen log and sat him on it so that I could get a good look at him.

When I touched him my amulet buzzed gently and felt slightly cold. Something wasn't right. My ring buzzed as I put my left hand on his forehead, he was icy cold.

My ring! I'd forgotten what my mother had told me. I opened my neckline a little so that I could bring the ring into contact with my amulet.

'*Mother!*' I thought as I touched the ring to the amulet.

I counted to ten inside my head and then repeated my call. Both the ring and the amulet chilled.

'*Yngvild! Where are you?*' The words were recognisably Lady Helga's.

'*On our way to the Sierra Cobre. I need your help.*'

'*What do you need?*'

'*Rojden put a geas on Noren. I got him away, but he's ice cold and won't speak or eat.*'

There was a pause.

'*Noren must be fighting the geas. You need to persuade him that he's obeying it.*'

'*Is this how geasa kill people?*' I was really worried

now. I'd done things against my will to free Noren, and now Rojden's geas was robbing us of Noren's life.

'People usually can't resist a geas like this, but Noren is stronger than most. Get him somewhere he can seem to obey the geas and it will stop.'

'I'm not taking him back to Rojden.'

'You don't need to. Just persuade Noren he's doing what Rojden wants.'

'Is there any other way to stop this?'

'Rojden could release him, or it might expire.'

'That's not very likely.'

'No. It isn't.'

'I'll look after Noren, can you contact me if you find out any other way?'

'I can, and I will. Stay safe Yngvild.'

I let go of the amulet, and instead touched Jafnadr. *'There is another way. You need to find someone more adept than Rojden and repeat the ritual for removing involuntary geasa.'*

'Do you know the ritual?'

'Only that it is possible. Alfarinn knows it.'

I placed my hands either side of Noren's face and knelt so that we were eye to eye. I imagined a spark inside him was still listening, and battling the geas.

'Noren, listen to me. Rojden said we could go because he has another mission for us. We're taking a message to your mother for him.'

I looked into his eyes searching for the spark, willing it to brighten and bring back my Noren.

The longer I looked the more I welled up. Our bond was blocked, I searched his eyes in vain.

A year went by. Tears flowed down my cheeks. I leant forward and rested my forehead against Noren's as I cried helplessly.

'He isn't dead, my lady.' Jerre gently pried me away from Noren. 'But we need to get help.'

I felt ashamed, yet grateful to Jerre for his humanity. I had an urge for human contact and hugged Jerre tightly. I was comforted when he held me. Jerre felt alive, warm, manly. There was a burn of desire inside me, which I struggled to suppress.

I broke the embrace, I knew it would be very wrong to give in to that desire. I just needed to feel wanted and attached to the rest of humanity.

'My lady, you might want this.' Jerre held up a piece of leather thong.

I looked at it, uncomprehending.

'For an amulet. It might protect Noren?' he said.

'I don't think giving him mine would help.'

'Remember the coin? From Beretha.'

I'd thought the coin would make a good amulet, but I didn't know how to turn it into one.

'Do you know how to make an amulet?'

'Maybe you pray over it and call on the gods to bless it for you?'

'Worth trying.' I dug the bent coin out and pushed it to bend it further round the leather.

Once I'd got it mostly closed I put it round Noren's neck and tied it at the back. Then I opened his collar and held the coin in my left hand, enclosing it with my fingers. I did the same with my own amulet in my right hand.

'Malfin, I vowed to pray to you first among the gods when I was bestowed with my amulet. Please intercede with your brother Jorunn to bless this amulet that I bestow on my brother, Noren.'

I paused and concentrated on the coin, imagining it closing around the leather, and taking on power.

'Jorunn, my brother Noren is lost, let him be found and protect him so that he may protect the little people from those that seek to do them harm.'

I let go of my amulet, and then placed Noren's against his chest. I kept the palm of my left hand against it, and covered it with my right. I looked Noren in the eye and spoke.

'Noren, I live for you, and protect you.'

I felt Noren's new amulet buzz under my hands. I caught him as he collapsed and gently laid him down next to the log he'd been sitting on. He was warm again and breathing like he was asleep.

'I hope you've saved him, my lady.'

'Yngvild.' I said 'Call me Yngvild, you helped save Noren too.'

~

I took first watch, there was no way I was going to sleep until I knew whether or not we had actually saved Noren. A little after Jerre fell asleep Noren grew restless. He still slept, but there were shakes of the head, and his eyes moved under the closed lids. He murmured indistinctly in his sleep. I leant in to listen, but couldn't make any of it out. I held his hand, happy that he was warm again.

Although it was still late summer it got properly dark in the Cobre Forest. Back on Straven at this time of year the sun went below the horizon, but it didn't get properly dark like it did in winter. Maybe it was the combination of clouds and the tree canopy.

The forest around us was mostly quiet, there were owls hunting, and small nocturnal prey scurrying in the brush to avoid becoming the owl's next meal. It was a long night, but I resisted waking up Jerre, and I resisted sleep. Noren felt like he might wake up soon, and I wanted to be at his side when he woke.

Eventually the sky brightened again and the birds started to sing. Noren slept on.

The horses started to shuffle and snort. Jerre had hobbled them when we stopped by tying two legs loosely together so that they could walk but not run. He'd also run a rope at chest height round several of the trees in the clearing to discourage them from straying too far.

I found my head nodding. I shook my head to fight the sleep.

I needed to stay awake until Noren woke. How long was he going to sleep for?

I let go of his hand and stood up. I rolled my shoulders round and stretched to wake myself up.

We'd need to eat breakfast. Maybe I could collect some wood for a fire?

It was getting fully light, and I noticed Jerre was restless too. One of the horses was slowly working its way towards Jerre, taking mouthfuls of grass along the way.

I looked around for wood, and started collecting it up a few feet from where Noren lay asleep. I didn't want to go too far from him in case he woke.

Jerre startled me. I hadn't noticed him getting up.

'You should have woken me, my lady. Sorry. Yngvild.' He said.

'I want to be here when he wakes up.'

TEN

ᚳᚢᚱᛋᚢᛁᛏ ᚠᚪᚾᛞ ᛗᚠᛋᛁᛟᚾ

PURSUIT AND EVASION

Jerre decided to check on our trail now that it was daylight while I lit a fire to cook breakfast. I was shaving some dry sticks for kindling when Jerre reappeared, wide-eyed.

'Stop lighting the fire. We need to move.' He pointed away from the road we'd come off.

'What?'

'There's a cavalry squadron approaching, I saw them come over the ridge on the other side of the valley.' Jerre was untying the ropes he'd slung round the trees to stop the horses from straying.

'How long have we got? Noren's still asleep.'

'They were moving at a slow canter, maybe ten minutes?'

I threw the saddle on Whiteface and tightened it as fast as I could. Then I did the same for Noren's horse. Even at my fastest I was no match for Jerre's expertise. He'd coiled the rope, loaded it on one of the pack horses and saddled the three spare horses before I'd done two saddles. I left him to finish the last two while I helped Noren onto his saddle.

Noren still slept. 'Noren, wake up!' I tried shaking him awake, but it had no effect.

A bugle sounded, a dipping and rising signal. I looked to Jerre. He stood stock still and held up his hand. When the bugle stopped he said. 'That's the signal to trot, they're at the top of our hill.'

'Can you help me with Noren please?'

'Leave him be, they're passing through.'

'How can you tell?'

'There would have been a different bugle call if they'd wanted to spread out and search the woods.'

'We still ought to move on. Farther away from here. We should follow the stream. Round the other side of the hill.'

'That might be good, but let's wait until this squadron have moved past.'

Jerre was staring at me. I stared back. Jerre started to smoke. It was billowing off him. He was smiling. Didn't he know he was on fire? He started moving towards me. Maybe he wanted help?

The trees were dancing now. Whirling green around my head.

Jerre caught me in his arms and held me tight. Smelt delicious. My toes tingle. So does my face. No more fire. No smoke.

~

Smoke. Fire crackled. Not a hallucination. My eyes were still closed. I could feel heat on my face, external heat. Not embarrassment. Although embarrassment followed fast on the thought. I opened my eyes to twilight, or was it just the leaf canopy dimming the daylight?

'Yngvild, you're awake!' Jerre jumped up from the small fire he was cooking something on.

'What happened?'

'You fainted, and stayed asleep.'

'And the cavalry?'

'They've gone past, a dozen squadrons through the day.'

'Is Noren awake?'

'Not yet, he sleeps still.' Jerre nodded at Noren's sleeping form. 'When did you last sleep Yngvild?'

'Three days before I fainted. I spent the first night

infiltrating Beretha, the second getting us back to the Citadel at daybreak, and the third watching over Noren. I dozed a bit in the breaks, and when I could in the saddle.'

'I think we can stay here a bit longer, get some rest for you and give Noren a chance to wake.'

'I made arrangements to meet with the Board of Trade people from Beretha a bit North of here. Near an old temple a few miles from a fork in the River Cobre.'

Noren wasn't getting any better and I had no idea what to do about it. Jafnadr couldn't help, and I doubted my mother would be able to either. So I did what I always do when I don't know what to do. I prayed. I prayed for inspiration. I prayed for a sign.

I left Noren and Jerre and the horses and went away from the camp into a clearing where I could see the sky. I sat cross legged on the floor and looked up into the almost cloudless blue sky.

'Malfin, my most favoured goddess, help me save Noren.' As I spoke out loud to the sky I spotted a dark dot circling above me. I watched it for a minute before continuing.

'Jorunn, Noren is one of your people, he is lost. Help me find him.' The dot seemed to grow bigger.

I watched it.

I stared and stared. It wasn't my imagination. It plummeted towards me, resolving into a large black and white bird.

It looked familiar. I'd seen birds like this before.

It came closer, gliding down in a spiral.

I recognised this sort of bird. I'd seen them before swooping down into the sea for fish.

The bird landed in the middle of the clearing and stared at me. Even when I stood up it stayed staring, turning it's head to put first one eye and then the other on me.

'Jerre! Come see this.'

It's head was part turned to the left, and it kept one eye on me. I felt it boring into me.

'That's a magnificent bird, what's it doing here?' Jerre whispered into my ear.

'I was thinking that. How far away is the sea?'

'The sea? Two or three days ride, maybe more.'

'It's a long way from home, I wonder why the gods sent it here?'

As I finished speaking the bird flapped its wings and appeared to grow.

Jerre and I involuntarily stepped backwards, away from the bird.

It continued to grow, the wings and the body thinning while the legs and head thickened.

'I was looking for you Yngvild.'

I stared open mouthed at the dark skinned woman with white hair standing where the bird had been.

'What? How?' I said.

'Relax, I'm a friend. I've come to help you get back home.'

'Are you from Malfin or Jorunn?'

'If either sent me it would be Jorunn, but the Board of Trade sent me first, I've been looking for you for almost four days.'

'Do you know anything about breaking geasa?'

'Most people think that it's impossible.' The woman smiled.

'But you don't?'

'Maybe we can talk about that later. We need to get moving fast. They're searching for you.'

'How did you find us?'

'Finding people is a special talent if mine, and Noren lit up very brightly the night before last. It's taken me a while to get close enough.'

'Does that mean Rojden will be able to find us?'

'I don't think so, he's descended from Meniaxter, not Jorunn.'

'What's your name?'

'Inibrakemi Funeresdottir'

'Well met, Inibrakemi. This is Jerre, he's been helping Noren and me.'

Jerre straightened up and bowed from the waist as I mentioned his name. 'At your service, my lady.'

'Well met. Where's Noren?' Inibrakemi said.

'He's not well, resisting a geas. That's why I asked.' I said. 'Come see.' I lead Inibrakemi to where Noren lay under a blanket in a semblance of sleeping.

She knelt next to him and touched his forehead. After a moment she shook him gently by the shoulders. 'Noren. Noren, can you hear me?'

Noren lay unresponsive, even to her vigorous shaking.

'He's been like this for a couple of days. We can't wake him, but he'll eat and drink if we sit him up and spoon it into his mouth.' I said.

'We need to move him. There were lots of soldiers looking in the woods, and they're coming this way.'

The green dappling in the forest that had seemed a comfort that hid us had become a dark threat that concealed our enemies.

'Jerre, are the horses ready?'

'Almost, Yngvild, I started while you went to pray.'

'Good. Let's tie Noren onto a saddle and move away from the soldiers.' Inibrakemi said. 'Once we're going we can talk about how to help Noren.'

I helped Jerre with the saddles, and collecting up the rope we'd used to help stop the horses straying.

Once we were ready Jerre and I carried Noren onto a horse and tied his feet to the stirrups. Then we tied him round the waist and the high backed saddle so that he couldn't fall out. In the distance horns sounded, I only heard them because they sounded several times.

'We need to go this way.' Inibrakemi indicated deeper into the forest. 'Probably best to go at a walk in single file. Stick to the leafy areas to minimise tracks.'

We went off, Inibrakemi leading on foot, with Jerre following leading the horse Noren was strapped to. The other horses were tied along the rope to follow one another.

I brought up the rear with my bow strung and an arrow knocked just in case.

We walked for a couple of hours before stopping in a grassy area near a stream to let the horses graze and have some lunch. We laid Noren down in the sunlight on the grass.

'Yngvild, we need to get more fodder for the horses.' Jerre held a large sack of oats. 'this is all we've got left.'

'How long will it last?'

'Two or three meals for the horses.'

'It might be best to cut your spare horses free.' Inibrakemi said. 'I have two colleagues with a train of pack horses coming from Beretha. We can meet him in a few days.'

'How far away is your colleague? Could we meet him by tomorrow afternoon?' Jerre said.

'No, they're on a different route, we'll meet them after we cross the river. There's a market at the fork of the Cobre.'

'These are cavalry horses, if I cut them free they'll likely just follow us.' Jerre said.

'Maybe that could work for us. Would you be willing to give them to another group and direct them away from us?' Inibrakemi smiled and touched Jerre's arm. 'You are dressed as they are.'

'I'm just a trooper, they won't listen to me.'

'They don't need to, you could be passing on a message and some spare mounts for the prisoners.'

'What if they want me to join them?'

'Tell them that your HQ asked you to report back when you'd delivered the horses.'

'That should work.'

We set to unloading the horses we'd give away of food, water and anything we'd find useful. Only three were kept. Inibrakemi said she'd fly some of the way when we were able to mount up.

It didn't take long. Inibrakemi scouted the area and tied back a couple of young trees and a bush at the edge of the clearing. I lead whiteface through, ducking her head as she passed into the canopy. Behind the bushes the ground was brown, mostly leaf litter and twigs. It was darker in here too, the higher branches had heavy leaf cover, although the lower branches were sparser. Visibility wasn't long, while it was easy to walk between the trees their irregular spacing and closeness meant that nothing could be seen more than a hundred yards away. Even that would be glimpsed in vertical stripes through the gaps.

I tied whiteface to a branch and put her nosebag on. It would keep her there long enough for me to return. Jerre met me halfway with the other horse, which had borne Noren. Inibrakemi was finishing a stretcher from a couple of saplings, a blanket and some rope when I got back into the clearing. Noren laid on the grass next to her.

'Yngvild, can you help me roll Noren onto the stretcher?'

'What do you want me to do?'

'If we roll him onto his side we can put the stretcher under him before rolling him back. Can you get his leg and waist?' Inibrakemi pointed.

~

213

Wide gnarled pillars supported the verdant sky. Skeletal brown fingers and arms rose out of the leaf litter on the floor. Nothing moved, except the dappling shadows. A susurration of leaves in the wind provided a backing to invisible birdsong. The smell of the forest was damp, yet fresh, a feeling of reassuring calm.

I'm calmer than I've felt in a long time. Since before I left home. I take a moment to think of when. It was after the First Night celebration when I fell asleep cuddled into Noren. The world had felt just right then. Before the Mangandlese ship called in at Straven.

I walked through the wood. Stepping round the fallen branches and patches of bracken. There must be deer in these woods. I couldn't see them, but there were droppings on the ground. There were also no branches with leaves below my head height. So I didn't need to duck and I could see a fair distance ahead.

Nothing moved, yet I was aware of someone behind my left shoulder. Turning I found a dark skinned woman with lustrous straight black hair. Her eyes were black, the pupils took the whole colour and sucked my gaze. She smiled at me. I felt a thrill that sent a shiver through me.

'Well met, my daughter!' She said.

'Well met, my lady.' my response was instinctive. I felt that I knew this woman well, yet I couldn't quite put my finger on who she was.

The light dimmed, like a cloud had covered the sun, unseen above the green leaves. In the distance bugles blew, hunters looking for prey. For me.

'Time is short. You need to pay attention. Don't worry about the hunters. They won't catch you as long as you follow the path.'

'Where's the path? I can't see it anywhere.'

'You need to find your own path and follow it well. Ignore the distractions.'

Bugles blew behind me, seeming close enough to see the hunters. I looked over my shoulder, but the forest was still empty, save for trees and dead-fall.

'What distra—' I stopped when I realised she was gone. She'd disappeared when I'd turned my head.

Behind me the noise of galloping horses grew.

I dashed for the nearest tree.

The bark smoothed. The branches were all beyond reach. I couldn't get purchase to climb.

The ground vibrated as a horde of blue coated cavalry closed on me.

My vision blurred and shook.

I could smell the horses.

The closest cavalry trooper launched himself at me, grinning as he swung a curved sabre.

I ducked under the blade and went for his throat with my bare hands.

He didn't seem to be expecting that. The grin disappeared, replaced by a choking grimace.

'Stop!' he gasped, grabbing at my fingers round his throat.

We rolled away from the tree.

A horse whinnied.

I felt for my dagger with one hand.

The green blur reduced.

'No! Yngvild, stop!' hands came away, palms facing me. The face contorted.

How did he know my name? I paused, dagger under the chin, ready for a quick thrust upwards.

'Jerre! Gods. I'm so sorry.' I dropped the dagger and rolled away. 'I dreamt the cavalry caught me.'

'We're not out of the woods yet, my lady.' Jerre stood up, brushing leaf litter off his clothes.

'Are you well?'

'It was just a very realistic dream. I'm really fine.'

ELEVEN

ᚠᛟᚱᛗᛋᛏ ᛟᚠ ᛞᚱᛗᚠᛗᛋ
THE FOREST OF DREAMS

Wide gnarled pillars support the verdant sky. Skeletal brown fingers and arms rise out of the leaf litter. Nothing moves, except the dappling shadows. A susurration of leaves in the wind provides a backing to invisible birdsong. The forest smells damp, yet fresh, a feeling of reassuring calm.

I walk through the wood, leading Whiteface. Stepping round fallen branches and patches of bracken. There are deer somewhere in the woods but I can't see any of them, only their tracks. There are no branches with leaves below my head height. So I don't need to duck and I can see a fair distance ahead.

'We've been here before Jerre.'

'I don't recognise it, Yngvild.'

'It's familiar. I've seen these trees before.'

'The ground is soft Yngvild, and if we'd been here recently you'd be able to see the tracks.'

I looked at the ground, it was soft in places, I could see the hoof prints behind us when I looked back. Was I losing my mind? Maybe I'd spent too long wandering in the woods and it was all blending into one.

'Maybe I still haven't recovered from the lack of sleep. I'd have sworn that we'll pass a fallen tree on our right just as we come to a shallow stream.'

'Perhaps you should nap when we next stop?'

'We don't want to stop for long. The further we get the less chance there is of them catching us.'

We push on while I puzzle over it. Every step seems familiar. With each passing yard I'm more sure that I've been here before.

But Jerre is right. There are no horse or human tracks amidst those of the deer. Before we've gone more than a hundred yards I see a patch of forest ahead where the sun shines brighter. It's a break in the canopy, and as we get closer I see a fallen tree to our right.

Then I hear the gurgling of water over the stones.

'The Goddess!' It hits me why this is familiar. 'She told me to find my own path, and to follow it well!'

Jerre looked confused.

'I know where we are now. Just follow me.'

Without waiting for a reply I follow the path I've followed so many times in my dreams. Calling it a path is stretching it. There's no actual path on the forest floor, but I recognise the trees and know which way to go.

Our walk is accompanied by birdsong, and after a while the gurgling of a brook that we follow down a gentle slope. We stop for a rest where an outcrop of rock sticks through the forest and the stream falls from a cleft in it to form a pool circled by boulders.

Jerre and I feed the horses from the last of the feed bags after we've lifted Noren to the ground and propped him up by a tree. Jerre fills our water bottles from the flow while I rummage in saddle bags for something for us to eat.

'There's not much left that doesn't need cooking properly.' I held up some stale bread. 'Just some bread and a bit of cheese.'

'I think we can do better than that.' Inibrakemi appeared from behind me.

'Inibrakemi!'

She smiled and embraced me. 'Well met, Yngvild!'

'Well met indeed. Are we close yet?'

'The temple is a couple of days away, but you seem to have lost your pursuers when you crossed the ridge.'

Jerre returned with the filled water bottles.

'Inibrakemi.' He nodded.

'Jerre, come here.' Inibrakemi held her arms wide to hug Jerre.

He put the water bottles down and hugged Inibrakemi, lifting her off the ground.

'That's a proper welcome!' she said when Jerre put her back on the ground.

'I'm not alone, I met some of your other friends Yngvild, and they have supplies.' Inibrakemi said.

Jerre looked around, staring into the trees. 'Where are they?'

'Not far, a mile or so through the trees there's a major road out of the Cobre Mountains.'

Knowing that friendly company was nearby we cut our rest stop short and moved to join them. Inibrakemi stayed with us to lead the way. Apart from Noren, we all walked to avoid pushing the horses too much.

The road was a little more than a wide clearing. Maybe a hundred yards between the woods and a slow moving brown river that was wider still. Grass grew between the waggon ruts, and there was plenty of evidence of horses that passed either way. As we broke out of the wood we saw several groups of travellers, some with lines of pack horses, others driving mules and a handful of waggons going in both directions.

Over the river in the near distance, maybe several miles off, was a small city. It had high walls and more than one watchtower. The land across the river was mostly open fields, crops I didn't recognise stood tall and green in the closest ones.

'So where are they?'

Inibrakemi pointed to a string of horses grazing near a waggon, with two men lounging on top of unloaded pack saddles.

Within a few moments we were practically on top of them. Close enough for me to recognise Olaf and Erik from Beretha.

'Well met!' I called 'How fares the road?'

Olaf grinned, looked around, and when he was sure no-one else was in earshot spoke. 'We haven't had any bother from Rojden's people. Although I'm sure that might change.'

'Let's hope not!' I said.

We all laughed a bit. I think we were all happier to be in a larger group. We fed our horses and then put some tents up. It wasn't long until night, and I wanted to skirt the city up ahead. It would be difficult if we were recognised by a sentry.

After a conversation we decided that my idea that Inibrakemi and I could take Noren on ahead during the night wasn't going to work. The river was too deep to cross safely without a boat, and we needed to go upstream on the other side of the river. The city of Minhaton sat astride the fork, and the river below was deep. Olaf and Erik had spare clothes so we could change our appearance, this meant Jerre could ditch his cavalry uniform. Inibrakemi and I could both dress as men. Then we would bring the waggon and horses through the city and across both bridges to the other side. If we hit it early in the morning we ought to get lost in the traffic.

Once we were over the river Inibrakemi and I could take Noren ahead, we'd move much faster than the waggon could. The men would take the waggon and walk the horses at a more leisurely pace and meet us when we were finished. There was an Inn nearby they could stay in for a couple of days without attracting suspicion.

We were only a mile from the south bridge at Minhaton. Most of the groups in front of us would have made it over the river before the gates closed at dusk.

Nonetheless I insisted that we strike camp at first light so that we were at the head of the queue the moment the gates opened.

Inibrakemi and I shared one of the tents. I would have been happy with a blanket, but at least the tent gave us privacy for our transformation. I decided to practice before I bedded down for the night. Inibrakemi sat on a couple of blankets and watched me.

I spread the clothes Erik had passed me on the groundsheet. There was a woven wool cap, gathered into a band that just fit round my head when I tucked my hair inside it.

A second, or maybe third-hand, long sleeved doublet was made from light brown linen canvas. I laid it out to examine, feeling stiffer patches at the right cuff, under the arms and a new collar that didn't match the interior lining. It was thicker still at the back where it had been inexpertly taken in by overlapping the two back panels. My fingers traced the darker areas along the panel edges, finding the odd loose thread where someone had removed ribbon. The lining was a soft pink linen, more like the material I'd use for making a shift.

Some short breeches were cut from the same cloth and had hooks and eyes round the waistband to fix them to the doublet.

It looked pretty ordinary, I'd seen others in Beretha wearing the same sort of clothes.

'Do you think these are what the locals are wearing?' I turned to Inibrakemi.

She just smiled.

'I worry they're looking for us.'

'Of course they're looking for us. But you don't need to worry.'

'Are you sure we won't stand out?'

'Yngvild, this isn't my first trip to Trollheim. I have been doing this since before you were born. You just need to make yourself look different, wear the clothes and play along.'

'That's what worries me, up close they'll know I'm a woman if they are paying attention.'

'They won't. Because you can look like anything you want to.' Inibrakemi shimmered a little.

I blinked, and looked closer at her. Her cheeks were fuzzed with a close cropped beard. The white hair contrasting with the darkness of her skin.

Looking down her chest had flattened and her waist thickened.

'How did you do that?'

'Same as you do everything else. Have a clear picture in your head of what you want to happen and then will it.'

'I'm not sure I can change my body the way you can. We're all good at different things.'

'This is something we can all do, although it helps if you can clearly imagine it.'

'How come no-one talks about this in the sagas?'

'They do, all the time, you've just not been paying attention if you've missed it.' she paused, and not getting the expected response, Inibrakemi filled the silence. 'Snorri Bearshanks? Or Gudrid the Gull?'

'I thought those were just nicknames, not actual shapeshifting. Not everything in the sagas can be literally true.'

'Mostly. Often an understatement because the real truth would be unbelievable for those that weren't there.'

'Ptchah! Next you'll be telling me Old Bjorn is a thousand years old!'

'I haven't been around that long, but it wouldn't surprise me if it was true.'

I stripped off and practised looking like a man, while Inibrakemi made helpful suggestions. It took about twenty changes for me to get the image clear in my head. Once I'd got it down I put on the clothes Erik and Olaf had brought for me.

'Nice. But don't pack away your own stuff yet.'

I stopped midway through rolling up my skirts. 'Why?'

'Are you planning on getting any sleep?'

'I thought I might just sit here and doze until it was first light.'

'It takes a fair bit of practice to keep a different shape while you sleep. You might be more comfortable changing back first.'

I relaxed my mind and thought about my usual body shape. Slowly I flowed back into my curves, the clothes slackened across my shoulders and waist. The contours on my chest and hips changed a bit, but I was still smaller as a woman than I had been as a man.

'I think I can get away with packing my own clothes up.'

'Looks that way.' Inibrakemi nodded sagely. 'I'm going to get some rest now, we've an early start.'

It seemed like only the briefest sleep before Erik spoke to us through the tent canvas.

'Time to get up!' Erik's wake up call was accompanied by creaking noises as he climbed off the waggon he'd been sat on for his turn on watch.

'I'm awake!' I spoke loudly enough to be heard through the canvas.

'Morning, Yngvild!' Erik said.

'I'll wake Inibrakemi and we'll be out as fast as we

can.'

Before I woke her I thought about the form of Ingwald, I'd decided to go by the name I'd used when we got on the ship to Grunwald. That seemed an age ago, yet it couldn't have been much more than a moon.

I concentrated on being a man, and felt my chest grow tight as other parts of me stretched. I hoped I'd remembered correctly. Once the feeling of strangeness had mostly subsided I gently shook Inibrakemi's shoulder.

'Wake up, it's time to pack up.'

Inibrakemi rolled away and sat up. A moment of shock crossed her face as I registered with her.

'Did I do it right?'

She paused before answering. Her gaze dropped from my face and flowed over my body, examining every part. She lingered longer in places I hadn't expected before delivering her verdict.

'You are a very handsome and well constructed young man. Possibly too handsome for a crew like this.'

'What have I done wrong?'

'Absolutely nothing. You're a perfect specimen. If you could see yourself you'd be delighted.'

I raised an eyebrow.

'That. That's a woman. You've got the look, now you need to learn the behaviours.'

Jerre, Erik and Olaf barely gave a second glance when I came out of the tent. Jerre and Olaf were focused on saddling the horses, while Erik helped Inibrakemi and I with the tents. We packed our kit and loaded it into the waggon. Noren lay on top, covered with a blanket. With the horses saddled and the waggon loaded in the faint grey light we were ready to go before the sun rose over the trees.

The hardest part I found was getting used to the

completely different body shape. It made me walk differently, and moving needed more thought than usual. I was just about getting used to it when I mounted the horse, and a sharp pain shot through me. I'd trapped a key piece of anatomy, the saddle had formed a Yngvild shaped space that Ingwald didn't fit into comfortably. I stood in the stirrups for a moment for the flash of pain to subside.

Inibrakemi looked at me and chuckled.

I shot a pained glare at her.

'Sorry! Should have warned you about that. You'll want to adjust the blanket and sheepskin.' She gestured at my saddle.

I got back off and pulled the sheepskin off. Under it the blanket had been rolled behind where I'd been sitting, making the gap between the pommel and cantle smaller. I guess the cavalry troopers who'd prepared the saddle for me had made allowances for my smaller size.

Jerre rode over while I was tugging at the saddle.

'Do you need any help, Yngvild?'

'It was a bit tight, Jerre.' I stopped fluffing and looked up.

Jerre looked back, his jaw slack and eyes wide.

'Part of the cover, call me Ingwald.'

Jerre shook his head. 'Never seen a disguise that good. Sorry. What?'

'Inibrakemi is very skilled, she showed me how.'

'Very skilled. Well done Inibrakemi.' Jerre half bowed to her, twisting to the side of his high cavalry saddle.

'My pleasure, Jerre.' She nodded her head in acknowledgement of Jerre's bow.

Jerre took the blanket from me and shook it into place. I passed the sheepskin up to him and he carefully smoothed it into the corners of the saddle.

'That should give you some more room. It's the way

our corporal taught us for the remounts.'

I swung up into the stirrups and carefully lowered myself into the saddle. 'Thank you, Jerre, that's much roomier than before.'

We set off at a walk as the sky brightened above us. We couldn't see the sun just yet, but it wouldn't be long until it was above the trees. When that happened the gates of Minhaton would open.

~

The gates of Minhaton proper lay on the other side of the river. A massive stone gatehouse towered over the river, three stories high and two taut chains joined it to the wooden drawbridge that sat on stone piers in the river. It was wide enough for two waggons, although the wide gateway into the town was closed by two sturdy iron bound gates.

On the near side a smaller gatehouse lead to an open area inside a wall. Two buildings guarded the stone pier of the bridge. They sat diagonally to the bridge and funnelled anyone that approached towards it. A loose wooden barrier lay across a paved section of road leading to the bridge.

A short queue had started to form while the guards checked people and cargo. There were a couple of waggons, and several people with handcarts with vegetables in them.

Over the river on either side of the gatehouse a stone wall surrounded the town of Minhaton. Mostly just blank wall, there were a few arrow slits near the bridge, but practically no windows at all. Downstream, where the two parts of the river met, was another tower, and built up fortifications. I could see people on the ramparts.

Above the wall a keep dominated the town. At the confluence of the rivers the lower part of the wall was sheer rock jutting out of the water.

As we got closer to the bridge end I realised that there were several guards. Four were moving through the queue, in pairs looking at the cargoes. A couple of guards stood behind the barrier, armed with halberds.

It was almost full daylight by now. Looking away from the town the road that came from the south was more lively than our river hugging approach from the East. A number of waggons and pack trains were either moving towards Minhaton, or getting ready to move from their overnight stop.

The doors opened as we reached the end of the queue. The barrier was swung to the side and the front of the queue ushered forward on the left of the bridge. A couple of the guards made the rest of us move to allow the outgoing traffic to flow. Even this early in the morning there was a stream of pack horses, waggons, horse riders and people on foot going south.

We shuffled forward until a pair of guards turned their attention to us. Erik was up front in the waggon with Noren in the back. Olaf and Jerre were leading the pack horses with Inibrakemi and I at the back. I was too far back to hear the conversation with Erik and the guard.

The second guard had a look in the back of the waggon before walking down the pack horses and looking in some of the packs they were carrying. It was just a cursory check, he barely paused in his walk along the train.

'This all your horses?' the guard gestured at the horses in front of us when he got as far as Inibrakemi and me.

'Yes, just those.' Inibrakemi answered.

'Where you going?'

'Wherever the boss takes us.'

'You aren't the boss?'

'He's the boss.' Inibrakemi pointed at Olaf.

'Where would he say you were going?'

'Somewhere up river towards the Cobre Mountains where they need to trade.'

'Got any plans to stop in town?'

'No, straight through.'

The guard nodded and walked back up the line to his partner.

Erik had dismounted and was talking animatedly by the side of the waggon.

I craned forward to listen more carefully. Erik was saying that Noren was sleeping because he'd been on watch all night.

The guard we'd spoken to stopped by Olaf for a moment and waved to his partner before speaking to Olaf.

'What do we do if it's not all good?' I put my hand on Jafnadr.

'Relax Ingwald, the boss will handle it.' Inibrakemi put her hand on my sword arm. 'Watch and see.'

There were shaking heads and serious looks up front. Erik looked worried.

'Maybe we should go join in?' I said.

'Wait. Look calm.' Inibrakemi said.

'Listen to her, getting involved now will just raise suspicion.' Jafnadr said.

The other pair of guards came down the line as the waggons in front of us moved onto the bridge. They stopped behind Erik.

'Maybe they're already suspicious?' I thought.

'If they are talking will be easier than fighting. Look at those walls.' Jafnadr said.

The other pair of guards carried on past us to the caravan behind us. I took my hand off Jafnadr.

Our guards waved Erik back onto the waggon and we started moving forward. They led us onto the bridge and raised a yellow flag as we passed by.

'Don't stop in Minhaton for anything.' the guard

said as we passed him.

'No problem.' Inibrakemi said.

Ahead a couple of guards stood waiting in the gateway across the bridge. One carrying a spear with a yellow flag mounted on it climbed onto the waggon as it passed through the arch. The other fell in behind us with his loaded crossbow.

He stayed several feet behind us as we passed along a wide broad curving street. On both sides were lines of shop fronts, with Inns interspersed. Side streets led off left and right, although mostly to the right. The citadel was on the left.

There were plenty of people around, although not so many as Kronstadt or Beretha. They gave us a wide berth, the yellow flag warning them off.

After a few minutes walk we passed through the market square, some of the people we'd seen with barrows were setting up stalls. There were interesting things on the stalls, but when I paused to look the guard reminded me to keep moving.

Not much further on the docks appeared on the left, inside the walls. A massive water gate stood open against the river. There were three bays in the basin, two of which had ships in them. Dockers loaded and unloaded cargoes as we passed by.

Upstream of the docks was another bridge. Barges passed under its arches, laden with stone. Once over the bridge the guard dismounted from the waggon and spoke to the guards. Our friend at the rear stayed on the Minhaton side when we crossed the bridge.

Once we were over the bridge an expanse of farmland lay in front of us. The main traffic bore right and followed the river upstream, in the distance we could see the Cobre Mountains. A couple of smaller paths went other ways, one inland away from the bridge, and another followed the river southwards.

Erik steered the waggon along the main road with the bulk of the traffic, I guessed he was avoiding suspicion by blending with the flow.

'Where's the temple?'

'It's west of here.' She gestured between the road and the track that lead directly away from the bridge. 'Slightly north of due west. I usually fly.'

'You come this way a lot?'

'Minhaton is the closest major town to the temple, so when I need some human distraction this is where I come.'

'How far is it?'

'About an hour on the wing.'

'You going to teach me how to fly?'

'That's an interesting idea.' Inibrakemi nodded her head. 'Maybe I will.'

'I'll hold you to that.'

We rode past fields being harvested, and others with leafy green vegetables in them. Most of the fields on the riverside were pasture, with horses or cows in them.

Coming towards us, out of the mountains, the waggons and pack trains mostly seemed empty, the weight of metal meant they couldn't fill the space.

Several pillars of white smoke rose on the horizon like fingers of the fluffy clouds feeling the texture of rough uplands.

'Is that normal?'

'What?'

'The smoke.' I pointed at the horizon ahead.

'Those are the smelting pits. Where they turn the ore into copper metal.'

'Do they burn all the time?'

'Why do you think there aren't any trees for miles? They cut them all down to make charcoal to keep the furnaces burning.'

'I thought it was just cleared for farming.'

'The furnaces use a lot of fuel, it comes up the river on boats, and then gets swapped onto barges at Minhaton.'

'Have you ever visited the smelting pits?'

'A couple of times, a while back there was a dispute about adulterated silver that someone was trying to pass off as red gold.'

'You got sent to resolve it?'

'That I did.'

A few miles out of Minhaton, once it was too far for them to see us, Erik pulled the waggon over just short of a track leading away from the river.

'This is where we part ways.' Inibrakemi said when we caught up to the others.

'What do you need to take with you?' Olaf said.

'Just Noren. He'll need a horse, a mare ideally.'

'Jerre, can you sort out one of the mares?'

'Yes, Olaf.' Jerre strode down the line and started to unload one of the pack horses.

I dismounted and went to help Erik unload Noren from the waggon. I climbed over the tailgate, and knelt by Noren's head. Reaching down to stroke his face I felt the heat radiating from him. He was hot to the touch, although not flushed red like you'd expect if he had a fever.

'Inibrakemi, Noren's hot!'

'He is, isn't he?' Inibrakemi chuckled.

'Not like that, he's burning up.'

'Is that what the guard was worried about earlier?' Inibrakemi asked Erik.

'He was worried that Noren was sick because he couldn't rouse him. I tried to persuade him that he was a really heavy sleeper and had been on watch all night.'

'Did he feel hot earlier?'

'I don't know, I didn't touch him.'

'Did the guard?'

'Yes, the guard tried to shake him awake.'

'Right, that changes things. We need to get moving faster.' Inibrakemi said.

'Should we come with you?' Jerre said.

'No, it's too dangerous for you.'

'Isn't that an argument for having an escort?' I said.

'It isn't dangerous for you or me, Yngvild, but it is dangerous for Jerre, Olaf and Erik.'

'What about Noren?'

'There's a risk, but we can sort that out when we get there.'

'Why is it dangerous for us?'

'The Temple at Estreham was cursed by the Clewgists when the Quirinites came for them.' Inibrakemi said.

'Oh. I get it.' Jerre took a step back. 'We don't want to go there, I heard the stories in my father's tavern as a boy. They gave me nightmares.'

'You can tell Olaf and Erik later, Jerre. We need to get going as fast as we can.' Inibrakemi said. 'Let's get Noren on that horse and get going.'

Jerre brought the horse to the back of the waggon and held it while Erik and Inibrakemi helped me manoeuvre Noren out of the waggon and over the back of the horse. He wasn't responding like he had been earlier, so we draped him over the saddle, belly down. Jerre fashioned a harness with some rope to secure Noren, said he'd learnt it for tying casualties to the horse as a cavalry trooper.

Inibrakemi and I mounted while Jerre tied Noren to the saddle. As soon as he was done we left.

'We'll meet in the Riggin Dale, in four or five days. Wait for us at the Wheel.' Inibrakemi said before we rode away on the track that led us inland, and towards the temple of the Clewgists at Estreham.

We moved at a fast canter to Estreham without stopping. The fields gave way to low hills, with pasture, and then groups of trees, and finally the return of the forest. Housing stopped fairly abruptly, apparently people didn't want to live to close to a cursed temple.

~

We crested a curved ridge and saw a bowl shaped valley below, a white domed building amidst a circle of twelve large chestnut trees about half a mile away. The trees sat in the middle of a large cleared area, with a crystal pond or small spring-fed lake on the western side.

Smoke drifted lightly from the centre of the dome, someone was in the temple, and they were burning something. Inibrakemi drove us on, breaking into a gallop now that the destination was in sight.

My attention was focussed on staying on Whiteface, I'd not ridden this fast before. So I missed the bear until Whiteface reared. Thankfully my concentration on holding on for dear life meant that I stayed on her back when she kicked her front legs in the air. By the time I regained control the bear was gone, and Alfinna stood in her place.

'Alfinna! How many times have I told you not to do that?' Inibrakemi dismounted, letting her confused horse go free.

Alfinna dissolved into laughter. 'Your face!'

Inibrakemi tried to look stern but ended up laughing with Alfinna as they embraced.

I dismounted and got hold of Noren's horse while they calmed down.

'Yngvild, I think you've met Alfinna before?'

'Yes, on Grunwald, near Knarvik. In the woods.'

'I like those woods.' Alfinna said.

'I need your help, Noren isn't well.'

'My brother? You brought him here?'

'On the other horse.' I said. 'Can we take him inside, he needs help.'

'It might not be best to take him inside'

'Relax Alfinna, we can protect him.' Inibrakemi caught the rein to lead Noren's horse.

'If the curse of Clewg strikes him down—'

'—Rojden is to blame.' Inibrakemi finished Alfinna's sentence. 'Let's get him settled.'

I unlaced the knot holding Noren's legs to the saddle. Alfinna gave up arguing and got to work on the other side of the horse from me. Together we gently lowered Noren from the saddle onto the soft short grass just outside the circle of trees. Noren shivered as we laid him down, yet he radiated heat like hot rocks after the fire had gone out.

'He's been like this since early this morning, before that he'd do things when you asked, but didn't speak or respond to anything.' I said.

'What happened?'

'Rojden had us, and sent me to end the war. I don't know what he did to Noren, but he put a geas on him, and he hasn't been the same since.'

'Has he been like this for the whole time?'

'No, it was only after I took him away from Rojden, and made him an amulet with a silver coin I found in Beretha.'

'The amulet might not be helping. Or at least not helping enough.' Alfinna said.

'If we take it off Rojden will know where he is.' Inibrakemi said.

'He can't do anything about that. Unless he's found out how to become an adept of Clewg.' Alfinna said.

'No-one knows the ancient rites of Clewg. It's not even written in their books, and they had a lot of those.' Inibrakemi said.

'Yngvild, you need to break the cord holding the amulet.' Alfinna said.

I loosened the top buttons on Noren's doublet and pulled the shirt neck open. The folded coin sat in the hollow where his chest met his neck. The coin glinted in the sun. It was beautiful. I didn't want to destroy my good work.

What if Rojden's army rode in here and massacred us all? He surely couldn't be happy with me. Probably had a special death planned, something slow and excruciating.

'No. I don't think we should remove Noren's amulet. As soon as Rojden knows where we are his army will massacre us.' I said.

Alfinna leaned forward, putting her hands on my shoulders and her mouth next to my ear.

'Yngvild. Listen. That amulet is powerful. Take it off.' She leaned back.

I couldn't move my arms. Had they been turned to stone? Was this the curse of Clewg?

Inibrakemi lifted my left hand and put it on the pommel of Jafnadr.

My mind cleared.

'Use me. It needs a drop of your blood before you cut the cord.'

I stood and drew Jafnadr. I touched the tip of Jafnadr with the little finger on my left hand. *'Bleed me a little.'* I thought. I barely felt anything as Jafnadr drew blood.

I dropped the point to touch the amulet. As I saw the blood drip onto the coin I spoke.

'Noren, I release you from this amulet, but you stay under my protection.'

My ears filled with a keening, rising to ululation as I dropped Jafnadr's point behind the cord and sliced it away from Noren's neck.

It got so loud I dropped to my knees and fell across Noren's chest. I let go of Jafnadr and the noise stopped. My left hand dripped more blood on his face. It sizzled.

His eyes fluttered.

'Noren! Noren!' I held his head in both hands and willed him to wake up.

He thrashed for a moment and lay still. I could see his chest rising and falling with each breath.

'Well done Yngvild, I think that helped.' Alfinna hugged me from behind. After a moment she pulled me away from Noren.

'I'll get some help.' Inibrakemi turned away and went into the temple building.

Noren cooled off when I removed the amulet. Some of Alfarinn's household brought out a bed and set it up before moving Noren onto it.

I found the amulet in the grass. What had started out as a two siller coin was now a melted triangular lump of silver. More like an arrowhead than a coin folded in half.

Alfarinn visited Noren and laid her hands on his head. She commanded her daughters to prepare something in the main temple. When they'd done this she had them strip Noren down to his shirt. Alfarinn didn't look at me though. Nor did she return after visiting Noren.

Inibrakemi and Alfinna came back to where I sat once Noren had been moved onto the bed.

'I've got a plan.' Inibrakemi said.

'That's what you said last time. It better work.' Alfinna crossed her arms.

'Remember the prophecy? The one that made your mother come here?'

'That won't help, it's rather vague. It could mean

anything.'

'It could.'

'What prophecy?' I asked.

Both Alfinna and Inibrakemi were facing me. Despite the different skin tones and hair colours I could see similarities in them.

'You're related to each other?'

'She's my Great-Aunt.' Inibrakemi pointed to Alfinna.

Alfinna nodded. 'I'm so much older than her.'

Inibrakemi raised an eyebrow.

'Which is why you should listen to me.' Alfinna said.

'What's the prophecy?'

'It's an ancient one, Alfarinn thinks it's about her, and that her son will bring an end to the dominance of Skyss.' Inibrakemi said.

'It's why she famously only bears daughters.' Alfinna said.

'Noren's her son?'

'Yes. Although it took her a while to admit to it.' Alfinna said.

'Do you know how we can break the geas?'

'Alfarinn said only death can break that geas.'

~

It had all been for nothing. I could have stayed with Rojden and enjoyed time with Noren, the actual functioning human. Instead I'd grabbed him and ran away. My selfish act had condemned him.

I turned and walked away from everyone, out of the circle of trees. I needed time to calm, so that I could plan how to enlist others to help me secure Rojden's death.

I stopped at the first tree that I came to. It was a huge gnarled old tree, bigger than any others I'd seen. The trunk was wider than the alley at Straven. Birds nested high in the canopy. Putting a hand on the trunk, feeling the roughness of the bark, I traced a circle round the tree, stepping over the massive roots that stretched out of the bottom into the leaf litter. It took forty eight steps before I came back to where I'd started.

Under the canopy green spiky lumps lay on the ground, I guess those were seeds. Looking up into the branches more were on the tree. I noticed the canopies for each tree slightly overlapped. There was a continuous circle of trees around the temple.

I followed it round, measuring each tree as I came to it. The birds sang happily above my head. On the fourth tree I felt a jolt of recognition, the pattern of bark seemingly familiar, but I couldn't place it.

By the sixth tree I was certain that the temple was off centre, it was oval rather than circular. The middle of the circle of trees was a small steaming pool, lined with smooth pink rock. It fed the lake by a small stream between trees six and seven.

At the seventh tree recognition came again, this time stronger, although I couldn't place it. I carried on. Birds landed on the trees, they sang on the wing as they approached, and fell silent as they landed.

As more birds appeared I was aware that they were forming a ring behind me. My progress measured by a line of birds of all different kinds. They sat on the same level, and I could see that at least one branch per pair was braided to physically join the trees and making a continuous circle.

While I transited the twelfth tree Alfarinn and her daughters drifted into a demi-circle facing the first tree. Alfarinn was equidistant between the temple door and the first tree.

The birds hadn't formed a full circle. So I carried on to the first tree. Standing outside the circle I put both hands on the tree and knelt before it.

'Clewg, I promise to keep your secrets if you help me to remove Rojden's influence.'

A single bird chirped.

'I will make sacrifice for you, and preserve your temple, second only to Malfin.'

Another bird chirped.

'I shall strive to be the best I can be, to help others be their best, and to push forward the boundaries.' I had no idea why those words came.

The birds spoke as one. The harmonics made the voice vibrate. 'Rise Yngvild! Clewg welcomes you. Seek the Chestnut Lodge.'

The birds rose, flew round the circle and then sped off in every direction at once.

I stood looking back at the temple, and Alfarinn standing with the other women looking at me. None of us moved. I could feel the wind blowing from behind me, lifting my hair and billowing it out on either side. I'd undone my braids when I'd tucked it into the hat.

Alfarinn walked towards me, arms by her side. She was barefoot, dressed in a light linen tunic that came to mid-thigh. She held my gaze. Her dark hair showed no sign of grey, nor her face any wrinkles. Yet her eyes showed a depth of experience only the oldest widows had.

'Sister.' Alfarinn reached out and put her hands on my shoulders. 'You are truly blessed.' She smiled with her whole face, her eyes glowed and rogue black hairs floated around her head.

There was a charge, a connection, between us. Like lightning had struck us both. For a moment I smelt the sea, and the forest, and the heavy smoke of wet wood. All at the same time. I felt joy and terrible loss, like I knew everything in the world.

As soon as the sensations washed over me they were gone. Alfarinn let go of my shoulders, and the weight of the world left me. The wind stopped and my hair fell down my back like always. I was just

Yngvild again, a lost young woman looking for her place in the world. Ordinary like everyone else.

'You are no ordinary woman, Yngvild.' Alfarinn shook her head. 'You are the bringer of justice in the night.'

'Jafnadr.'

'More than that.' Alfarinn picked at the buttons on the doublet that I wore. 'Be yourself again, we have work to do, you and I.'

I stripped the doublet off and tossed it aside. It was warm at Estreham, and all the other women, save Inibrakemi, wore the same short, sleeveless tunic that Alfarinn wore. The grass was soft and cool between my toes when I pulled the shoes and hose off my feet. I tossed them in the same direction as the doublet before losing the breeches too. I brought Jafnadr, still in her scabbard, when, clad only in my shirt, I followed Alfarinn into the temple building.

Alfinna waited to greet me at the entrance. 'Whatever happens in there, Yngvild, just play along, I believe my mother has an idea, but she rarely shares them'.

While I'd been losing my manly disguise the other women had lined up either side of Noren and hoisted him onto their shoulders. They carried him into the temple, feet first, between two of the immense pillars that ringed the building. There was a step up into the temple. The floor was slightly cool, and smooth. Smoother than anything else I'd ever stood on.

Inside an altar made of a single large piece of black rock stood directly in front of the entrance, and midway between there and the pool I'd seen earlier on my traverse of the grove. It was surprisingly light inside, the temple was open at both ends for the entire height of the pillars, I could see that the walls were raised, like sails, at the southern end where the pool was. Looking round more ropes were secured on the pillars. Only the bottom yard wasn't a sail.

Wicker hurdles blocked the gaps, except those along the East-West axis of the temple.

There were eight women carrying Noren. Four on each side. Alfinna took position at his head next to a woman I didn't know, but who could have been her twin sister. Alfarinn was behind them, I followed them in, and Inibrakemi brought up the rear. Like me she'd discarded her travelling clothes. Although hers were neatly folded, and she had changed into a dark blue tunic in the same style as the others.

The women turned sunwise when we were all in the temple. Noren's head now towards the pool, they laid him gently on the altar and stepped back.

Alfinna nodded when they set him down and stepped back. Nine surrounded him, and I realised that their otherwise identical linen tunics bore the colours of the gods on their ribbons.

Gods! This was a funeral. Noren's funeral. My knees buckled and I sank involuntarily to the floor.

He wasn't dead. Noren was fighting the geas.

It wasn't time to give up.

There had to be other things we could try.

My head rested on the cool polished stone floor. I could hear the words above me. None of them properly registered.

My Noren wasn't gone, that just couldn't happen.

A wave of guilt passed through me. Had I made this happen? What if I'd stayed with Noren and Rojden? I could have persuaded Rojden to release Noren, he'd said we could go.

Why hadn't I believed him? If...

Sobs replaced coherent thought, tears flowed freely and spattered on the stone floor.

~

I sat on the base of the first tree I'd touched and let the night air chill me. A full moon in the cloudless sky and the temple area was bathed in light. Small flying creatures flitted between the trees, catching moths in flight. Crickets chirped in the longer grass, clear above the susurration of insects. Further away owls hunted, hooting to each other.

I'd come out here when I'd stopped sobbing on the temple floor. Inibrakemi and Alfinna had both tried to comfort me, but I'd waved them off. I wasn't in the mood for talking. Noren lay on the bier in the temple, he wasn't dead, but he wasn't moving or responding either.

The further I'd taken him from Rojden the worse he'd got. My attempt to protect him had made it worse. I'd thought Alfarinn would have known how to break the geas. Old Bjorn had said she was practically a demi-god, and older than anyone else alive. Yet her words had rung true when she'd said she didn't know of any way to break the geas short of death, or Rojden releasing Noren.

Rojden had promised me that he would let me and Noren leave. But the effect the geas was having on Noren was proof of the lie. Jafnadr said she didn't think I could kill Rojden myself. Not without lots of practice, and probably some help. So those weren't options for freeing Noren. At least not soon enough.

A procession of robed people entered the opposite side of the circle. Each bore an armful of wood. They were silent, not even disturbing the night wildlife. Their leader knelt near the pool at the edge of the temple. There was a slight clatter as the wood hit the ground.

Without any words being spoken the leader stacked the wood from each one in turn. Each turned and left as the leader took their offering. In a fairly short time they'd stacked wood to about mid-thigh on their leader, and two yards long. When the last of them turned away the leader looked straight at me and beckoned me towards them.

I wasn't sure that they could see me, I was in the shadow of the tree and hadn't moved while they'd been there.

They beckoned again.

My curiosity got the better of my desire to be left alone. I stood and walked toward the robed figure. They were taller than me, and a loose, flowing, hooded robe covered their head. As I got a bit nearer the leader threw their hood back, revealing close-cropped silver hair and an un-bearded face. A rich warm smile welcomed me, and open arms invited an embrace.

I stopped just beyond arms length and took a closer look.

'Welcome Yngvild.' The voice was friendly, at least on the surface.

'I don't think we've met before?'

'Clewg sent me. I am Wall.'

I looked carefully at Wall. Their face was smooth, with no sign of being shaved. The hair was a close cropped iron grey. Broad shoulders and muscular build. The flow of the robes made it hard to tell whether they were male or female.

Wall watched me watch them. Hands still spread for a welcoming hug.

After a minute I broke and accepted it. I missed the human contact I got from Noren. As Wall held me tightly a warm feeling spread through my body. Wall squeezed the tension out of me.

'What is your objective?' Wall said.

'I want Noren back.' We sat on the grass while Wall told me more about Clewg's teachings.

'Commendable, but not a suitable life objective.'

'I want to make the world a better place.'

'Define better.'

That was a hard question.

Wall looked at me inscrutably. I was pretty sure Wall would win a staring contest.

What did I want with my life?

I'd never stopped to think about it. I was growing up to enjoy time with Noren, helping my crew feed and clothe ourselves, and maybe in a decade when I'd enjoyed being an adult I'd have a couple of kids.

That wasn't going to happen now though. I'd ignored Noren's caution and dragged him away from the comfort and safety of the world we'd grown up in. Where did my idiotic quest to meet Noren's mother come from? It had dragged us through a war, and got Noren into trouble.

Worse than trouble really. If I didn't find a way to break the geas then Noren was going to die.

'Why can't I have saving Noren as my objective?'

Wall looked up and pointed at the full moon. 'Before this moon has waxed half away Noren will be saved or beyond help.'

'You've seen this before?'

'Not exactly this, but when people can't or won't eat, they don't last long.'

'I'm not giving up on Noren. I'd rather die first than not help.'

'Everyone has their time, Yngvild.' Wall looked me directly in the eyes. 'You need to prepare.'

'I'll stick with it for now. I can think up a new objective when I need it.'

'That's not what I meant.'

'Do you know how to end an involuntary geas?'

'There are three ways to end a geas.'

'Three?'

'The easiest way is for the geasor to relinquish their hold.'

'I don't think Rojden would do that, besides I don't have any way to ask him.'

'If Rojden were to die it would also release all those that he has bound of their obligations.'

'What is the third way?'

'Divine intervention.'

'Go on.'

'You need to sacrifice something very dear to you while calling on an appropriate god to help.'

'Does Clewg do this sort of thing?'

'I think another god would be more appropriate, perhaps one that had an interest in Noren and Rojden.'

'Will it work?'

'There are few certainties. You need to consider the options and pick the one that seems most likely to help you meet your objective.'

'If I do nothing then Noren will certainly die?'

'We all have our time. Heroes are hard to kill, but it seems more likely than not.'

'Do you know where Rojden is?'

'Unless he enters the sanctuary of Estreham I have no way of knowing where he is.'

'Can other gods act here?'

'I've never had reason to call on any other gods. Perhaps Noren's mother will know.'

I went back to the tree and sat cross-legged with my back to the trunk facing the centre of the oval. Jafnadr lay across my knees, my hands rested on the sword, one over each knee. Anyone watching would think I was meditating on the problem.

'*I need to kill Rojden. You said I'd need help. What sort of help?*'

Jafnadr didn't reply immediately. '*Training in how to fight would be one thing. I can help the sword work, but you need to fight him with your brain as much as with a sword.*'

'*He drugged my father, could I do that to him?*'

'Possible, but unlikely you'll get an opportunity. Rojden tricked your father because your father trusted Rojden. The drugs didn't kill Oddmundr, they just stopped him defending himself properly.'

'So I need a way to create an element of surprise?'

'You also need to strike a killing blow before he can recover.'

'Can you help with that?'

'Heroes are very hard to kill. They heal even from mortal wounds, so you need to make sure.'

'Like cutting his head off?'

'That would probably work. As long as you made sure the head was kept away from the body.'

'Do you have any idea where Rojden is?'

'You aren't ready to fight him yet, unless you can get Old Bjorn or someone experienced to help you.'

'Noren won't last that long.'

'Nor will you if you try to fight Rojden alone.'

'I'd rather die trying than not try.'

'Killing Rojden isn't the only way to remove the geas. Wall told you that.'

'Was Wall telling me the truth?'

'Wall was hard to read, everything they said was true, although I got the impression that there was a lot that wasn't said.'

'Do you think Malfin would break the geas?'

'I can't speak to the minds of the gods, but she's the one you have the most powerful connection to. However neither Noren nor Rojden do.'

'How does calling on another god to help fit with my obligation to pray first to Malfin?'

'You could call on her to intercede on your behalf.'

'Is it possible to see a geas?'

'I'm aware of them, you could perceive them too, if you focused enough.'

'Show me, please.'

~

Everyone else seemed to have left the temple area. I walked softly into the temple. The combination of moonlight and the candles burning round Noren made it as bright as day for my eyes.

Noren lay still on the bier. Incense from the candles scented the air when I got close enough. The air was still, and the candle flames went straight up, without even a flicker. Only when I laid a hand on Noren's forehead could I tell that he wasn't dead, because he was burning hot.

I focused like Jafnadr had showed me. It turned out easier than I'd expected. Noren's geas was powerful, and shone like the Moon when I concentrated enough on being able to see it.

Light shone round his head, neck and chest, like a hauberk. Only this one wasn't protecting him, it was suffocating him.

I spread my arms over Noren's form and spoke quietly. 'Malfin, my Lady, I pray to you as your champion. I seek guidance and help to free Noren from a geas unjustly laid on him by another.'

I put every ounce of my will into the prayer to Malfin. 'I call on you to intercede with Meniaxter.'

The candles extinguished as one. I should have known Malfin would prefer it dark.

Nothing moved, yet I was aware of someone behind my left shoulder. Turning I found a dark skinned woman with lustrous straight black hair. Her eyes were black, the pupils took the whole colour and sucked my gaze. She smiled at me. I felt a thrill that sent a shiver through me.

I dropped to my knees, and bowed my head.

'Rise Yngvild.' Her voice was smooth and made my body move before I understood her words.

'I have need of service from you, and Noren.'

'I will do anything in my power, my Lady.'

'Indeed you will. You have my daughter's sword.'

I drew Jafnadr from the scabbard and offered her to Malfin.

'You must use Jafnadr.'

I reversed my grip and rested Jafnadr's blade on my right shoulder.

'Offer Noren to me as a sacrifice.'

I spent a moment looking at Malfin. I wasn't compelled to act like the previous two instructions. It didn't make sense, but who was I to argue with a goddess? I remembered the lamb we'd sacrificed for the first night celebration earlier in the summer.

'Malfin, I offer this man to you as a sacrifice, for your continued protection of us, and in honour of your power over the darkness.'

I pulled Noren's chin up with my left hand to expose his throat, and then hooked Jafnadr's tip under the edge of the shining geas and pushed her up and forwards.

A great red fountain sprayed from Noren's neck, covering me, Malfin and Noren in hot blood. I could taste it.

The geas flickered, and shimmered as the blood stopped flowing. Slowly it faded and sputtered out. Noren's eyes were unfocussed and glassy. I let go of Noren and stepped back. The geas was gone.

Looking down the blood ran off the altar into the pink pool. It spiralled where it mixed with the warm clear water from the spring.

Malfin had gone.

So was Noren. I killed him.

I dropped the sword and threw myself on his body, grief, guilt and disbelief clashing for my senses. My tears splashed on his face, washing away the blood.

I needed to clean us both up. I couldn't leave Noren on his own, and I couldn't leave us both covered in his blood. I stripped my clothes off and, except for my linen shift, I threw them aside.

I knelt at the pool edge to rinse my shift to use as a cleaning cloth. I took off Noren's shirt, working up the hem on both sides until it was under his neck. I raised his arms to get each sleeve free, and then pulled it all over his head.

I rinsed it several times in the pool and rang it out. It was far from clean, but the colour was more evenly spread, and it looked less dramatic than it had when he was wearing it. I draped it over a wicker hurdle on the edge of the temple space.

There was so much blood on Noren.

It covered his hair, and the top of the bier was slick with it.

It would be easier to wash him in the pool.

I pulled Noren's arms to get him off the bier.

He was heavier than I expected him to be.

Slowly he moved towards me, closer to the pool.

I staggered under the weight when he got more than halfway and gravity pitched us into the pool.

I was underwater, held down by Noren's body. I needed to breathe, his weight held me down.

I pushed frantically to get out from under him. Water splashed as I kicked and pushed.

My forehead cooled where it was out of the water, but my nose and mouth stayed below the surface.

My lungs started to burn.

Spots floated in front of my eyes.

The bottom of the pool was too smooth, and the sides curved gently up. There was nowhere to get leverage. I tried rolling in the hope it would dislodge Noren.

The urge to breathe in was strong.
I couldn't resist it any longer.
My strength deserted me.

The warm water filled my nose and mouth.
I coughed, but it only served to let more water pour
down my throat.

What happened to heroes are hard to kill?

Everything went black.

I deserved this.

Maybe in death we would be together again.

TWELVE

ᚷᚮᛁᚾᚷ ᚠᛖᛋᛏ

GOING WEST

'Yngvild! Yngvild! Can you hear me?'

Even without opening my eyes I knew it was fully daylight on a warm day. Someone was rocking me in their arms. It was too bright to open my eyes fully.

Everything hurt.

My head pounded, my chest tight, my nose felt like smoke had been blown into it by a gale. Surely the afterlife should be better than this? Was I being punished for what I did to Noren?

'Mm.' Even my voice wasn't working.

'Give thanks to the gods, you're awake.'

That was Noren's voice.

My heart leapt.

I struggled to open my eyes, blinking in the bright light.

'Noren?' my voice was hoarse, and it hurt to talk.

'I'm here, Yngvild. Are you okay?'

I looked up at him, bare chested, muscles still spattered in dried blood, but no sign of his throat having been cut. He smiled at me.

'Whatever you did, Yngvild, it worked.' He kissed me on the forehead. 'We need to clean up, there's blood everywhere. What did you sacrifice?'

I pulled myself up from where I lay and hugged him. 'Malfin asked me for a sacrifice.'

Noren hugged me tight into his chest, and I felt warm where we came into contact, against the chill where the water had cooled now that I was out of it.

'You saved me, Yngvild, and I'm grateful.' Noren moved his feet together, making it easier for me to sit on his lap.

'It was terrible, I thought I'd lost you forever, and I never want to have to do something like that again.' I snuggled in, wiggling closer, and wrapping my legs round him as well as my arms.

I pulled back slightly and kissed him.

~

Once my glow subsided I padded out into the warm morning sun. It was pleasant, and enhanced my mellow feeling of satisfaction. Just outside the trees I found my clothes, someone had picked them up, neatly folded them and placed them on top of my saddle-bags. Next to them were Noren's clothes, save for the shirt that hung to dry over the hurdle. They were also neatly folded on his bags.

I dug my spare shirt out of my bag and looked in vain for Noren's, his saddlebags were all but empty. I settled for taking his outer clothing back to the temple so that he could at least wear something. The last thing I wanted was him to get sunburnt.

Alfinna found us asleep under one of the south-eastern trees. Noren and I were both exhausted and we'd picked the sunniest spot we could find to fall asleep, basking in the late summer sun.

'Yngvild!' She shook me awake. 'Yngvild!'

'What?' I didn't open my eyes.

'We've got to get him back.'

'Yes. Definitely. Am planning that.' I nodded.

'How did you get Noren out here?' Alfinna's tone was like she was talking to a small child.

'He walked.' I made big eyes at Alfinna and mimed walking with my fingers.

'He walked?' Alfinna's eyes half-lidded.

'Yes. He walked.' I nodded my head in emphasis.

'So who helped you?' Alfinna stood back up, and planted her feet, her fists on her hips. Clearly she meant business.

'Malfin.'

Alfinna gave me a hard stare.

'Seriously. I prayed to Malfin to save Noren.'

She raised her left eyebrow. 'And that was enough to break a geas?'

'Not on its own. I had to make a sacrifice.'

'I see.' Alfinna crossed her arms. 'And what, exactly, did you sacrifice?'

'The thing I hold most dear. That was what Malfin asked of me.'

Noren stirred from his sleep, our voices must have woken him. Alfinna's jaw dropped as he stretched and yawned. I hugged him again, he'd saved me from some hard questions.

'My apologies, Yngvild, I never thought it was possible to break a geas. I've never known anyone do it.' Alfinna pulled me to my feet and hugged me.

Noren used the tree to push himself upright, and joined our hug. 'Yngvild has always been special, she never gives up once she's set her mind to it.'

We stayed there for a few moments before Alfinna broke, 'we need to go tell the others.' She grabbed us both by the hand and tugged us away from the Temple. 'Come on.'

Alfinna lead us over the short cropped grass around the Temple. About two hundred yards across the open field the semi-circle of forest that formed an outer boundary for the Temple had a gap. This lead to another clearing with huts in it, where everyone had gone overnight.

When we got closer a combination of woodsmoke,

the sizzle of frying bacon, and the smell of baking bread greeted us. I noticed a woman milking a cow towards the back of the clearing, while a couple of others attended to the fire, and food preparation.

Things stopped when they realised Noren was walking amongst us. A dark haired woman left the cooking and dashed into the closest hut, shouting for Alfarinn. Inibrakemi came out of one of the other huts, and ran to meet us.

Noren stopped as Inibrakemi threw herself into him, hugging him and crying out to thank the gods that he was living. The other women I'd seen yesterday all came out too, shouting with joy about the miracle that had saved him, and hugging him, me, and each other. We were swept round in a whirlwind of celebration.

Alfarinn came out and wept on the step. She held her arms out in benediction, and a path cleared for Noren to walk to her.

'Mother. I have missed you so.'

'Noren, my son, my beloved son. I am sorry I ever doubted you.'

Noren enveloped Alfarinn with his arms and held her tight to his chest. It struck me how much taller and wider he was than her. Noren straightened up and spun round, trailing Alfarinn's feet round in a circle as he lifted her. She laughed.

After a large breakfast of fresh bread, fried bacon, cheese, milk and eggs, and telling the story, with some of the details left out, the conversation turned to what we should do next.

'We're going back to Kronstadt. We've got a rendezvous in the Riggin Dale, and then we're meeting the Seagull off the West coast.' I said.

'We need to initiate Noren before you go. Rojden will be able to track him if he isn't protected.' Alfarinn said.

'If Rojden can track him, don't we need to move quickly?' I said.

'We're safe here, no man that isn't an initiate of Clewg can come here.'

'Are you sure about that?'

'We've found the bodies of men that got lost when prospecting nearby a few times over the years.'

'So the curse is real?'

'Very real. You heard Clewg yourself via the birds. He still protects the Temple.'

'How far does it run?'

'I don't know. But far enough. All the ones we've found have been a few miles distant.'

'That's good to know. But Rojden knows we're here, he'll be sending people to find us.'

'Do you have the amulet you made for Noren?'

'I do, but it's melted and unrecognisable.'

'Maybe you could craft it a bit while we make arrangements for Noren's initiation?'

'I think I've got an idea about that. Alfinna, could I borrow you to help me a bit please?'

'I'd be happy to help, Yngvild.' Alfinna said.

Alfarinn took Noren off to her hut on his own after we'd finished eating. A couple of her daughters and granddaughters cleaned up.

~

'Do you need to borrow any tools to craft the amulet?' Alfinna asked.

'No, we just need some where quiet.'

'I think I know just the place.' Alfinna took me into the woods to another clearing.

'Is this quiet enough?' she asked.

I looked around. The clearing wasn't huge, it had been made by a couple of fallen trees, judging by the sections of trunk that had been sawn and stacked at the edge. The roots weren't in the ground, so blown over rather than cut down.

'It'll do.' I sat on one of the log piles. 'Would you mind turning into a bear please?'

'Sure.' Alfinna blurred briefly and stretched, getting darker and browner as she did. It was the first time I'd properly watched someone transform from a human into an animal.

I took a good look, and tried to fix the form of the bear in my head. I wasn't quite sure how to do the crafting. I expected that I'd need to imagine what I wanted the coin to become so that it would take on the new shape.

I pulled the deformed two siller coin out of my pouch, and held it in palm of my left hand. Putting my right hand over the top I focused on the coin and it becoming Alfinna's bear.

It felt hot in my palm. At first I thought I was imagining it, then the pain started. I dropped the coin with a yelp onto the clearing floor. It landed on a drier patch of brown grass, which started to smoke. I stamped down hard on it.

'What's up? Did something sting you?' Alfinna had turned back into her usual form.

'No, it got hot, and I thought it was setting the grass on fire.' I stepped off the coin and tentatively touched it with a finger. 'Have you got any water?'

'You haven't done this before, have you?'

'Does it show?'

Alfinna laughed and I couldn't help but join in. Everything suddenly seemed absurd, and I fell to the ground laughing so hard that tears streamed out of my eyes.

When I'd recovered my composure Alfinna leaned down and pulled me back onto my feet. Looping her arm through mine. 'I think I can help you, let's go to my hut, it's a better place to work than here.'

We walked arm in arm through the forest, Alfinna

pointing out some of the different sorts of trees, and calling attention to the multitude of wildlife that lurked at the edges of sight. This forest was way more alive than the ones we'd been through on our journeys from Straven to Estreham. Or maybe Alfinna was better at showing me how to see it.

I knew which hut was Alfinna's before we got close. Amongst the group of huts in the clearing one had several sculptures outside it, including a huge black bear.

'Did you make those?'

'Yes, my dad taught me was I was about ten.'

'Your dad?'

'He was an epic craftsman. Had a workshop in Kronstadt.'

'For some reason I thought you wouldn't have known your dad either.'

'Alfarinn chooses carefully, usually at any rate. Most of us have known our fathers, even if they haven't been around all our lives.'

We got to the door of the hut, the windows were on the other sides of the wooden building, this side was dominated by a very wide double door, comfortably taller than Noren. It went up to the eaves of the sloping roof. Alfinna pulled both doors open, the ground sloped imperceptibly away from the hut, so they swung open easily. As she fastened the first door against the wall I got my first view of the inside.

Inside the hut was a riot of colour. The walls were covered with paintings, drawings and pieces of intricate metalwork. A large mirror, bigger even than the one I'd seen in the palace at Kronstadt drew my eye. Surrounding the glass was a silvery filigree frame that shimmered with every colour in the rainbow as the light hit it. When I moved my head the colours changed.

'How does it do that?' I pointed at the mirror.

'Years of study and quite a lot of hard work.' Alfarinn opened the other door.

There were even more items inside, every one a work of art. Along the shorter wall was a work bench, with an array of tools on a rack that spanned the full length. A half sized anvil sat on the bench, and there were several clamps along the front edge, as well as evidence of cut marks, burns, and splashes of colour where things had been spilled. At the end of the bench were a lot of bright metal leaves, in silver, gold, brass and the duller grey of iron. Several logs stood upright in the middle of the floor space, scattered randomly it seemed. On them were a helmet, the boss for a shield, leather straps with brass plates, and several small statuettes.

'Did you make all this?'

'It's what I do most of the time.' Alfinna waved for me to go in. 'Making things is my gift.'

I went in and wandered through Alfinna's wondrous creations. The whole hut was crammed with them, apart from some spaces around the workbench at one end, and a bed at the other.

'Grab that stool next to you and bring it over to the bench.' Alfinna said.

I brought the stool over to sit next to Alfinna. On the bench was a large stone, and on top was a thick black iron bowl.

'Put your coin for the amulet in the bowl.'

I fished it out of my pocket, it was no longer recognisable as a coin. It had fused into a cylinder with irregular edges, and there were specks of mud and leaf litter stuck to it. It tinkled when I dropped it into the shallow black bowl.

'So what did I do wrong?'

'What did you do?'

'I started with trying to memorise the shape that you had as a bear. I focused on that, and imagined the coin flowing into the same shape, only smaller.'

'Did anyone show or tell you how to make things?'

'Not like this. Old Bjorn had me make my own shield, and Arne showed me how to make arrows, bowstrings, and a bow. I also watched the smith when he came to work in the forge on Straven a few times. I've seen him fix armour, make hooks, and one time I watched him make a cooking pot.'

'Those skills are all pretty useful. The easiest way to make stuff is to combine the physical with the divine. You shape your materials with the same tools that the ordinary craftsmen do, but you also bend your will to making them flow.'

'So I should have used some tools?'

'When you watched the smith, how did he shape the metal?'

'He heated it in the forge, then he pulled it, hit over the anvil and kept turning and tapping it until it was just right.'

'Exactly, so you need to do that too, although you can probably dispense with the fire.'

'Why don't I need the fire?'

'The smith uses it because it's the only way they can make the metal flow. But you have other ways to make that happen.' Alfinna reached across the bench for a tiny hammer and tongs, like a small child's version of the tools I'd seen the smith use. 'Shall we try it?'

It took me a couple of attempts to co-ordinate my mental image of the bear and my physical shaping of the metal. It grew hot, as it had when I held it, and I pinched it with the tongs while hitting gently with the hammer. Once I'd got the measure of how gently I needed to do it, the shape took form. Alfinna talked me through the process and guided my head more than my hands. When I had a wonderfully detailed silver bear she suggested I enamel it the colour of the large bear out front.

Over the day Alfinna guided me to make a very lifelike pendant about the size of the top joint on my little finger. She had found a silver chain to hang it from and we took the finished amulet to where everyone was congregating for dinner.

Dinner was served on a couple of tables arranged in a line in the middle of the clearing. Benches ran along both sides, in much the same way that we did in the hall back on Straven. The only real difference here were that we were outside, and some of the food was quite different. I guessed Estreham was too far from the sea for fish to be the main staple, but there were a lot of red coloured dishes, and also some strange green and black fruits on the table in little pots next to oil and bread.

Noren was back with Alfarinn, although she took a seat at the other end of the table from me. Inibrakemi and Noren sat with Alfinna and I. Although unusual, I enjoyed the food, and quite enjoyed the rather salty green and black olives as well as the oil and vinegar they dipped the bread into.

'We're going to need some help on the way.' Inibrakemi said when we were nearly finished eating. 'I've asked Alfauda' Inibrakemi waved a red-headed woman to join us, 'and Gefjun' she beckoned a darker haired woman 'to help us with it.'

Both Alfauda and Gefjun shuffled onto the end of the bench opposite me. Alfauda looked about my age, with very similar colouring to me. Gefjun looked old enough to be her mother, although I was learning that not everything was as it seemed.

'Rojden's going to be looking for you. He'll be using every method he has to try and track you.' Inibrakemi pointed at Alfauda. 'You're cousins, you share a grandfather, and it won't take much for Alfauda to be mistaken for you.'

'Rojden knows Alfarinn, they were close friends until Noren was born, so he knows she lives here in the winter, and travels through Caratis when she goes North for the summer. He'll be expecting you to do the same.' Gefjun had a soft, lilting voice, softer than the others.

'We're not going that way are we?' I asked.

'No. You are going to Ocaso. It's an abandoned coastal fort on the west coast. Alfauda and I will be going to Caratis with a few of the Clewgists. We'll leave just before you, and be just conspicuous enough to confuse the scent.' Gefjun said.

'I'd rather you didn't take risks on account of us.' Noren said. 'We can take care of ourselves.'

'There's no real risk to us, we're all able change our forms, and they won't be able to find us unless we let them. Gefjun is a master at this sort of thing.' Alfauda said. 'Besides, we want to help you. Mother wants revenge on Rojden for everything he's done.'

'You're sure?' I said.

'Absolutely. We wouldn't offer if we weren't certain we wanted to do it.' Gefjun said.

Alfinna stood. 'Yngvild, you'd best make sure you're packed and ready to go. We need to prepare Noren too.'

The others all left me at the table. I tried to help the two women who were clearing up, but they swiftly shooed me away to a sparsely furnished hut that had mine and Noren's bags in it as well as two sets of bunk beds. There was a roll of woven linen in the corner, and I decided to make Noren a couple of shirts to replace the one that I'd ruined earlier.

~

The amulet wasn't the only thing I'd made for Noren. The two siller coin I'd originally picked up in Beretha during the siege was unrecognisable. After being bent when I'd first turned it into an amulet, and then warped and half melted when I cut it off. It had resembled an arrowhead that had hit armour when I picked it up from the grass.

Alfarinn had used the amulet I'd made when she'd initiated Noren into Jorunn's mysteries. The amulet would protect him from future attempts to involuntarily bind him with a geas.

I didn't get to see the ceremony, not being an initiate of Jorunn. So I'd made two new shirts for Noren, the one he'd had on was never going to be clean again. I cheated a bit when making them, channelling Frijdodr to make the ends knit together like they'd been woven on a massive round loom. It made a change from the extra panels that his previous smock had needed to cope with his huge muscular frame.

Two days after I'd arrived at the Temple we left for Riggin Dale. Riggin Dale was over a ridge, about thirty miles north east of the Temple.

We left mid-morning, shortly after Alfauda and Gefjun had left in the company of four Clewgists. It had been strange to see Alfauda dressed identically to me, with my shield, bow and wearing a sword that was superficially similar to Jafnadr. One of the Clewgists had a similar build to Noren and was wearing very similar clothes, although they were far easier to tell apart than Alfauda and I.

Noren rode next to me, and we found Alfinna a horse so that she could accompany us to the coast. Alfarinn had asked both Alfinna and Inibrakemi to escort us to the rendezvous with the Seagull at Ocaso. It was in the opposite direction from where we'd last seen Rojden, and further from Kronstadt. The four of us rode out to the meeting place where we'd find Jerre, Olaf and Erik.

It was late afternoon on the second day when we

crested the ridge and saw the river Riggin meandering northwards and glittering in the distance. The Dale was mostly grassland, with patches of trees and widely scattered buildings. Across the area were many herds of cattle and horses. A wide muddy swathe followed the river north on its western side.

'That's the Great North Road. Or at least where they think of round here when they use that name.' Inibrakemi said. 'But it's not the greatest or the longest of the Great North Roads.'

'Looks like it sees quite a bit of traffic.' Noren said. 'There's a lot of mud down there.'

'It's mostly cows and horses. This area is renowned for them.' Inibrakemi said.

'So where are we supposed to be meeting Jerre, Olaf and Erik?' I asked.

'There's an inn, called the Wheel. Down there, where the road forks.' Inibrakemi pointed. 'We can probably make it before dark if we push on.'

The Wheel had a large wheel on the roof line, which they'd painted gold. This was bigger than anything that I'd ever seen on any cart, at least three people tall and visible from miles away. We saw it well before we were close enough to make out any detail, and before it was dark.

We didn't quite make it before dark, but fortunately the moon was still almost full and it shone brightly enough for us to keep going without me having to help anyone's vision.

Inibrakemi rode her horse between mine and Noren's. 'Yngvild, Noren. Before we get there some words of warning about the Wheel.'

'It's dangerous?'

'Not exactly. We'll be seen by people, so when Rojden's folk come asking questions they'll be told we were there.'

'So why are we going in?' Noren asked.

'We need to be positively identified here, and Alfauda and the others will be seen further up the north road over the next few days.'

'Is this where we're turning West then?' I asked.

'Yes, and when we leave tomorrow, you will all need to look different. So they see Alfauda's party going North.'

'Is Alfauda in there already?'

'No, they're camped in a copse just behind us. They'll sneak in before it gets light.'

The Wheel was surrounded on all sides with large fields fenced off from the road. We spent several minutes riding past the fields. Six of them had animals in, four with cattle, and two with horses. Most of the occupied fields had tents at their edges. Once I saw them I noticed spaces on the others where the fences took a bite out of the field so that tents could be pitched, or in one case a couple of waggons parked.

It was past sundown when we got up to the Wheel Inn itself. However, there was plenty of light shining through windows and open doorways from the collection of buildings.

The rhythmic clang of steel being worked slowly overtook the sounds of the cattle as we closed. The sharp tang of animal dung was replaced with the clear burning smell of charcoal as we rode past the orange glow. Whinnies of horses, and shouted instructions, competed with the hammers. The smith was working with two farriers and several grooms to replace horseshoes. A queue of horses waited to be seen to.

Near the forge, but outside the main inn complex, were several smaller wooden huts. One familiar looking two story hut looked like it ought to be blue in daylight. The main inn building was much-extended, with three stories and a large sloping roof where the enormous wheel had been mounted. Behind it the stables were far larger than the inn itself, and fairly full. I recognised the cart our friends had been travelling with standing amongst several other carts parked nearby.

I scanned the main room when we went in for Jerre, Olaf and Erik. The place was lively, there were about thirty people in the main room. Inibrakemi put her hand on my arm. 'Don't go over, don't show any recognition. We'll catch them on the road tomorrow.' She spoke quietly and without looking at me.

'There's a good table, near the window.' I said loudly, and pointed to an empty table on the other side of the room from where I'd seen our friends.

Noren strode towards it with his usual long paces and claimed it by dumping the saddle bags he carried on one of the seats. Inibrakemi carried on towards the bar. When I hesitated Alfinna hooked my arm in hers and dragged me after Noren.

I casually put my hand on Jafnadr's pommel. *'Are there any particularly interesting people in here?'*

'Depends what you mean by interesting.'

'Anyone that might work for Rojden, or that you can't read, or who could be a spy.'

I sat facing Noren, with my back to the room, and made a thing of looking out the window. Alfinna sat next to Noren.

'Jafnadr is checking the room for us.' I leaned across the table and spoke quietly.

'She says that there are two Board of Trade agents in the room, one of whom she can't read.'

'Is it a problem if she can't read someone?' Noren asked.

'What you can't read, you can't know. It's always wise to be wary of the unknown.' Alfinna said.

Inibrakemi joined us with a tray bearing four metal

cups of ale. 'Not much variety on offer tonight, beef, cheese, bread and beer.'

She chose the seat on the short end of the table that faced back towards the door. She set the tray on the table and passed the cups round.

'One of the Board of Trade agents is sitting with Olaf, Erik and Jerre, he's recognised them as Skyssian, but not that they aren't cattle merchants.'

'What about the other one?' Noren tried his ale.

'He's sitting with the Cottalemnese cavalry captain, who's trying to do an overly complicated deal to buy horses for the army that will also make him rich.' I said.

'I see him. Blond guy with a moustache and a dark blue jacket. On my left, halfway between the door and the fireplace.' Alfinna said.

Noren glanced leftward and nodded.

'Anyone else of interest?' Inibrakemi asked.

'There's a table of four in the middle. Two men, a woman, and someone she can't even identify. Very strange indeed.' I said.

'Can she describe them a bit better?' Inibrakemi asked.

'The strange one is aware of being read.'

'Let me try.' Alfinna closed her eyes for a moment, and then shook her head. 'That's an interesting sensation. I think we might be fine.'

'What?' Inibrakemi said.

'Have a look.' Alfinna took a swig from her cup. 'Mmm. This is nicer than I expected it to be!'

I tried some too. It had some sort of fruit brewed in it, giving it a nicer flavour than most of the ale I'd ever drunk.

'Oh! Not seen one of those outside the woods. How did it get here?' Inibrakemi said.

'Is it dangerous?' I said.

'Probably not to us.' Inibrakemi said.

'Unless someone says what it is and starts a riot.' Alfinna added.

'You'll have to tell us later then. I've had a look and I've no idea what you are talking about.' Noren shrugged and drank his ale.

A man came over with a basket of bread and placed it in the middle of the table before returning to the bar to ferry over a board with a chunk of cheese on it and four plates for us. His last trip brought a cast iron pan that sizzled, when he took the lid off the aroma of fried onions, beef and hot oil made me realise just how hungry I was. All conversation ended as we dug in to the food.

More ale arrived as we were eating, and as soon as it was all gone we went upstairs to two rooms that Inibrakemi had ordered with the food. Noren and I were in one together in the roof-space, and Inibrakemi and Alfinna shared another through a wooden wall.

~

Inibrakemi shook me awake just as it was getting light outside. She put a finger to her lips to shush me. She whispered 'Get changed, like you did at Minhaton, make your hair dark. Then come next door. Let Noren sleep a bit longer.'

I wriggled free of Noren's arm and covered him with the blanket in the hope that he would stay asleep. I rummaged in the bag for the breeches and doublet. It took a moment to check the hooks and eyes were attached all the way round. I pulled the breeches on over my hose before putting my arms in the sleeves to keep them from falling back down. I didn't have a mirror, so I couldn't check to see what I looked like.

I focused on what it felt like when Inibrakemi showed me how to change outside Minhaton, and imagined myself in that shape, with shorter black hair, and brown eyes. As I concentrated on the shape I wanted to be my shoulders filled into the doublet, and my waist thickened. I stretched up too, bringing the bottom of the breeches from halfway down my calves to just behind my knees. When I was done I picked up the shoes and quietly slipped through the door Inibrakemi had left ajar.

Next door the room was crowded. Three other people were with Alfinna and Inibrakemi. I recognised Alfauda, who had changed herself so that it was like looking in a mirror. There was a tall Clewgist, and Gefjun. Alfinna took the Clewgist next door while Inibrakemi took a good look at me.

'Not bad Yngvild. If you can make your skin and hair a little darker, like mine, then that will help.'

I concentrated a bit more, looking at Inibrakemi's hair, mentally editing it to be more male in style, and felt a blushing sensation as my skin darkened.

'Well done. Gefjun, your turn now.' Inibrakemi stripped off her outer garments and turned to face Gefjun, who had also taken off her outer layer.

'On three?' Gefjun said.

'Together. 1 - 2 - 3.' Inibrakemi paled and morphed.

Gefjun got darker and a little shorter, and her cheekbones became sharper as she started to resemble Inibrakemi.

Within a count of ten the two women had switched likenesses.

'I'm guessing the plan is we stay in here while the others leave?'

'Got it in one.' Gefjun who was now Inibrakemi said. 'Andy has gone to become Noren, and I'll leave with him and Alfauda.' She pulled Inibrakemi's dress over her head. 'Once we're clear you, Noren and Inibrakemi can leave in different shapes and anyone that sees us will think you've gone north.'

'Wouldn't be better for us to leave first? Then you can tell if anyone tries to follow us?' I asked.

'That's a good idea, but we were hoping any followers would leave with us.'

'How were you going to solve the horse problem?'

'We were going to sell them to your friends with the cart. Then rent some of the post horses so we can move faster.'

'You can still do that. Sell them our saddle bags, shields and horses. We'll slip out and walk along the west road. When they finally catch us up we'll be mounted again.'

Inibrakemi, now looking like Gefjun, had stuffed some more clothes in a sack while we were talking. 'Wait here Yngvild, I'm going to go out to the privy and change again.'

'Why not change here?'

'Gefjun was seen coming up the stairs, so she needs to be seen going back out. When you see me through the window go outside and wander west, looking like you're appraising the horses in the field.'

'What about Noren?'

'Alfinna will get him clear. We'll meet up further out. Just keep going west.'

~

It wasn't the first time I'd made an unobtrusive exit, but it was the first time I'd sneaked out in full daylight. I reckoned the best thing to do was just to walk confidently down the stairs and out of the door.

I watched out the window until I saw Inibrakemi cross the courtyard at the back of the Wheel to where the privies were. Once she was inside one I pulled the room door open and went into the corridor. I put my hand on Jafnadr as I went down the bit of corridor to the stairs and asked her to make us both as unremarkable as possible.

I made it down two flights of stairs before I saw

anyone else. In the main room there were still several people having breakfast, although it wasn't anywhere near as busy as the previous evening. None of them were paying me any attention. So I carried on across the room to the main door.

The door opened before I reached it. I stepped sideways to let the two men coming in pass me. One was the cavalry officer Jafnadr had mentioned. He was too busy talking to his companion to see me.

'Careful. That's the agent I couldn't read.' Jafnadr warned just as the other man stopped facing me.

'Excuse me.' He said to the cavalry officer. 'I need to have a word with this young man outside.' He put his left hand on my right shoulder and gently pushed me towards the door.

'I'll catch you up for breakfast. Order for me.' He said as he followed me out of the door.

'I think you've made a mistake.' I said when we were outside.

I took an extra pace and spun to face him.

He smiled at me. 'No. I really don't think I have.' His hands rested on his hips, and I noticed that he was wearing a sword, and a larger dagger than was needed for cutting meat.

I edged backwards slightly, watching him carefully and saying nothing. I focused slightly on seeing if he had a geas. *'He has three geasa!'*

'Look. We're almost certainly on the same side. You have Kronstadt written all over you. Summer Isles kid with a Skyssian accent. It's not subtle.'

'That's probably why I can't read him.'

'I should make a resolution to be less obvious.'

'When did you get here?'

'I'm literally just passing through, and I'll be gone before the sun is over the roof line.'

'Where are you going? I might be able to help you along the way.'

'Thank you, but that won't be necessary.'

'It would be no trouble, and probably more interesting than marking Captain Corruption and his dubious horse swindle.'

'Why don't you go back inside and do what you need to. I've got to visit the privy.'

'I could wait for you, and then we could go have a chat in my office.'

He was more insistent than I'd hoped. He probably wasn't just a Board of Trade agent either.

'No. I promise that I'll see you in your office when I'm done. What did you say your name was?'

'I'm Ormrun.'

'Well met Ormrun, I'm Arne Revnasson.'

'Arne?'

'My mother named me for her father. My father wasn't around to see my birth.'

He shifted slightly. Softened a little. 'You best visit the privy. My office is the blue building over there.' He pointed.

I ran for the privy I'd seen Inibrakemi enter. There were seven wooden doors in a row, all on a wooden platform with a step up to it. I tried the door she'd gone in and it was locked. So I took the one on the left. It opened easily, and I pulled it closed behind me and locked it.

Leaning against the shared wooden plank wall I knocked it a couple of times with my knuckles.

'Is that you Ingwald?' I said.

'Jafnadr, can you tell if Inibrakemi is in there?'
'She is.'

'It's your friend from the Summer Isles.' I said.

Inibrakemi realised what was going on. 'Ah. Who might that be?'

'Arne. Arne Revnasson. I've met a mutual friend. Ormrun would like me to visit him in his blue hut.'

'That's interesting. I think that we should go see Ormrun together.'

'I'm sure he would be happy to see you too. He likes making promises to people.'

'Give me a minute, I'm almost ready.'

I realised when Inibrakemi had stopped talking that I did actually need to use the privy. By the time I'd finished and tidied up Inibrakemi had finished her changing. The door banged open as I was fastening my breeches back up.

Inibrakemi was only recognisable because she, or rather he, was stood outside the privy door waiting for mine to open. He was half a head taller than me, and a typical Skyssian with blue eyes and fair hair with a bushy beard. Grey ran through the fair, making it paler. His skin was also the typical pallor of the Northern Skyssians. In fact Inibrakemi was about the opposite of how she normally looked.

'Call me Sven.'

We walked over to the Board of Trade office.

'Have you met Ormrun before, Sven?'

'No, never heard of him, but that's not a surprise. There are thousands of agents.'

'I don't think he's completely trustworthy, he's got more than one master.'

'He wouldn't be the only one. It's easier to subvert people when they're far away from oversight.'

Ormrun was waiting for us when we arrived. After I'd introduced Sven to him as my colleague he took us upstairs, where he said it was more private. There was no sign of his partner, and the office was empty apart from the three of us. Unless someone was hiding behind the furniture or in the roof space. Neither seemed likely, but I had Jafnadr check just in case.

Ormrun had used the few minutes we'd spent

preparing to do some of his own preparation. There were some refreshments, just milk, fresh water and ale. He found a third cup and sat us round their discussion space, clearly the agents were used to entertaining people in their outpost.

'Look, I'm sorry if I was a bit too direct earlier. I know you are Skyssians, and my job here is to offer what official assistance I can.'

'We understand, Ormrun.' Inibrakemi/Sven looked around and then leaned forward. 'My colleague was worried about the wrong ears hearing about our very sensitive mission.'

'So what can I do to help?' Ormrun asked.

'Well, a couple of days ago we got an urgent message from our master. He'd lost track of something special to him, and he wanted us to find it for him.'

'I think I've also had the same message.' Ormrun said. 'That's if the special package was a young man, accompanied by his abductors.'

'I think it's safe to say, between these four walls, that we all serve a common master.'

Ormrun nodded in response to Inibrakemi's statement. 'Sven, I think we do.'

'We happened to be nearby for reasons that I won't go into. Yesterday we spotted a small group that met the description travelling North on the drover's road. We think they stayed here overnight, and our plan is to follow them north and keep giving updates on their position.'

'I saw them too last night, in the main room.'

'Do you have anyone watching them just now?'

'It doesn't do to betray one's sources, but I'll know which way they go, and whether they're all accounted for properly.'

'Do you know if they've made any contacts while they were here?' Inibrakemi/Sven asked. 'I'd be worried if they'd recruited help.'

'No. The only person that went to see them was a maid, and she came back out with a bag of washing. Last I heard they were inside eating breakfast.'

'We've got a couple of people watching them too. We heard they were planning to sell their horses and use post horses so they could outrun pursuit.'

'That's interesting information. The only post route from here is North to Caratis.'

'It could be a ruse, they were talking where we could overhear.'

'True. Some of them are wise in the ways. However I expect they're looking to get a ship for home, and Caratis is the closest port.'

I finished up the cup of milk I'd taken, and set it down significantly.

Inibrakemi took the hint. 'I think we'd best see to our own change of horses so that we're ready when they are.' She stood and offered a hand to Ormrun.

Ormrun and I both stood, and we all shook hands.

'What are we going to do?'

Inibrakemi looked more relaxed than she had on the way in, I couldn't quite see how we could get out the trap. She strode purposefully away from the Board of Trade's blue two storey hut back towards the Wheel.

'What we always planned to do.'

'But he's got people watching.'

'He does.'

'So he'll know we didn't go north.'

'No. All he'll know is that he doesn't know where we've gone, and that we're not here any more.' We got to the back door of the Wheel, and Inibrakemi stopped and turned to me. 'Do you have anything that you need before nightfall in your saddlebags?'

'Not unless I need to get changed again.'

'Good. We can leave now then.' Inibrakemi turned

north and started to walk.

I followed her across the yard, past the privies and behind the stables. Inibrakemi stopped in a corner where we could see the fenced in animal enclosures, but were screened from the Wheel by the outbuildings.

'Have you tried any animal forms?'

'No.'

'That's a pity. It's always easier to assume a form when you've done it before. Animals are much harder than people.'

'Maybe I could copy your bird?'

'No. We don't have time for me to teach you how to fly. It needs to be land based, and local.'

'What about a horse?'

'People aren't used to seeing horses run about on their own. Someone would try to harness us. It needs to be something that won't cause enough interest in anyone to do anything that would get in our way.'

'Maybe a dog?'

'Do you have a picture of one in your head?'

'It would be easier if I could find one to work from, I've never really studied how a dog looks.'

Inibrakemi nodded. 'Me neither, I've never had to become a dog. Birds are more useful.' She looked around. 'Let's scout about until we find some.'

We started a purposeful circuit of the area round the Wheel. It didn't take long to find the midden, and with it a couple of dogs. Their shoulders were about mid-thigh on me, and the ears stuck straight up were almost at waist height. One of them was a sand colour, and the other had a reddish hue that was almost brown. Both had noticeably broader shoulders with a fuzz of hair, and slimmer rear areas, with a bushy tail.

'You need to think about how their hind legs are different from your legs, and imagine how your arms need to change to become their fore legs. Don't forget how the head goes, and the tail. The tail is really tricky, you don't have anything like it, but you won't be able to balance without it.'

We went back to the quiet corner to make the change. Neither of us got it right first time, but we got there after a few attempts. The two things that really stood out for me were the changes to sight and smell. The world looked different, and smell was as important as sight.

Things I hadn't noticed before became significant, I could tell the people apart just by their smell patterns, and I could practically see where the other dogs had marked their territory. It took an effort not to cover their marks with my own.

The other thing that surprised me was that I could still understand Inibrakemi. I wasn't hearing words, and it was more than just sound, but I knew what she meant. The messages were more direct, and less complex, but the meaning was clear.

After sniffing around, to train my sense of smell with our horses, we moved northwards. Most of the animal pens were empty by now. The drovers had started moving as early as they could. Only those collecting up animals were still here.

Inibrakemi pointed towards our doppelgangers. We followed them at a discreet distance until they made a mid-morning stop. Inibrakemi and I lay in the long grass and watched. I noticed with satisfaction that they had picked up a couple of followers, both of whom stopped when they did, and started again when they moved off.

We watched until they were too far away to see, and while we did a third watcher seemed to follow behind the first pair. When they were out of the way we turned west for a bit and walked for a mile. Once we were far away from the drover's way we turned south west and ran as fast as we could.

It was exhilarating running on all fours. I don't know if dogs are any faster than humans, but being closer to the ground it felt a lot faster. A blur of smells went past us too. I could tell where other animals had passed, dogs especially, but also rabbits, cows, horses, deer, and a whole host of small creatures I didn't recognise by their smells. It was a riot of tones, like every instrument we owned in Straven were all trying to play the same tune at the same time, even the ones that didn't have the range for it.

Just as I started to tire a familiar scent drifted faintly on the breeze. The wind was blowing it towards us, and Inibrakemi smelt it too. We both slowed to a walk and sniffed the air to get a better feel for the direction it was coming from. I couldn't see any people or horses, but I could smell Whiteface. I'd sort of known her horsey smell as a human, but as a dog it was way more distinct from the other horses I'd been around. Without consciously thinking about it I knew the way to go, and went at a run.

The scent got stronger and stronger as we closed on the others. It was approaching noon, and the shadows were short. I felt thirsty, and hungry. But there was neither food nor water nearby. I felt myself slowing, tiredness, hunger and thirst were making it harder for me to keep going.

Inibrakemi pulled ahead. I followed her as closely as I could, but she was still moving faster than I was. The scent of the others was very strong now. The grass was shorter too, and bare patches showed hoof prints. The smell told me that many horses had passed here. We were on the road. Behind our friends.

Turning west I tried to catch Inibrakemi, she'd stopped slightly ahead. I slowed as I got close. Suddenly her dogginess left my nose.

'Yngvild, time to change back.' Inibrakemi was

back in Sven's body. 'They're just ahead, and we'll spook the horses.'

I turned back into the last form I'd had, realising that the clothes I'd had on wouldn't properly fit my normal body, and also I didn't know if anyone had followed our friends.

~

Jerre, Erik and Olaf had stopped just after a copse on the road west from the Wheel. They'd let their string of horses graze while they made lunch and waited for us all to catch up with them. As we walked towards them I could see Jerre sorting out saddles while Erik was building a fire. Olaf had a small axe and was chopping a fallen branch into smaller pieces.

'Hello there!' Inibrakemi called when we were still fifty yards off.

All three stopped what they were doing and looked in our direction.

I waved and smiled. It was good to see them again. 'How are you?'

'Well met.' Olaf stepped away from the branch, keeping a hold of the axe.

Erik stood too, putting his left hand on the pommel of his sword as he took a couple of steps towards us.

'Would you mind if we joined you for some food?' Inibrakemi said.

I noticed Jerre looking around.

'We can help gather wood for the fire, and we can entertain you with some stories.' Inibrakemi had her arms wide palms out.

'I'm not sure we've got enough spare. The rest of our party is out collecting wood.' Olaf gestured into the copse. 'They'll be back any moment.'

'We're the people you're expecting, Olaf.' I said.

Olaf gaped at me.

Erik drew his sword.

Jerre dived over to a saddle for his sword.

'Stop!' I flourished Jafnadr.

Inibrakemi changed back to her usual self.

The swords went down.

I turned back into my usual self, and used one hand to prevent tripping myself up on the now too long breeches.

'My apologies, I didn't recognise either of you.' Olaf said.

'I thought we'd been followed by two of Ormrun's agents.' Erik said.

'We saw you come out of his hut.' Jerre added.

'It's okay, we should have agreed a recognition signal or something.' Inibrakemi said. 'You might still have been followed, so Yngvild and I should stay in disguise until we're sure.'

I hugged each of them in turn. I was so pleased to see them again. Especially Jerre who had looked after me so well when Noren had been at his worst. I held him a little longer than the other two.

'I couldn't have helped Noren without you, Jerre.' I said while we embraced.

'It was the least I could have done.'

We resumed our disguises and helped with firewood and cooking. Jerre saddled one of the sleeker looking horses and rode off to look for Noren and Alfinna ahead of us on the drover's way. We'd warned him that they wouldn't look like themselves. I suggested that since they wouldn't recognise him either that he should ask any pairs of people that he met if they had spotted any bears, saying that he'd heard that there were two in the vicinity. I figured that would be enough to make them curious enough to speak more openly to Jerre.

In the end though, they were far behind the rest of us. They came from the direction of the Wheel just at the point when we thought we were going to have to start moving on. With Jerre's assistance, Olaf and Erik had used most of the money they had brought with them to buy extra horses, grain and fodder. The cart was full with provisions and had four horses pulling it, they'd extended the bar at the Wheel. This made it faster than it had been. We also had three horses each, two mounts and a pack horse. There were four spare horses too, in case any became lame.

We were able to spend longer moving, because we could switch horses. Jerre showed us how the cavalry did forced marches. We alternated walking and trotting, with short stops for water and grain, every hour. By nightfall we were thirty miles away from the Wheel Inn. We didn't stop at any of the inns we passed. Now we had provisions and the cart we kept moving until nearly dark, although we did a second long stop in the afternoon to let the horses rest again and for us to have a hot meal. We then carried on until it was twilight.

'How long until we get to Ocaso?' I asked while we were taking saddles off the horses.

'If we keep going at today's rate, then it's about four more days.' Alfinna took the bridle off her horse and replaced it with a feed bag.

'We can probably go slightly further tomorrow.' Jerre said. 'We won't need to wait so long to start, and the load will get lighter, hut we'll need to let the horses rest a bit the day after.'

'I thought we'd sell some, and the cart, when we got to the market outside Dacidade.' Olaf said.

'Not sure we want to go that close to Dacidade, it'll be crawling with people.' Alfinna said.

'I'm with Alfinna in this. We're better staying well away from lots of people. Less chance of someone recognising us.' Inibrakemi said.

'I appreciate the risks. I thought of that too.' Olaf said. 'If anyone asks what we're carrying then prime horses to Dacidade makes sense. It was the only cargo I could think of that sped us up rather than slowing us down.'

'That's a fair point. We could use it until we need to turn off the road.' Alfinna said. 'But we do need to turn off before the market.'

'What will we say if we get stopped by a patrol after we've left the road?' Noren said.

'We'll tell them we're taking them to a client just up ahead. I know quite a few of the farms on the way.' Alfinna said.

'Where's the best place to strike off?' Olaf asked.

'If we stop for the night at the Troll's Head, just outside Campedra, we can ditch the cart there. Then it'll be easier for us to cut across country.' Alfinna said.

'How far is it from there to Ocaso?' Olaf said.

'Maybe fifty miles, we usually take two days to cover it.' Alfinna said.

'You've done this route before?' Olaf said.

'Not recently. When I was younger we made a few trips to the Southern Isles, and we went from Ocaso because it was quieter.' Alfinna said.

'Why is an Inn in the middle of Cottalem called the Troll's Head? We're over a thousand miles south of Trollheim.' I said.

'It's run by a couple of Skyssians. It's a long story, maybe I'll tell you tomorrow while we're moving.'

We took turns being on watch overnight, but it passed without incident. Erik had the last watch and he woke us all at first light so that we could pack up and start moving as early as we could. Noren and I needed to transform again, neither of us had a clear enough sense of our disguises to keep them up while we slept. We ate breakfast five miles or so down the road while the horses got a breather after cantering all the way. That was to become the pattern of the day, canter as far as we could, then walk for the same amount of time, stop for water and food, swap riding horses, continue until it was too dark to carry on.

After breakfast I pulled my horse alongside Alfinna's.

'You said you'd tell me about the Troll's Head.' I said as our horses fell into step. 'Why is it safe for us to spend a night there, and not one of the inns we've passed already?'

'The Troll's Head is run by old friends.'

'Wouldn't Rojden know to have agents there?'

'These people are no friends of Rojden.'

'That won't stop the agents though, would it?'

'It won't stop them trying, but Eskil would spot them, and Arinhildr would make them disappear without trace.'

'They're heroes?'

'Yes. Arinhildr is descended from Aeolf and Meniaxter, so she's pretty deadly. Eskil is mixed, but more Jorunn than anything else, he's a cousin.'

'Is that why he's here and not in Skyss?'

'No. Although it is how I know him. They've been in Cottalem since before I was born. I spent time with them when I travelled. Eskil has Frijdodr in him and is good with making things, and enchanting them.'

'Like Jafnadr?'

'He's not good enough to make something as complex as Jafnadr, Frijdodr herself made Jafnadr.'

'So what sort of things does he make?'

'One of his specialities is finding things, and he can make items that can find things.'

I frowned. 'How does that work?'

'Well he can attune an item to react to the

presence of something. Like making a box that will rattle if it's near someone with a geas.'

'He makes geas detectors?' my eyebrows rose.

'The Troll's Head is littered with them. All round the Inn above all the doors and the area around it. Eskil will know if someone under a geas arrives.'

'Can he do other things?'

'Yes. He makes dowsing rods as a sideline, usually attuned to find water, but sometimes for other things. People pay good money for those.'

'I bet they do. Sounds really useful. Do you know how to do that?'

'Yes. Although I'm not as well practised as Eskil.'

'I think there's a lot I need to learn when we get back to Skyss. Can you teach me some more?'

'One day, maybe, but I'm not coming all the way.'

'You're not?'

'Inibrakemi and I have other things to do. Alfarinn asked us to make sure you made it to the coast. After that we—'

'Cavalry!' Jerre shouted back along the line from where he was leading.

Sure enough when we looked to the front there was a group of fast moving horses coming towards us. The rider of the second to lead horse had a guidon snapping in the wind from a lance.

The cavalry patrol was coming on fast, they were going somewhere in a hurry. Jerre kept us walking, but pulled the line of horses to the left of the track to make room for the cavalry to pass us.

With twenty-four horses we took up quite a length of road. There was a similar number of horses in the cavalry patrol, except that every one of theirs had a rider.

They swept past us without stopping. Not even a sideways look.

'Just as well that we moved fast yesterday and

started early this morning.' Alfinna said as the cavalry passed into the distance, and the dust they'd kicked up had settled.

'How so?'

'I think the reason they didn't stop was because they don't expect us to have got this far yet.'

We saw two more cavalry patrols before we were questioned, just as we made our evening meal stop. Six cavalry, an officer, a trumpeter and four troopers, rode into our makeshift horse lines. The officer dismounted to speak to Olaf, who was apparently the one that most looked like he was in charge.

'You there!' the officer pointed his white gloved hand at Olaf as he came closer. 'Where have you come from?'

I kept my head down and busied myself with splitting some wood for the fire. Noren was digging a small pit to light the fire in, and Jerre and Erik were sorting out the horses with Alfinna. Inibrakemi was organising some food to cook from the back of the cart.

'We've come from Caratis, by way of the Riggin Dale.' Olaf replied.

'How long ago were you in the Riggin Dale?' the officer stopped two yards from Olaf, one hand holding his cavalry sabre sling so that it didn't trail on the ground.

'It's been been three nights since.'

'You're Skyssians?'

I chanced a sideways look at the officer, his tone seemed suspicious.

'I am, but we're a mixed company.'

'What sort of business are you in?'

'Horses.' Olaf waved his arm expansively at the line of horses Jerre and Erik were feeding grain to.

The officer's eyes followed Olaf's gesture.

'You look like you appreciate a fine horse?'

'You do have some fine looking horses, but I'll wager they're not trained as cavalry mounts?'

'Not yet, captain.'

'Where are you bound?'

'Dacidade. We thought it the best place to get a good price for these horses.'

'Speak to Javier Caballero when you get to the horse market, he trained many of our mounts. I'm sure he'll give you a good price.'

'Thank you kindly, sir.' Olaf bowed his head. 'I shall be sure to do that.'

The officer nodded in acknowledgement and then turned back to his horse.

He mounted it, and looked around, his horse jogging sideways as he did.

'One more thing. Are any of you from the Western Isles of Skyss?' the officer seemed to be looking straight at Noren and me.

Olaf cocked his head to one side. 'Fishing folk?'

'Two. Highly dangerous. They'll stop at nothing.'

'No man here like that.' Inibrakemi said, with what I assumed was a Summer Isles accent.

'But if we see any we'll let the nearest guard know.' Olaf added.

'Have a safe trip then.' The officer nudged his horse and it trotted off down the road towards the Riggin Dale followed by his trumpeter and troopers.

'They're definitely looking for us.' Noren mopped the gravy from his stew with a piece of bread.

'They didn't have a description though.' Olaf said.

'We still need to be very careful.' Alfinna scraped some leftovers from her bowl into the fire.

'Should we keep moving?' I asked.

'Best to stay here tonight in case that officer wants

to come back.' Alfinna said.

'Isn't that a reason to keep going?' Noren asked.

'No. He'll only come back if he's suspicious. If we're gone then that will confirm it. Every cavalry trooper in Cottalem will converge on us.'

'Alfinna's got a good point. I think we need to stay here tonight.' Olaf said. 'But we should move early.'

'The horses will benefit from a longer rest.' Jerre said. 'Then we can go a bit faster in the morning.'

'One night here, then we'll be at the Troll's Head, after that we can dash for the coast.' Alfinna stood. 'I think I'll get some sleep in while I can.' She put the bowl back in the basket on the cart and started putting up our shelter.

'Noren, Yngvild, you're on first watch until midnight, if the cavalry come back it will be before then, and you won't need to change.' Olaf said. 'Wake me if they arrive. Inibrakemi can take second watch with Erik. Alfinna and I will take third, and we'll wake you all just before first light.'

The cavalry didn't return that night, although a headquarters group, complete with the mobile kitchens we'd seen when Rojden caught us, rolled past and set up half a mile down the road. A small town of tents appeared, with fires and lanterns lit. We could smell the mobile kitchen working while we looked after the horses. All the way to midnight a steady stream of riders came and went from both directions on the road. I saw our officer return about half-way through our turn on watch.

When the time came I passed on everything that we'd seen to Erik and Inibrakemi. Then I gratefully clambered into the shelter fully clothed and fell asleep.

It was still dark when Alfinna shook me awake.

'Don't get up until you've changed.' She whispered

in my ear. 'The cavalry bosses all seem to be outside.'

I felt down and kicked my feet free from the shoes that were too big for me in my usual body. It was getting easier to imagine myself as a dark skinned young man having spent almost two whole waking days in that form. When my clothes fitted me again I sat up and put my shoes back on.

'You might want to look like you need a shave.' Alfinna said. 'Check out Erik if you need to see.'

I put my hands to my face, and it was as smooth as always. Erik had two days of dark stubble colouring his lower face. I imagined mine being the same, and felt the furze appear under my fingers.

'Maybe not. Or maybe you should just shave.' Alfinna said.

'What's wrong with it?'

'It looks too soft.' Alfinna ran a finger along my jawline. 'It needs to be a bit scratchier.'

'Maybe I'll stay clean shaven for now.' I thought about how smooth my face was, and willed that to be the case. The fluff on my chin disappeared.

'That's better. If anyone asks, you're still 15, so your beard doesn't grow fast.'

'Do I look like a 15 year old?'

'One of the bigger ones.'

Outside there were even more tents with the cavalry headquarters. The traffic was less than it had been, but there were still plenty of signs of life. The mobile kitchens were still cooking, only now the smell of fresh bread scented the air.

Our fire was still burning, Olaf had a kettle on it, and there was some porridge in a pot on the grass.

'Eat something. We can't start until first light.' Olaf said.

I looked over to the East, where we'd just been.

The sky was slightly brighter on the horizon than it was to the West, although maybe only because I was better in low light.

'Will they be suspicious if we move too early?' I ladled some porridge into a bowl.

'Not if we wait until it's light enough to see well.' Alfinna sat on the ground near the fire.

I passed the steaming bowl to her, and filled another. 'If we all eat first it might look better?'

'Good idea.' Olaf accepted a bowl from me.

I filled others and passed them round. We sat round the fire and ate in silence. The porridge was creamy, and whoever made it had added honey to it, so it was sweet as well. By the time I'd finished my bowl it was definitely first light. Everything was a monochrome grey, but distinct.

Noren and I sorted out the fire, and cleaned the cooking pot and bowls with hot water from the kettle. While we did that Jerre, Erik, Inibrakemi and Olaf saddled all the horses, and Alfinna packed away the shelter. Before the sun was visible over the horizon we were all packed up and ready to leave. As the top of the sun appeared, and the day become coloured, we rode off with it at our back. We started at a walk and moved to a canter when the cavalry headquarters was out of sight.

We stopped twice to rest the horses on the way, they needed a break more than we did. Unlike the previous two days we didn't try to cook meals. We ate the bread, cheese and ham that we'd brought with us in the cart. The road was easy, and we passed several caravans going the same way as us, and more cavalry went the other way. We counted over three hundred.

No-one said anything, but none of us wanted to stop longer than we had to. Even the horses seemed to sense that, although it might have been my imagination. It felt like they cantered faster and for longer. A couple of hours after noon we saw a small village ahead, clustered around an Inn. The open grassland started to turn into farmed fields. Mostly standing crops that I didn't recognise, and orchards with old gnarled trees with small dark fruit. I saw sheep, goats, and cows. The Inn had a painting of a person with a golden circle behind them. Not the Troll's Head.

A couple of miles down the road was another small hamlet, this one had the coat of arms of Cottalem on a board above the door. Over the farmland to the north and south we could see other buildings. Some of them were farms, or barns, but there were smoke stacks on a few too, signalling a forge, or perhaps a pottery.

Before long we started to be aware of traffic moving from north to south in front of us. When we got to the junction our road turned south to join the other road. We went straight across.

~

In the near distance was another small hamlet, nestled in the loop of a wide stream that looked easy to ford. A low wooden bridge, with a stone ramp on each bank, spanned the stream.

The Troll's Head was mounted on a pole on the near side of the bridge. The pole was thicker than my wrist, but the same length as a long spear, with the severed head jammed on the top. The other end was firmly embedded in the ground. A wire fence, with waist high posts and four strands of wire, started on the bridge and went all the way round the buildings that served as the Troll's Head inn. A large three storey steep roofed building dominated the centre of the space. There were a forge, two open sided wood stores, four terraced cottages, stabling, and an assortment of other outbuildings, including some privies at the downstream end of the stream that went round the hamlet.

We were met at the entrance by a white haired but clean shaven man. He was wearing a farrier's apron, which was well worn, and holding a hammer in his right hand. It looked like he'd just stepped away from the anvil on the stone flagged area, but there were no horses in sight other than ours.

Alfinna, who had been leading, dismounted just before the bridge.

The rest of us came to a stop behind her.

'Eskil!' Alfinna threw her hands up and moved quickly onto the bridge.

Eskil squinted at her, half twisting.

Alfinna changed when she was half-way over the bridge, her clothes got baggier as she walked.

'Alfinna!' Eskil ran forwards and swept Alfinna off her feet in an enormous hug, spinning her round.

He set her back down when he'd completed the circle. 'Who have you got with you?'

'One old friend, and several new ones. Can I bring them in?'

'Of course.' Eskil turned back to the forge. 'Dagmar! Jorge! Ketil! Albrecht!'

Eskil waved us to come forwards, as four people came out from the Inn and the forge to help us unload the horses and stable them. Several others joined in when we got round the back to the stables. I noticed that Inibrakemi had returned to her usual self when we passed the bridge, so I changed back too when I dismounted, and nudged Noren while I was taking my shoes off.

Eskil said to leave the stabling to his team, and we should join him inside. The ground floor of the Troll's Head was a maze of linked rooms joined by dark wood panelled corridors. It was like a darker version of Straven, although with several stone chimney breasts that the house on Straven lacked.

Eskil brought us into a room with three windows

that looked out to the side of the main building. There were two doors on opposite ends of the room, and a third in the middle wall surrounded by a waist high bar. A stone chimney breast took up most of one wall, the fireplace was set but not lit. Under each of the windows was a table with bench seating under the window and on both sides. Wood dividers separated the tables, with fretwork on the upper parts so that the light could spread.

No-one else was in the room, and with an extra seat on the fourth side we were all able to sit at the same table. While we were shuffling round the table onto the benches Dagmar appeared with a tray full of tankards of ale. She put it down and went back through the gap in the bar and out the door.

'So Alfinna, are you going to introduce your friends?'

'Everyone, this is Eskil. Eskil owns the Troll's Head —'

'—co-owner. I share it with Arinhildr.'

'I stand corrected, Eskil is one of the owners of the Troll's Head, we'll meet Arinhildr later. Eskil apprenticed me for a bit in my youth.' Alfinna said. 'Olaf and Erik joined us a couple of weeks ago to help us to escape from Rojden. They've organised most of this trip.'

'Well met.' Eskil nodded at both Olaf and Erik.

Alfinna pointed to Jerre, 'Jerre is a former cavalry trooper, without his help Yngvild and Noren wouldn't have got away.'

'My house is your house, Jerre.' Eskil said.

'I shall treat it well' Jerre bowed as well as he could with a table in the way.

'This young lady is Yngvild Helgasdottir, also known as Yngvild the Fierce. She carries Jafnadr, and she broke a geas.' Alfinna said.

Eskil's eyes went wide. 'You carry Jafnadr?'

In answer I drew Jafnadr and laid her on the table

between us. 'I do.'

Eskil put his hands behind his back, as if to resist the temptation to take the sword. 'I've only seen her once before, in your grandfather's time. Leif used to put it on the table facing the accused when he sat in judgement.'

'You met my grandfather?' I said.

'Only once, and briefly at that. I was a small boy, and sent away on an errand. When I got back he was long since gone.' Eskil said.

'Inibrakemi you know.' Alfinna said.

'Indeed I do.' Eskil said.

'So that leaves my brother Noren. He grew up with Yngvild on Straven under the watchful eye of Old Bjorn. He's the reason we're all here. His father is chasing us to get him back.' Alfinna said.

'Your brother?' Eskil's eyebrows were practically in his hairline.

'Alfinna is most definitely my sister.' Noren said. 'Even if you find it hard to believe.'

'That would certainly explain all the excitement these last few days.' Eskil said.

'We could do with some help in that regard.' Alfinna said.

'If it's putting one in Rojden's eye, then I'm glad to help.' Eskil said. 'What can I do?'

'We want to leave some things with you so that we can travel lighter tomorrow.' Alfinna said.

'I might want some help strengthening my skold in return.' Eskil said.

'I'll help with that after dinner, Noren and Inibrakemi will too.'

'So what are you leaving behind?' Eskil said.

'Nothing dangerous, just the cart, and some of the horses, and the provisions we can't carry. You can dispose of them as you like. Put it on our account.'

'I will be happy to do that.' Eskil finished off his

tankard. 'Would you like something to eat?'

Eskil took his leave of us and we stayed at the table to wait for dinner to be served. It wasn't long before Dagmar and another dark haired young woman came through the middle door with bread, olives and oil. More ale followed swiftly on, and then a steady stream of small dishes appeared. Some were highly spiced, others red, orange, or green. There were baked eggs, chicken, fish, and other unfamiliar dishes, including some very chewy fish, and rather more garlic than I was used to. It tasted great though, better than the food we would have had on the road, and someone else was cooking it and cleaning up afterwards.

I was fit to burst, and ready for an early night. It was just as well I was wearing the wrong clothes, these were baggy around me. I think if I'd had my skirts on then my belly would have been under too much strain.

Alfinna leant over and whispered in my ear. 'When we're helping Eskil, get Dagmar to show you the bath house. You'll enjoy it.'

'Can you send Noren over when you're done?'

'I'll see what I can do.'

Alfinna was right. The bath house was amazing. It was right next to the forge, and the water was brought up from the stream by a wheel into a pipe that wrapped round the forge's chimney and then flowed into a tank that was against the fire in the forge. So the water flowed in hot to fill an azure tiled pool set in the floor. Steam gently floated on the surface of the water. The pool was stepped, so you could sit in it comfortably, or move into the centre to submerge your whole body. There were shutters on the roof, when they were open the sky was visible when you lay in the hot pool.

A second pool was cooler, fed directly from the stream, with wire filters to stop flotsam from filling the cold pool. Dagmar left me with a towel and a clean shift. I hung them on the pegs on the opposite wall, opened the ceiling shutters, and then stripped off. I started in the cold pool, using the soap and wash-cloth to clean my body. Then I soaked myself in the hot pool until my skin flushed pink all over.

Just as I was about to give up on Noren there was a knock on the door. I got out of the water and went over to unlatch it. Through the crack in the door I saw Noren outside. I opened it up just enough to put my arm through and grab him.

'You need to wash, my love, let me help you.' Pulling him in I kissed him. I closed the bath house door behind us and latched it.

I got a good night's sleep, in a proper bed, and dressed in my own clothes for breakfast. Noren had shared that we were going to make a dash for the coast, and that Alfinna believed we'd be past the area that Rojden's army was searching.

There were only six of us at breakfast though.

'Where's Inibrakemi?' I asked Alfinna when we'd finished eating.

'She left at first light.'

'Without us?'

'She's gone ahead to contact the Seagull, so they make landfall where we need them.'

'Flying?'

'Yes, much faster and safer than riding there.'

The best horses were saddled and ready for us. One mount, and one spare each. All the pack horses and the cart were staying behind. Both sets of horses were saddled for riding, and we cantered as far as we could, and then switched horses, walking for a mile or so before cantering some more. By the time we stopped for lunch we were only a few miles short, but the horses were lathered with sweat, and they needed to rest before we could go any further.

~

"Look! The sea!" Jerre pointed.

"The Sea!" Erik stood in his stirrups and stared at the sliver of sparkling blue between the rolling hills on our left. We'd just come out of the forest on the track that would take us through the fields to our rendezvous with the Seagull.

I felt relief when I followed Erik's finger to the horizon and saw the sun glittering on the waves. We couldn't be much more than a mile from the sea.

"Keep going." Alfinna spurred her horse into Erik's. "We'll have plenty of time to look at it later."

I realised we'd stopped to look at the sea. I felt guilty as I nudged Whiteface with my heels to get her moving again. We met a farmer's track that was heading towards the sea.

Sheep grazed in a field to our left, the forest curved back towards the sea, and our track, on the right. Fences kept the sheep from straying too far, that wasn't something we worried about on Straven, the island wasn't so large that you could lose sheep.

When we met the Seagull I'd get to go home. I missed the simplicity of Straven. The safety of my childhood, the warmth of the fire in the old hall where the children ate. My excitement when I'd finally been old enough to eat in the new hall with the adults. I'd be back there in time to help prepare for the winter. Probably before—

A horse screamed and crashed.

I looked up to see Jerre rolling away from his mount, which was on its side thrashing its legs on the track.

Whiteface raised her front legs and whinnied, I held on tight and leaned forwards into her mane.

On the right, coming out of the woods, were dozens of soldiers. Archers. They were shooting at us as they came.

I pulled on the reins to make Whiteface turn away, and pushed her at a low fence. She launched herself over the fence and away from the noise.

Looking behind me I saw Jerre scrabbling onto a spare mount, urging the others to follow me.

I reined Whiteface up and turned her round to get a good view of our ambushers.

We were now out of bowshot, they'd started shooting a bit too soon. I strung my bow anyway, getting ready to shoot if the archers got closer.

They came out of the wood to close the range and carry on shooting arrows at us.

I picked the lead archer and drew my bow up to aim at him. He's shouting at the others, and I put the tip of my arrow to the top of his head and loose it. He's some way off, and I channel Kari to make the arrow hit him.

While I'm watching the arrow drop the lead archer, unbidden my hands find the next arrow and nock it. I repeat my motions, taking aim at another archer that's trying to take the initiative and lead his comrades towards us.

Jerre is leading the other spare horses. Olaf, Noren and Alfinna race past me, spurring their horses on over the next fence. Erik is struggling, but close behind.

The Archers are still coming, two casualties isn't enough to stop them.

Erik's horse goes past me, he's taken an arrow to the shoulder, and there are three more embedded in his shield, with a fifth in the back of his saddle.

I draw, nock and loose three more arrows at three different archers. Their shooting slackens, but now it's all aimed at me.

I turn Whiteface and follow the others.

A horn sounds to my left rear, it's answered by another over to the right. I don't look back.

My heels encourage Whiteface to run faster. Her ears are flat, and her mane waves in the wind as we race to catch the others.

Out to sea there is a ship with a blue circle on its sail, that must be the Seagull.

Just to the right, a few hundred yards ahead, a jumble of grey stones forms a line across a headland. It's the sea fort where we're supposed to meet the Seagull.

Jerre's in the lead. I'm closing, he's slowed the horses to let Erik catch up.

Erik topples off his horse, just short of the fort. Noren stops to help. Alfinna wheels round.

I haul on the reins to stop Whiteface before we crash into Alfinna.

'We need to hold them off a bit!' Alfinna pulls a short bow from her saddle as she dismounts.

We're about a hundred yards from the relative safety of the fort. About half a mile from the ambush point. To the right, there's a cavalry troop lining up for a charge in front of the woods we came out of. They're about four hundred yards away. As soon as they decide to move they'll be on us in less than a minute.

'You're an exceptional shot, Yngvild. Shoot their trumpeter, and the officers. That should slow them.' Alfinna knocked an arrow. 'I'll just aim for the middle, they're too far for me to hit them.' She lifted the bow and loosed an arrow into the air.

I scanned the line of horse soldiers. A couple were standing forward of the others, and a few more on the flanks facing the line. A glint of sun reflected off something metallic.

I focussed on that soldier and aimed an arrow at the man. Kari, help me. I stilled my mind, and hopefully the air.

The arrow sped away.

A glint of sun flashed through the air above as the blue coated trooper tumbled off the back of the horse. The line moved back a bit and one of the horses broke out of it.

I picked another target, one of the officers I hoped. The blue coat was covered by silver braid, or maybe mail. They wore a shiny helmet with a red plume, definitely not an ordinary soldier. I chose one of the bodkin points. If that was mail, rather than braid, the bodkin would slice through it.

As I aimed he started moving across the line. I followed him with the bodkin point. A second trumpeter appeared from the end of the line to meet the officer.

Kari guided this arrow better than the first. It went right through the officer's chest and came out the other side. The trumpeter he was talking to squeaked his trumpet as the arrow hit his chest.

'Yngvild, back!' Alfinna shook my shoulder.

Suddenly I became aware of arrows in the turf in front of me. Our erstwhile ambushers had crept closer while I was shooting cavalry officers.

Alfinna stopped and loosed an arrow at a couple of archers that were shooting at us before carrying on towards the fort.

The cavalry were moving towards us at a walk.

Everyone else was in the fort. Noren was moving some wooden beams to block the entrance.

I ran after Alfinna.

Arrows thudded into the ground around us.

I passed Erik's blood-stained cloak, where he'd fallen off the horse.

The ground was shaking. The arrows stopped coming in.

I turned to loose another arrow at the cavalry. Seeing a horizon filled with a wall of horses. I drew Jafnadr. If I was going to die I'd take some with me.

'Run, Yngvild! Run!'

I obeyed Jafnadr's instructions and dashed for the fort. I could feel the hot breath of the horses on my neck. My back itched in anticipation of being scratched by a sabre.

Then the screaming started. It's not a sound I ever want to hear again. Horses screaming.

Alfinna had pulled her bear trick again. Six bears stood tall with their sharp claws ready to disembowel anyone that closed with them. A seventh bear had charged the cavalry and was tearing into the mounts and troopers alike.

Horses and men screamed. Blood and guts spread over the ground. The wounded horses thrashed and rolled, kicking anyone close. Men crawled away from the line. Others tried to regain control of their frightened horses.

What had been an orderly line of cantering horses had become a maelstrom of dancing and rearing hooves. Horses galloped in different directions, anywhere away from the bear, many of them riderless. Men also ran, the less fortunate lay still, or were crawling away.

'Did you know she was going to do that?' I thought at Jafnadr.

'I felt her change. It's in her character.'

'Yngvild, let's go, before they recover.' Noren pulled at my arm.

I took one last look round, the only enemy that weren't running away were in no position to pursue us. Putting Jafnadr back in the scabbard I followed Noren to a slightly tumbledown section of the wall. He put his hands on my waist and lifted me up, Olaf reached down to help me over the wall. Once I was up I helped Olaf with Alfinna, and then we all helped Noren.

'How long do you think we've got?' Olaf said.

'Maybe an hour?' Alfinna shrugged. 'They'll realise

we aren't running after them, and that the bear's gone. Then they'll come back to pick up the trail.'

'They'll be a lot more cautious when they do though.' I said.

'There's only one way into the fort. I checked after I blocked the gate.' Noren said.

'Where are Jerre and Erik?' I said.

'Erik went to signal to the ship.' Olaf said. 'Jerre went with him.'

'We need to guard the fort until the Seagull can take us off.' Alfinna said.

'Let's take turns watching until they come back, I'll go first.' Noren said. 'The rest of us can move everything to the landing point.'

It took longer than two hours for the enemy to creep back into range of my bow. In the meantime I watched one of the wounded cavalry troopers limp between the fallen horses and put them out of their misery by cutting their throats. Once he'd done that he checked the fallen men, dragging his left foot as he moved from body to body. I hoped that they rewarded him for his devotion when he got back, and that I wouldn't need to shoot him.

The cavalry started to re-form on the field in front of the wood. It was about half a mile from us. Well out of bowshot. They spent at least half an hour lining up. There were quite a few missing. A little later archers appeared in the fringes of the wood. Over on the left more cavalry appeared, a mile or more distant.

'They're surrounding us landward.' Alfinna spoke from behind me. 'They're making sure we can't get away before attacking again.'

'We've probably got until nightfall then.' I said.

'We'll be gone by then. The Seagull is loading the horses.'

'How are they getting the horses on board?'

'There's a jetty, and the Seagull has an empty cargo hold.'

'They're docked?' I was surprised.

'Yes. That's why I'm here. We're the rearguard.'

Alfinna and I watched the enemy make sure they were all round us to landward. As we watched more soldiers marched up, spearmen with shields. They stayed well out of range, even for me.

Noren appeared. It was time to go.

The Seagull was already untied from the jetty and waiting with oars shipped for us. The moment my foot was on the deck two sailors were hauling the plank inboard. Oars were already out of the rowlocks and used to push the Seagull away from the jetty.

A little sail was unfurled because the wind was blowing offshore. Using both oars and sail we put distance between us and the shore. As soon as the ship was far enough out more sail was put on. The oars were shipped and sailors climbed the rigging to get full sail.

We were out of sight of land before the enemy did anything. By nightfall we were heading north.

Only when it was dark and I was in a bunk did I start to relax. I hadn't realised how tense I'd been for the last couple of weeks until I hit the bunk. They woke me for dinner the following day.

ABOUT THE AUTHOR

James Kemp has been writing stories for over 30 years, sometimes he has even written (non-fiction) for a living. James Kemp is a Glaswegian with a strong talent for telling stories. He has studied Creative Writing with the open university and also has a BSc from the University of Glasgow. He writes a variety of fiction, non-fiction & poetry. His first published story, Crisis Point, came from taking part in the National Novel Writing Month (NaNoWriMo) in 2012. He has also written about his experiences as a creative writing student.

Almost 30 years after he went to work full-time for the UK civil service in London he is now back in his native Scotland as a senior civil servant. Living in Angus with his fantastic wife and youngest child. James is also an explorer scout leader training teenagers for the Duke of Edinburgh Award.

All author royalties from the sales of his books are donated a variety of charities.

For more of his writing you could have a look at his blog. You can also sign up to receive very occasional news on new releases and special offers at http://www.themself.org/james-kemp-books

If you liked the story, please leave a review, or at least rate it, on Amazon, Goodreads, the Storygraph or wherever you bought it from. If you thought there was room for improvement, then he'd love to hear from you.

Blog: http://www.themself.org/
Mastodon: @themself@mastodon.scot

That's all. Thanks for reading.

§

NB the runes round the cover show Gudrid's prophecy when transliterated into English.

Milton Keynes UK
Ingram Content Group UK Ltd.
UKHW010308010624
443378UK00004B/211